Lee Hunt
Private Detec

CW00797577

5 Murders and Counting.

The Lee Hunter Crime files.

Second Edition.

Many thanks to:

Yuki Muraille - Proof Reader
Andy Rymer - Technical Content.

A word about the author.

I live in breathtaking Abruzzo, southern Italy. The views of the magnificent mountains, rolling countryside and the Adriatic Sea are a great inspiration for my work.

I have been here for several years now with my wife and our ten dogs, enjoying the atmosphere, the people and the wonderful traditions of this little-known region of Italy.

I would normally write adult fiction, of which the Peter Parker series is one, although I do occasionally write for children.

My latest children's book is "Popysan, the Green Dragon". Have a look at that book and the other books in this series on Amazon.

I also have a Facebook page, Russell B. Smith Author. This contains my latest releases and information, such as the map relating to the Peter Parker books.

Books by Russell B Smith.

The Peter Parker Series.
The Beyondness of Things.
(Published December 2020, available from all good book shops and from
Amazon books as an e-book or in paperback)
ISBN 978-1-8383146-0-6

The Beyondness of Fear.
(Published April 2021, available from all good book shops and from
Amazon books as an e-book or in paperback)
ISBN 978-1-8383146-2-0

The Beyondness of War.
(Expected winter 2022. ISBN 978-1-8383146-4-4)

The Beyondness of Peace.
(Expected 2022/23)

Children's books.
Popysan, The Green Dragon.
(Published March 2021, available from all good book shops and from
Amazon books as an e-book or in paperback)
ISBN 978-1-8383146-1-3

The Lee Hunter Crime Files.
Five Murders and Counting.
(This book is available from all good book shops and from
Amazon books as an e-book or in paperback)
ISBN 978-1-8383146-3-7

Characters in the book.

Lee Hunter.
Private Detective, Ex-Metropolitan Police Force.

Adele.
A client of Lee Hunter.

Gwen Walker.
Missing daughter.
Kim Walker.
Mother.
Simon Walker.
Father.

Mr Brau.
Gangland Boss.

Detective Inspector Deborah Smith.
Murder Squad, Merseyside Police.
Detective Sergeant Sharron Shacklady.
Murder Squad, Merseyside Police.
Detective Constable Mike Evans.
Murder Squad, Merseyside Police.

Kaye Marie.
Senior Scenes of Crime Investigator.

Inspector Marcus Cooke.
Thames Valley Police, C.I.D.

Detective Chief Inspector Mark Bruno.
Operation Elm Tree, Merseyside Police.

Detective Chief Superintendent Martin Kiff.
A Senior Officer, Merseyside Police.

Chief Superintendent Watkins.
A Senior Officer, Merseyside Police.

Ruth Davenport.
Lee Hunter's next-door neighbour.

Smelly Ken.
Drug addict and informant for Lee Hunter.

Mike Geil.
Manager of the Rehab Centre in Ormskirk.

This is Me.

You wake up some mornings, look in the mirror and wonder exactly what life has in store for you. To be honest, I wonder if life has a certain vendetta towards me. Things never quite go my way. I try my best, I've always had, but it's Sod's Law I guess - If it can go wrong, it normally will, and guess who finds himself in the way?

I am 55 years of age, an ex-police chief inspector, but more on that later. I am told that I cut a dashing image, well, my daughters say that. Shame no one else ever seems to think that way. It's been two years since my divorce and no other woman has ventured into my life. Perhaps that's not a bad thing. Not sure if anyone could actually put up with me!

Ok, I have got more of a food baby than I had twenty years ago, but hey, who doesn't? My hair is kind of thinning, I guess you might call it salt and pepper, my right knee hurts when it's cold and I can't remember things like I used to do. I have no sense of style - that's something else my daughters tell me. Perhaps that statement is true.

I love listening to Van Morrison and George Michael while sitting in a semi-lit room with a good bottle of wine. I guess sometimes life can be romantic, and when those moments roll up, I'd just sit back and enjoy. Like Van once said, *"when no one steps on my dreams, there'll be days like this."*

Anyhow, I now live in Southport. It's a large town on the west coast of England. Pay her a visit someday - plenty to see and do. Why Southport? Well, I lived in London for most of my life and the noise, people and 24-hour lifestyle just weren't doing it for me anymore. I had to get out and go somewhere where I could stroll along the beach and just relax. A place where no one knew my name or wanted to put a knife in my back!

So, I guess I am the man who picked up a shit hand of cards, just when the pot on the table exceeded my annual salary. I never really seemed to get lucky. I just get hit by life's many crosswinds. I have had my lucky breaks, don't get me wrong, but it never seems to turn out the way I expect or as good as other people's lives sometimes do.

Of course, you never really know what's going on in other people's lives. What you see is not always the truth. The things that go on behind closed doors would amaze you. They did me.

That's where I come in. As a private detective, I get to see what the real truth behind that suburban smokescreen is. People contact me because they are not certain about their husbands or wives. There are affairs, gambling, secret junkies, alcoholics, dating apps, all kinds of stuff. You would be surprised, perhaps even shocked, at the things hidden away, just waiting to be found.

Anyway, that's what I do. I burrow around in people's turgid and grubby little lives, trying to find a secret that will inevitably lead to unhappiness and maybe a trip to the divorce courts.

The trouble is, I have my own life to deal with, and I carry a considerable amount of baggage around with me, and it's bloody heavy, I can assure you of that.

It really began to go wrong for me when I started drinking. I mean really drinking. It was the first thing I thought about in the morning and the last thing I did before I went to bed at night. The problem was, the Met Police didn't appreciate one of their chief inspectors turning up pissed in the morning, especially when meeting the public.

So, after 25 years of service, several warnings, three rehabilitation courses and a period on sick leave, they asked me to leave. It was either that or they would sack me!

In the end, I agreed to retire early. Divorce quickly followed as my life started to fall apart. My wife took my two daughters, the house, the dog, and every bit of money I had. I don't blame her really. I was not the easiest man to live with. I used to work 20 hours a day, I drank too much and I had not led a completely honourable life with the opposite sex. Now I have no job, no future, nothing!

Anyway, you will be glad to know I have kicked the booze. Well, mostly, and it has been 24 months since my divorce, but who's counting? So, I decide to become a private detective and open my own business.

LEE HUNTER.
PRIVATE DETECTIVE.
All types of investigations undertaken.
By the hour, day or contract work.
Absolute discretion assured.
Full references available.
Contact 011743 65994 - 24 hours a day.

The mistake I made was presuming people would come flooding to my door and beg me to help them. I have had customers, but not enough, and that's where Tony Bianchi comes in, or Fat Tony as everybody calls him. My daughter told me not to call him that, it was disrespectful, and you shouldn't call people fat. Well, my take was, his name is Tony, and he is fat!

Anyway, I needed some money to set this business up. I had to lease an office, buy a car, mobile and laptop. So, I borrowed 20k from Fat Tony and now he wants it back, plus the 10k interest, total 30k.

I checked my bank this morning, total funds available - £115.67. I don't think that's going to help. It's certainly not going to stop Fat Tony from kicking me to death at the end of the month.

So, there you have it. Not much more to say really. I live in an ex-council flat on a rundown estate. My office is above a taxi booking office on Lord Street and I sometimes feel very lonely. Well, I often feel very lonely to be honest. I hadn't ever thought about loneliness before my divorce. I was never alone you see. A very busy job, a family life, mates down the pub and football at the weekend. You never really understand how much you miss people until they are gone - until they are all gone!

Oh yes, going back to the beginning, you might remember me talking about lucky breaks - it was on this particular rainy Wednesday morning, at 10.30am, that one of those lucky breaks came walking into my office. In addition, shortly afterwards, I received a telephone call, pleading for help from a distraught mother whose daughter had gone missing. Things were looking up...or so I thought!

The Lucky Break.
Wednesday AM

It was one of those disgusting English spring days, horrible, cold and pissing it down. The rain was hammering at the window of my office. It was impossible to see outside as the condensation painted a dirty grey gloss on each pane of glass. The water ran down the inside, forming little pools on the rotting windowsill, dripping onto the stained carpet below.

The phone sat silent and lifeless, as did my computer. There had been no calls or emails, not even a scammer promising great riches. If only they could have my bank details. Best of luck with that! They were certainly going to be very disappointed raiding my current account.

Unfortunately, the few customers I had were a distant memory - *'job completed'* - their files said - *'paid in full'*. The trouble was, Fat Tony's file said, *'pay me the 30k by the end of the month Hunter, or you're a dead man'*. I was fully aware what those fourteen words meant, and I can assure you they were not a suggestion. Fat Tony was never about subtlety and refinement wasn't his strength. Brutal torture and retribution were his forte, and he was good at it.

I scanned my email inbox just one more time - no further emails, no prospect of saviour. I sat despondent in my dim and dirty office and wondered if this, or the end of my career with the Met Police, was the worse episode in my miserable bloody life.

I looked around my office, noting every bit of furniture. It wouldn't be long before I handed the keys back and walked away. The office was not more than 20 feet square, with two sash windows looking onto the street below. The door to the office was set opposite my desk, which was a rather ornate and solid affair, with a worn green leather insert on top. Six filing cabinets lined the wall to the right and an old, but very comfortable, three-seater settee sat with its back to the window. Behind my desk was a workbench with cups, a kettle and tea and coffee jars. A small fridge sat underneath, gently humming, keeping the one carton of milk cool.

It just couldn't get any worse than this, could it? And another thing, I don't understand why this place smells of cigarettes. I don't smoke. At least that vice is not tormenting my conscious mind. I can't stop thinking about Fat Tony though and his threats. It's making my head throb and my heart palpitate. I can feel hot flushes race through my skin.

I looked down at the coffee-stained desk. I really needed to do some cleaning around here and get rid of the biscuit wrappers and the McDonald boxes. If anyone did actually call in, they would run for the closest decontamination centre, rather than engaging my services.

I was shaken out of my melancholy by a knock at the door, then a second knock followed. It needed two to shake me out of my inner feelings. They were followed by a third knock and then silence. A sensation of apathy swept over me. Why should I answer? It wasn't going to change anything.

OK, let's give it a go. It might take my mind of Fat Tony. I don't suppose it will be anything interesting. It's more than likely to be some pitiable wife wondering why her husband went out smelling of Luna Rosso aftershave and came back smelling of Chanel No5.

Why don't they ever ask them themselves beats me. I suppose it's easier to get me to dig about and see what I can find. Of course, she won't want to know the truth. She's hoping beyond hope that I won't find anything. Trouble is, I almost always do.

I pushed the chair back and stood up, stiffly extending my right knee. It clicked a couple of times before I felt confident enough to start walking. I hadn't taken more than two steps toward the door when it opened. It swished as it swung into the office, causing a rather nasty and cold draft to enter.

I must have looked a bit like a gawking idiot as the goddess who entered my office caused me to take a breath. She was a beauty - almost six feet tall, long blonde hair, legs going all the way to Scotland, and smelling of the headiest perfume that no doubt must have cost an absolute fortune.

I often speculated if such creatures actually existed. Perhaps in dreams. Maybe they were cultured in test tubes and launched at unsuspecting idiots, like me, to gain an advantage as I dribble down my shirt. Anyway, she strode purposefully into the office, seemingly occupying or at least owning the whole place.

Her face was a picture of perfection - brown eyes, red lipstick, carefully manicured eyebrows, perfect hair. Similarly, her clothes were obviously very expensive. They had that appearance of real quality and not something you buy from the local market!

She also spoke with a clear voice that had a very posh accent. One cultured from the very best of schools, not one you might hear at the Dog and Duck on a Saturday night.

"My name is Adele and I need your help."

For one moment I stood open-mouthed at the appearance of this woman. The grotty paint work, smelly carpet and empty cartons all came back into focus. Why the hell didn't I clear this place up yesterday? It only made her flawless appearance and the smell of her perfume, look even more perfect against the shabby nature of this dump. Her cut-glass diction rang over my senses like a summer shower on a hot and humid day.

"I assume you are the detective, or perhaps his assistant?"

"Sorry, madam. Yes, I am Lee Hunter, private detective. Pleased to meet you."

I held out my hand. She looked down at the offering and then back up at me, without responding. I am not certain, but I am sure she had that *'disgusting, I am never touching that'* look on her face.

"Yes, I have some work for you, Mr Hunter, but perhaps one might want to consider all the details of the offer, before agreeing to it?"

I was going to offer her a seat, but the smelly old settee would not be a place this lady would sit under any circumstances. I couldn't think of what to do next, so I ended up standing motionless in front of her. It reminded me of a visit to the headmaster when I was at junior school.

I had put a dead frog in Jacob Swanson's backpack. Suffice to say his parents weren't best pleased and they wanted some payback. I ended up having to stay in at break time for a month. That wasn't so bad. What was bad though was Jacob

Swanson's revenge. A few years later he stole some sexy underwear from his neighbour's washing line and put it in my backpack. He knocked on his neighbour's door and said he had seen me stealing it. Oh my, that took some explaining, and my parents never did forgive me.

Anyway, I drew myself up, looked Adele straight in the eyes and tried to play it cool.

"Well, I am rather busy at the moment, but I am sure I could fit you in. What would be the nature of the work?"

She looked around at the general state of the office, frowning from time to time.

"Well judging by the appearance of your business premises, I would suggest Mr. Hunter, that busy is perhaps not the right word. I would guess that I might be your only customer and therefore, I will have your full and undivided attention?"

I found it difficult to counter this. The place was a shit hole, so why bother?

"You will certainly have my fullest attention, Mrs...?"

"Adele, just call me Adele. That will suffice for now. There is a rather nice coffee shop just around the corner. Can we talk there? The coffee is just as I like it and the place doesn't smell of cigarettes."

I was embarrassed by the comment, but not totally surprised. Glancing towards the windows, I noted that the rain had abated somewhat and getting out of the office might be a rather nice distraction.

"That's a nice suggestion, Adele. Let's go."

I ushered her out of the office and down the stairs, past the entrance to the taxi office and out into the street. The pavements shone in the late morning light, the rain had now stopped and the sun was beginning to appear.

People scurried backwards and forwards, some still holding up their umbrellas, unaware that the deluge had ceased. Others were wrapped up in their coats, a young couple passed in front, holding hands, seemingly impervious to the inclement weather and the early spring cold.

"Follow me, Mr Hunter. It's only two minutes away."

She strode off purposefully. I turned and pursued her, trying to keep up, my right knee complaining all the way to the café. She pushed the door open and walked in, with a 'I own the place' attitude.

I followed dutifully behind her into the warm and inviting space. I felt like a servant behind my mistress, or perhaps that naughty boy following the headmaster, yet again into his office.

There were two young men working behind the counter, pulling the levers on various machines which hissed steam while they were sprinkling chocolate on the various types of coffee. They looked really smart in their white and dark blue uniforms. The place sparkled. Pictures of Italy adorned the walls, rich red leather seats and marble effect tables were everywhere. The place was busy, almost every table was taken. A very attractive waitress looked up and watched us all the way into the café.

"A table for two, sir?"

I felt somewhat embarrassed. Adele was clearly in charge and she was not the kind of woman who would accept the role of the 'subservient' in any relationship.

She turned and stared down at the waitress. Those liquid brown eyes of hers must have sent a very stern message to the young woman who took a couple of steps back.

"I do want a table for two", Adele spoke to her in a calm but very controlled manner, quickly and firmly grabbing control of the whole situation. I felt that red flush in my cheeks again.

"Oh, yes madam. Please, follow me."

I followed, feeling rather awkward and sat down as directed by the waitress. The warm and dry ambiance was enhanced by the aroma of coffee and freshly baked croissants. It was obvious why Adele rather liked this place. It was smart, as were the staff, and just about everyone in here too. It was in direct contrast to my office and if I was being honest, my life in general.

"Can I take you order, madam?"

"Yes, I will have a skinny latte and the gentleman will have?"

They both looked at me. I was surprised at the unexpected attention, but I managed to compose myself, I think.

"Cappuccino, and can I have a croissant? I am bloody starving."

Those rather clumsy words drifted out of my mouth, just like an unexpected burp, especially the one that appears when you are in company. It wasn't in keeping with the behaviour that women like Adele were used to, nor in a place like this. The young waitress turned and marched off towards the bar.

"Right, Mr Hunter. I have a proposition for you. Perhaps something you would not normally undertake, but one that will prove very profitable. This is not the place to discuss such things and I think you will need some time to assess and carefully consider my proposition. So, I have written, for your information, this document outlining the proposal, and the fees that I will pay you for said work."

She reached into her small handbag and pulled out a white envelope, put it onto the table and pushed it over in front of me. I remember thinking it felt like one of those spy movies, perhaps some evil menace was just about to blow up the world and I was the only person who could save humanity. Sadly though, it was more than likely to say, '*my husband is up to no good - find out who he is seeing and take some photos.*'

"In addition, Mr Hunter, this is a number of a mobile phone. It is a pay as you go SIM, so it's not traceable. And just in case you decide to '*talk to anyone*' about this proposition, I will simply destroy the SIM and disavow all knowledge of this or any further meetings."

Now that sounded a bit more exciting. Maybe Blofeld was just about to blow up the world?

"Do you want me to open the envelope now or later Adele?"

"I would suggest that you return to your office before opening it, Mr Hunter."

I wanted to ask more questions, but I couldn't think of anything useful to say. In any case the young waitress returned with our coffees and my croissant.

Back in the Office.
Wednesday PM

By the time we finished our coffees and chatted aimlessly about the awful weather, the rain had started again. Adele asked me to remain in the café for a few minutes so she could slip away. I wasn't sure why she would say that as it wasn't as if she was a wanted criminal! Hey, she was paying the bills, so who was I to argue?

Anyway, as I said, the weather had turned crap again. So, by the time I got back to the office, I was soaked to the skin. I grabbed the rather smelly towel from the tea making area and rubbed it through my hair. I quicky realised that it would make me smell just as disgusting as it did, and why did the bloody office stink of cigarettes?

Right, black tea, one sugar and where were the bourbon biscuits? I need a chocolate rush before I open the envelope. I had this horrible feeling of impending bitter and uncontrolled disappointment. Subconsciously, I had talked myself into a big pay day and getting Fat Tony off my back. However, I just knew the job contained in the envelope would be some *'cheap as you like'* week long spy job, £250 at best.

Anyway, at least I would be able to enjoy myself with the money before Fat Tony caught me. I would be able to die full of Pepsi, Galaxy chocolate and a vindaloo from Alerk's Indian Restaurant - what a way to go! I was just about to push my *'with love from Newquay'* paperknife under the back of the envelope when the phone rang.

"Lee Hunter Private Detective Agency, how can I help?"

"Are you a private detective?"

Now I know in times of stress, people don't think straight, but there's no helping some folks.

"Yes, madam. I am a private detective and my name is Lee Hunter. How can I help you?"

"It's my daughter. She is only sixteen and she has gone missing. Please help."

Now this was very serious. I had spent five years on the Missing Persons Team, or MISPER as it was known, and I know just how difficult this kind of situation really is.

I enjoyed working in that department, but unfortunately, I was transferred out. It wasn't my fault really. The boss came at me with a chair and I had to hit him. I was just defending myself. Fortunately, I wasn't on duty at the time, otherwise I would have been sacked. The truth was though, I was in bed with his wife at the time. So, to be honest, I couldn't blame him for trying to kill me.

"Madam, please can I have your name before we go any further? There are steps you need to take and people you have to speak to."

"Mrs Walker, Kim Walker."

"Right, Mrs Walker, you need to go into your local police station and report this. Time is of the essence. They have specially trained staff and all the resources needed to help you. If you don't know where your local station is, I can certainly point you in the right direction."

"You don't understand, Mr Hunter. I have already done that, but I need extra help. There are complications you see."

"Mrs Walker, I don't understand. What kind of complications? You need to tell the local police everything you know, no matter what else is going on, and you need to do it now."

"No, Mr Hunter, I can't do that. Please can we meet? I don't want to talk over the phone."

"Mrs Walker, this really is a police matter. Yes, I will meet up and give you all the help you need, but the local constabulary are the people who need to control this, all of it!"

"Thank you, Mr Hunter. Can we meet somewhere private where we can talk without being overheard?"

"The best thing to do is for you to come to my office. We can shut the door and talk as much as we need to. I must warn you, Mrs Walker, that I may end up either calling the local police or taking you there myself."

"I understand Mr Hunter, and I appreciate your advice regarding the police, but when you hear what I have to say, I think you will change your mind. I have your address. I found it on the internet. I will be with you in about thirty minutes. Is that OK?"

"I will have the kettle on ready, Mrs Walker."

By the time I finished speaking, she had already put the phone down. This lady was in a real rush and why didn't she want to tell the local cops everything?

People in this type of situation either don't want to or can't talk to the police, so they don't contact them at all. Or they call the cops, tell them everything, give them photos, get onto social media and try and attract as much attention as possible. People calling the cops and not telling them everything is very unusual. Wanting to keep things quiet and involving people like me - very strange!

I couldn't think of many cases like this. Even during my time with the Missing Persons Team. The only scenario that sprang to mind was one of a cover up. Perhaps they did know what had happened to their daughter, but didn't want the cops digging too deep, well not yet. Get some advice from me, buy a little more time before the spotlight turned on them. I needed to be very careful here. This was an easy situation to get tangled up in, make yourself look culpable, part of the cover up, even responsible!

Anyway, I had some time before Mrs Walker arrived, so I turned my attention back to Adele's glorious envelope - see what the job was. It felt a bit like a game show, should I open the envelope or take the prize? The only thing was, the prize was a kicking from Fat Tony, so I decided to open the envelope.

The Job.
Wednesday Evening.

I could smell her perfume on the envelope. I couldn't help holding it up to my nose for a sniff. Odd thing was, I looked around before I did so, just to make sure no one was looking. Why the hell did I do that?

Anyway, I am no expert on expensive perfume, but this smelt expensive - very, very expensive. I slipped my paperknife under the top of the envelope and sliced it open. Was this going to be a disappointment or the job of a lifetime? Well knowing me, it would be the former.

There was a small light blue piece of paper inside. I opened the envelope and it fell out onto my desk. The blue note was folded in two. I opened it up and read the typed message it contained:

Dear Mr Hunter.
I will be brief. I need you to undertake a very difficult and challenging job for me. I am certain that such a job would not be one you have undertaken before. The level of danger and potential outcome if undertaken would be severe.
I need you to deal with my husband and I want you to undertake this task on my behalf.
If you accept this job, I will pay you £20,000 straight away and an additional £10,000 upon completion.
If you decide to go to the police regarding this offer, I will simply deny everything, and my very expensive lawyers will tangle you up in litigation until hell freezes over.
I don't expect a reply any time soon, but I will need to hear from you by the end of the week.

I read the note several times. That was a joke, right? She wanted me to *'deal'* with her husband? What the hell did that mean, *'deal with'*? Put the frighteners on him so he left? Blackmail him out of her life? Arrange a honey trap so she could divorce him? Surely, she didn't mean kill him?

No, you idiot. She didn't mean kill him. You are a detective and not a very successful one. This is real life not a bloody film. I will ring the number she left me. I will do that after I have dealt with Mrs Walker.

That letter, however, had set off something in my turgid little mind. It was those numbers in the note, £20,000 and £10,000. Add those together and it came to, well exactly the amount I needed to pay off Fat Tony.

I couldn't help thinking of the magnitude of the offer, £30k! That was a hell of a pay day. OK, she is a rich bitch and money probably doesn't have the same meaning or value as it does for me, but nonetheless, £30k! What the hell does she want doing for that kind of cash? I was intrigued, but she would have to wait. First, there was Mrs Walker to deal with.

Mrs Walker
Wednesday Night.

I was on my third cup of coffee by the time Mrs Walker finally arrived. Having been watching out of the office window for the last thirty minutes, I saw her walking up Lord Street. There was a BMW X6 just behind her. It was driving really slow as if it was following her, rather odd. I do love that model. Unfortunately, I don't have the 60k to pay for one.

Anyway, I could hear her climbing the stairs up to my office, past the entrance to the taxi place. She didn't bother knocking. She just pushed the door open and walked in. She was an attractive woman. Perhaps forty or forty-five, auburn shoulder length hair, blue eyes and very well dressed and clearly very worried indeed.

"Mr Hunter, I came as quickly as I could."

She was red in the face. Perhaps the result of stress or the effort in getting here and up those bloody steep stairs.

"Please take a seat Mrs Walker. Try the old settee. Would you like a drink?"

"No thank you, Mr Hunter. I just want this sorting out as soon as possible."

She dumped herself down with an uncomfortable *'crunch'*. I carefully sat down beside her. This settee was not as strong as it used to be and I didn't want to initiate a rather embarrassing incident involving a collapsing, old leather sofa.

She spun around to face me. I didn't get the chance to speak before the flood of words assaulted me. The torrent was borne out of fear and the unknown, and of course the love for her daughter.

"You have to help me, Mr Hunter. I am beside myself. I don't know what to do best. Please say you will help. I will pay you whatever it takes to sort this out."

"Slow down, Mrs Walker. Let's start from the beginning and let's do it slooooowley."

"Sorry, Mr Hunter. It's my daughter. She has gone missing and I need to get her back."

"Yes, Mrs Walker. I understand that bit, but the police are always your best bet in this situation. They must always take the lead in cases such as this. I can certainly add to what they are doing, but they are always in charge of the case, not me!"

"I understand that, Mr Hunter, but I need some more help you see. It's not quite as simple as it seems."

I couldn't help myself from smiling. All those years as a cop taught me many lessons, including reading what was really happening behind the story.

"I thought as much, Mrs Walker. Please tell me everything and I mean the whole story. If you leave anything out, it could and probably will prove extremely serious. Let me assure you of my complete discretion in this matter. Anything you tell me will go no further, unless you want it to, and that includes talking to the police."

"Thank you, Mr Hunter, and call me Kim by the way. It's less fussy. Right, my daughter her name is Gwen. This is her photograph."

Her hands were shaking manically as she opened her light brown leather handbag and pulled out what looked like a recent photo. For a second or so she started to cry, but managed to hold herself together as she handed me the photo.

"This is Gwen. She is almost seventeen, our only child. She goes to Stanley Highschool on Fleetwood Road. Do you know it Mr Walker?"

"Sorry Kim, I don't. But please can we get back to your daughter. How can I help? We need to get things moving as time is of the essence in these kinds of cases."

I felt this upwelling of panic. All that time on the Missing Persons Team, the one thing it had taught me was about the first few hours. If you don't get things up and running quickly, it always was too late.

"Yes, Mr Hunter. She disappeared on her way home from school yesterday. She takes the school bus, which normally takes about an hour before she gets home, but she didn't appear. I phoned her friends, but they didn't remember her getting on the bus. None of them could even recollect seeing her at all once they left the school premises. My guess is she was taken as soon as she left Stanley."

"OK Kim, you said 'taken'. What makes you think she just didn't just wander off or run away from home?"

"I have been through this with the police, Mr Hunter. She was taken! She didn't run away, get on the wrong bus, fall into a ditch, get lost, move in with her boyfriend or get off her face on drugs and forget where she lived. She was taken and that's the only explanation. There is no other factor in play here, Mr Hunter."

"Right, so why would someone 'take' her, right in front of a school with goodness knows how many people buzzing around? If you wanted to snatch someone you wouldn't do it there, Kim. It's way too obvious. Are you sure she didn't just get into a car with someone she knew?"

"Mr Hunter, she was taken and that's that. Trust me, that's what's happened."

"I get the feeling there is something else to this story, something you aren't telling me Mrs Walker. I said earlier, you have to tell me everything or I can't help you."

She looked around the office, but she wasn't looking at anything specific. She was buying time. She stood up for a moment before sitting down again. There was no doubt in my mind that there was another explanation to this and I had to persuade her to tell me what it was.

"Look, Mr Hunter, it's very difficult. If I tell you what I know it might make this situation way worse. Please can you just ask around, try and see what you can find out? Perhaps you have other ways of finding information? Have different contacts than the police have."

"Listen, Mrs Walker, Kim, you have to tell me what going on here. If she's been kidnapped you need to tell me. Kidnapping is a very serious situation. I have to know what's going on."

"Mr Hunter, I will pay you whatever your daily rate is. Please just do what I ask. The police can do the rest."

I was tempted to say no. Let the police deal with the whole thing, but my appointment with Fat Tony at the end of the month kind of shaded it. So, like any desperate man I agreed to help her, no questions asked.

We signed the appropriate documents and agreed payment terms. She left me her details, some more information and that was it. She left the office no better off than when she had arrived. I would certainly do my best, but I failed to see what I could do above and beyond what the local police could.

Anyway, I had a couple of contacts. I would put the word out and see what came back. My guess would be a big fat zero. What the hell could be so important that she couldn't tell me?

My guess was a kidnapping, but Mrs Walker didn't seem the millionaire type, so it probably wasn't money. It could be debt of course, *'pay up or your daughter gets it'*. It wouldn't be the first time that had happened. She could just have run off with her boyfriend, but the police could find her, way quicker than I could.

Damn strange thing if you ask me. I could ask the local police, but they would just warn me off and tell me to keep my nose out. Then there were my contacts of course. I could get them to poke around. John Faulks was one, but it wasn't his kind of thing. He was a sleezy grease ball. Porn, exploitation and prostitution was his bag. Pete Anders was smacked out of his head nowadays, no point in going there. What about Jenks? Drugs and the underworld. He was pretty reliable, especially if you paid him enough. Trouble was, he was difficult to get hold of. This could be because he was in Strangeways Prison or someone had shot him, again. Worth a try though.

Right, grab the mobile, text Jenks and then get in touch with the beautiful Adele. Try and get to the bottom of this 30k offer. I remembered the old saying though - If it sounds too good to be true, it probably is!

Call Adele.

Thursday Lunch Time.

"Mr Hunter, thanks for calling me. Can I assume you are willing to talk further about my offer?"

She sounded just as sultry over the phone as she had when she walked into my office. Funny really, I could have sworn I could smell her perfume. I must be losing the plot, nothing new there then.

"Well Adele, it does seem a rather interesting offer, especially the details regarding payment. I think we need to get together again to develop things further. I am sure you don't want to talk about it over the phone."

"Absolutely not. I will send a cab over for you. We will meet in the Hesketh Arms. It's in Churchtown, opposite Saint Cuthbert's Church. It's lovely in there. We can have an evening snack, and then go for a drive in my car to finalise the details."

"Sounds perfect, I will keep an eye open. See you soon."

The phone went dead. I was looking forward to finding out what she had to say, but it made me feel somewhat vulnerable. *'Go for a drive in her car'* - I don't like being out of control. We could agree something, and I would have no proof that the meeting ever took place. Anyway, it was worth a punt, and with that meeting with Fat Tony bearing down on me like an out-of-control express train, I had to do something before it hit!

I stood watching out of my rotten and grotty office windows. The day had turned out rather well. Some late afternoon sun and it looked to be developing into a very nice spring evening down Lord Street. There were plenty of cars, people and even the odd bus running up towards the Monument - a rather normal scene.

Little did any of those people know about the events evolving in my day. Mrs Walker and her errant daughter, Adele, and well, goodness knows what. I wondered what their names were, what their lives entailed and if they had encountered the issues I had since I crawled out of bed this morning.

Almost opposite my window, a cab stopped. I could see the driver looking about. Someone tried to get in, but was obviously told to go elsewhere. I assumed it must have been the cab sent by Adele. I grabbed my coat, made my way down and crossed the main road.

The driver spotted me trying to cross Lord Street. He wound the window down and in a thick foreign accent, shouted my name.

"Mr Bunter is it, sir?"

"No, but that's close enough."

I rounded the front of the cab and got in, "The Hesketh Arms, please."

"That is in Churchtown, sir. It is a pub you know, are you loving it there?"

"If you mean it's in Churchtown and it's nice, the answer is yes."

"Good! We will be arrive in fifteen minutes."

Without really checking behind, he swung the cab around and sped off in the opposite direction. This caused a certain amount of alarm with the other road users, but their shaking fists and horns seemed to have little or no effect on my driver.

"It has not been raining, sir, not since the morning."

I really didn't want to engage him in any form of conversation. I just wanted him to concentrate on the bloody road. It was impossible though, constantly turning his head he was absolutely determined to start up a conversation and shortly afterwards, kill us both.

"You are not from Southport, sir. Your accent is foreign to me?"

I thought that was a bit rich, "No, I come from London originally. I have been down here for a couple of years now. It's really nice, lots more room to breathe and relax."

"I love it here too. It's good for my work, sir. Lots of tourists and people who are working in town."

We came within an inch of killing a cyclist and I swear he didn't see the old lady in the electric wheelchair. If he had got any closer, she would have been on her way to the Hesketh Arms, along with me!

My nerves were by now shredded, my palms were sweating and my shirt had stuck to my back. If he didn't start concentrating on the road in front of him, my worries regarding Fat Tony would be no more. He swung left and right through the traffic running yellow lights, and completely ignoring any speed limits.

It seemed like hours before we turned right at the lights on Cambridge Road, past Sunny Road and first left on the roundabout, past The Bold Arms on the right and pulled up in front of the Hesketh Arms. I had never been so thankful to arrive anywhere, ever in my life before! I sat there for a few seconds, trying to make a mental note of his face and name. There was no way I would ever travel in his taxi again. Not even if my life depended upon it.

"How much do I owe you?", I said with a trembling voice and a very dry throat.

"No, no, sir. This is on the account of the beautiful lady Adele. She has me working so much, my family are getting rich because of her."

Without speaking again, I opened the door and got out, much relieved to still be alive. It seemed like minor miracles do happen. The early evening had turned out rather nicely. It was considerably warmer than this morning and that cold wind had disappeared. I remembered thinking as I entered the front doors of the pub that spring was on the way and things were looking up. Maybe my life was about to get better.

Funny how wrong you can be. I remember my old man's favourite saying, well apart from *'don't tell your mother'*, was *'don't count your chickens until they hatch'*. How right was he!

I hadn't been inside the Hesketh Arms before. It was rather nice, a bit of character and a touch of the modern. There was a plaque next to the door and I stood for a moment. I do enjoy the history bit. Not something you get to see so much in the hustle and bustle of central London. The plaque read -

'As one of the longest established pubs in the area, locals have enjoyed coming to the Hesketh Arms (previously known as the Black Bull) for over 200 years. Guests

from local towns such as Ormskirk and Formby have returned time and time again, looking to unwind in historic settings after busy days visiting Southport's thriving shopping and entertainment attractions.'

That's nice I thought - 200 years! I bet many a scoundrel has drunk in here during that time! I wonder how many dodgy card games have gone on in the Landlord's little hideaways.

Anyway, I had an appointment with Adele. I pushed through the inner doors and into the main area of the pub. It was surprising to see how many people were in here. Several business folks in suits, a few older ladies doing dinner and sat by the fire, a couple holding hands. There were staff running about taking orders, a few guys stood at the bar having a drink, but I couldn't see the person I had risked my life to meet.

I spent a few awkward moments walking about the place trying to find her, with many an inquisitive look, especially from those people hidden away in corners, holding the hands of people who were not necessarily their partners! I have learned to recognise that look of panic, perhaps anxiety at being found out. It was part of my job to look for these cheaters. How easy it was to find them and how dumb they were thinking that sitting in a busy pub would be a safe place to meet?

I wondered how many of these people had made an excuse not to go home - *'just a quick meeting after work', 'it's so and so's birthday, so we are having a few drinks', 'a night out with the girls'.* None of that held very much water with their partners of course, and it made a living for me I guess, so I shouldn't complain.

"Mr Hunter, I was worried you weren't coming. Come over here and take a seat. We have a lot to discuss."

I looked behind me and sitting by an old fireplace was Adele, looking just as good as this morning.

"Sorry, Adele. It's a big old place. Lots of quiet little corners."

I ordered a couple of drinks from a passing waiter and sat down. It was a bit of a squeeze next to the fire with a little round table sat between us. She smiled and I would have done anything to make that a genuine gesture be directed at me personally, but I knew otherwise. She was a manipulator, used to getting her own way, partly because of her looks, partly because of her money, but she could play the game, better than most anyone else, I had to be careful.

"So, what's this all about Adele? 30k? I think you have too many noughts on that. That's a lot of money even in your world. You can get an awful lot done for 30k you know."

"I certainly do have the right number of noughts, Mr Hunter, and I would expect an awful lot from you for that money."

We both looked up as the waiter brought our drinks. "Will there be anything else?"

The young man looked at Adele with a large smile on his face and I knew exactly what he was thinking, and I was very certain that he wouldn't be getting it.

"No" she said, briefly returning the smile.

"Well Adele, I hate suspense. So, spill the beans. What do you want me to do?"

She looked around, trying to assess if anyone was within hearing distance. Assured that there wasn't, she turned back to me.

"It's simple, Mr Hunter. It's my husband. I want him gone. Will you take the job?"

"Gone? Gone where, Adele? Do you mean blackmail or putting the frighteners on him? What exactly do you have in mind?"

"I what you to kill him, Mr Hunter. I want him dead!"

That last comment seemed to bring the whole place to a stop. Like someone had pressed pause on a PlayStation game whilst they make a quick cup of coffee. I found myself laughing, although there was nothing to laugh about. I might be an ex-police officer, but I still thought something of the law and abiding by it. Murder, I don't think so. What the hell was she thinking?

"I don't see that there is anything to laugh about, Mr Hunter. I am very serious indeed."

"I don't doubt it, Adele, but I am a private detective, not a bloody hit man. You have got the wrong guy. I don't mind finding out who your husband is shagging, but I am certainly not going to kill him. Why the hell do you want him dead anyway? What's he done to you that's so serious?"

"It's a long story, Mr Hunter. Sufficed to say he is an animal. He treats everyone around him with utter contempt. He uses me as his private sex toy. Abusing me, for his own gratification. He plays sick games with me, never asking just taking, using my body for whatever he wants. If that wasn't enough, he rents women and men for sex. I hate to think how much they suffer. Then there are the beatings, Mr Hunter. For no reason he would attack me. I can't remember the number of days I have spent in hospital, broken noses, dislocated fingers, fractured ribs and that just the beginning."

There was a long silence. I looked at her. She wasn't crying, but I could tell the emotion of the last few seconds had taken its toll. It felt awkward starting up the conversation again. This kind of situation is very serious and from my experience in the Met, all too common.

"Listen Adele, I can't possibly imagine how you feel. What it's like to be abused, but you can't just kill someone because of it. There are ways and means to tackle this kind of thing. I know people in the police whose job it is to help in this kind of situation. They are trained and good at their jobs. Let me contact them, they will help you."

She was looking across the room and I could tell she wasn't listening to a word I had said. She had made her mind up. She wanted him dead.

"Drink up, Mr Hunter. We can go for a drive and we can talk more easily in my car, with no one earwigging."

"We don't need to talk about anything Adele. I am not going to do it!"

"Look, let me drive you back to your office. If you still don't want the job, no problems. You will never see me again and that's a promise. How's that, Mr Hunter?"

I still couldn't believe what was happening. Any minute now I was sure I would wake up and spend the rest of the morning laughing at the silly dream I had. Trouble was, it wasn't a dream. She was genuine. She really had asked me to kill her husband.

I was so shocked by what had just happened that I found myself unable to turn the offer of a lift down. In fact, I was so stunned, I couldn't really think of very much at all. I eventually decided to take that lift back to my office. Being with Adele in her car was preferable to that bloody taxi driver coming back. I had got away with my life once, I was certain I wouldn't get away with it again.

We exited the back of the pub and into the carpark. It was clear straight away which was her car - a rather stunning Maserati Ghibili Tofeo - bright red with cream leather interior, best part of £90,000, wow! We strolled out into the night without saying a word. I was looking forward to the ride when the phone buzzed in my pocket. I pulled it out and read the screen.

MESSAGE FROM - 'JENKS'
HI LEE, NICE TO HEAR FROM YOU AGAIN MATE. DON'T LEAVE IT SO LONG NEXT TIME.
THAT BIT OF INFO YOU ASKED FOR ON THAT GIRL WHO'S GONE MISSING. YOU WILL NEVER BLOODY BELIEVE WHAT I HAVE FOUND OUT. MAN THIS IS UNBELIEVABLE. I HAVE NEVER KNOWN THE LIKES.
CALL ME MATE AS SOON AS YOU CAN. IT'S EXTREMELY IMPORTANT.
JENKS.

Talk about eager. What the hell has Jenks found out? It wasn't like him to get overly excited. I usually had to give him a kick to get him moving, sometimes literally. It hadn't taken him very long either. It seemed odd that the old bill hasn't found anything of note, but Jenks had come up trumps in an afternoon. Odd that the little scumbag has something important to tell me, but the police had nothing to say to Mrs Walker?

Oh well, he would have to wait. I needed to deal with Adele first and try to stop this idea of murdering her husband. What the hell was she thinking and why had she chosen me? Did I look like a killer?

The car purred into life. The gentle smell of leather was wonderful, the whole motor exuded opulence and luxury. She gently engaged drive and pulled away, turning right out of the carpark and back towards town.

"So, Mr Hunter, I am not going to ask for your final answer. I would expect you want to think about the offer. Just to reiterate, I will pay you twenty thousand now and the remaining ten thousand upon completion. I will leave the place, time and method up to you. All I need is proof of completion."

"Adele, I have to tell you as an ex-police officer, I should be reporting this conversation to the local CID. I won't because…well, I just won't, but this can't go any further. I will not be killing anyone. I just spy for suspicious husbands and wives, I do a bit of work for the taxman, or jobs for employers spying on staff who are supposed to be doing one thing but are doing another. It's not exciting stuff, but it's honest work. So, you see, I do boring junk, not murder!"

"Mr Hunter, by the look of your office and the clothes you are wearing, I don't think you are actually doing anything at all. Now don't be silly! Go away, think about it and call me Saturday morning, say about 10am. If it's still no, then I won't bother you again. How's that?"

I wanted to argue with her some more, but it wouldn't have accomplished anything. I resolved to keep my mouth shut, leave it until Saturday morning and say, *'thanks, but no thanks.'*

Jenks.
Thursday Night.

I found myself sitting in my office with a hot cup of coffee steaming away on the desk in front of me. It has been sat there for fifteen minutes, waiting to be consumed.

Adele had dropped me off in front of the building on Lord Street, where my office was located. She hadn't spoken another word since leaving the Hesketh and I was glad about that. This was a crazy situation and one I was not going to become part of.

There was a dark part of me thinking about that 30k. Wow! I could pay off Fat Tony or simply take the cash and run, set up somewhere else. No, don't be so bloody stupid you idiot! You will spend the rest of your life in jail. An ex-cop in protection in Strangeways - wonderful!

If only there was a way though to get rid of someone without killing them. That way Adele would be happy and so would Fat Tony, and I would still be alive at the end of the month. Can't be done, can it? How the hell can you kill someone, but not actually kill them? How can you convince an intelligent woman like Adele that her husband is dead, so she pays the money?

There was no such plan. It was impossible, but there was something in the back of my mind, could it be done? I would need to act quickly before Adele went somewhere else or fat Tony came knocking.

By now the coffee was tepid at best. I needed to go home, make something to eat, get some sleep. Tomorrow is Friday and Adele's Saturday deadline was not that far away. I was just about to stand up when my phone buzzed again in my pocket.

Damn, Jenks. I forgot about him. I needed to reply and find out what he knows. I pulled the phone from my pocket. I guess he's texted me again, wondering where the hell I am. Perhaps he has got some more earth-shattering information. I popped my code in and selected 'text messages'.

TEXT MESSAGE FROM – O2.
Dear customer, please remember that you need a
minimum of £10 credit to get your next bundle.

Damn, that's not what I was expecting. Never mind, I need to call him and see what this is all about. I fumbled through the menus, looking for his mobile number...it was in here somewhere.

Select Contacts.
Names.
J-K-L
Jenks-MOBILE.
Phone Jenks-mobile.

I put my old Apple iPhone to my ear and waited for the phone to start ringing. It was a moment or two, but nothing happened. I looked at the screen to see if the call had connected. As I did that, I heard a click and I put it back to my ear.

"This number has been disconnected"

"What?", I redialled but the same bland response, "This number has been disconnected."

"Jenks, you bloody idiot! What the hell are you playing at? You need to put some credit on your phone. Ok, think, yes, he has a landline number. He might be home by now."

Select Contacts.
Names.
J-K-L
Jenks-HOME.
Phone Jenks-Home.

The line connected immediately and started to ring, "Come on Jenks, pick up! I need to know what you found out. This is important."

I hate it when the phone just rings and rings. I get that sinking feeling, I just know no one is there. What made this occasion worse was Mrs Walker and her missing daughter. The absolute panic on Mrs Walker's face was still clear in my mind. She needs my help. That idiot Jenks seemed to have something important to tell me, perhaps the answer to what had happened, and I couldn't get in touch with the scum bag.

"Pick up you……"

The phone clicked……. "Detective Inspector Deborah Smith, can I help?"

My mouth opened, but nothing came out. I expected to be talking to some minor drug dealer and sometimes a cocaine user, not a detective inspector.

"Hello, is anyone there? Can I help?"

I wanted to put the phone down. I guess it was a kind of fight or flight response. I didn't have a ready answer as to why an ex-cop, turned private detective wanted to speak to some local ne're-do-well smack head.

Ok Hunter, just say something. You need to find out why the hell a DI is in Jenk's place, and you need to do it now.

"That's come as a bit of a surprise, detective. I was expecting to hear from my friend."

"You know Mr Jenson then? May I ask your name, sir?"

"Sorry, my name is Lee Hunter. I am a friend of Jenks, sorry Mr Jenson. What's happened to him?"

"I am sorry to say that there has been an incident involving Mr Jensen. I can't be any more explicit at this time."

She had that well trained, *'don't give anything away'* inflection in her voice. I knew there was no point in asking anything else, but I thought I would give it a try.

"An incident, what sort of incident?"

"I am sorry Mr Hunter, but I can't say anything else at this time."

"I need to know. He is a very good friend of mine. Listen, I am an ex-DI with the Met Police. I know the protocol, but it's important that I find out what's happened to him."

There was a long silence and I thought I heard a muffled sound, like she had put her hand over the receiver and was talking to someone in the background.

"Mr Hunter, I can't be more explicit I am sorry, but if you call into the station tomorrow morning at about 9am, I might be able to help you some more. Just ask for Detective Inspector Smith. I will be there and we can have a chat. It's the large building at the top end of Lord Street. Do you know where it is?"

"Yeah, I do. What department are you in? Just in case they ask?"

"I am in the Murder Squad, second floor. They all know me there."

The shock ran through me like a bolt of lightning. She had said '*the Murder Squad*'. Murder! Jenks had been murdered? It wasn't a surprise I must admit. Low life drug dealers like Jenks die all the time. A deal gone wrong, someone after his money, in debt to the wrong person, dealing on someone else's patch. But this was Jenks, he was never a good guy, but he was my friend!

Thing was though, he was a very street wise guy. Just did enough to get by, never sticking his head too far above the parapet. He was a survivor, not some dumb junkie who thought he could make the big time.

The thought that had crossed my mind is that it could be the information he got for me. No, surely not. It wasn't that explosive, was it? He couldn't have come across something so dangerous that it had cost him his life, could he? No, I was just being paranoid. Putting 2 and 2 together and coming up with 5. The end of the month meeting with Fat Tony was beginning to make me jumpy. I had to try and relax, some bloody hope of that.

Go home, get some sleep and go see DI Deborah Smith in the morning. She will fill you in. It'll turn out to be a drugs deal gone wrong...mark my words.

Meeting with DI Smith
Friday Morning, 7:30am.

The alarm jolted me out of my dream. I couldn't remember exactly what it was about, but it did include being naked with my next-door neighbour. Rather strange really given that she had never spoken to me, even after living next to her for just over a month or so.

Anyway, I had to get up. DI Smith would not wait around all morning and I had to get over to the main police station as soon as I could. I tried to push myself out of that warm and comfortable double bed, but it was cold outside and I just couldn't manage it. I drifted back into that warm and safe place and fell into a deep sleep.

That bloody horrible noise shook me awake again - the ten minutes snooze timer had elapsed and I had to get up this time despite the cold. I swung my feet out and onto the floor. Now was the time, get up! I have never been a morning person. Much better in the afternoons or even in the evenings, more time to line your thoughts up for the day.

I blundered into the bathroom as I looked in the mirror. The news of the previous day came flashing back. Jenks has been murdered, or at least a detective inspector from the Murder Squad was at his place and it didn't take too much imagination to work out what had happened. The question was, why? I couldn't help thinking it was something to do with me. The information he had managed to acquire, what was it he said in his text, *"You will never bloody believe what I have found out, man this is unbelievable."*

So, what the hell had he found out? More importantly, how would I ever get to know? There was no chance of me ever finding out now. Damn it all! That must have been significant. Jenks never got excited about anything, except cocaine and cheap hookers. Still, perhaps this DI Deborah Smith might know something. Problem is, would she ever tell me?

I eventually found a parking space and made the short walk to the police station located at the top of Lord Street, in Albert Street. From the façade, it looked a classic 1930's build. Not the most imaginative by today's standards, but one that had clearly stood the test of time.

The desk Sergeant looked up as I entered the reception area. A man in his early fifties, grey hair, tall athletic build. He had that look of retirement being just around the corner, a look I had seen many times before. It was difficult to explain, but it was obvious his mind was more interested in his retirement home in Spain rather than the job in hand.

"Yes, sir. Can I help?"

"Certainly Sergeant. I am here to see DI Smith. She is expecting me."

Without replying, he picked up the phone, looked at the telephone list on the wall next to him and dialled the number. It was a few seconds before anyone answered and I was beginning to worry that no one was there.

"Hi Pete, it's Sergeant McDonald on reception. Is Deborah in this morning? There is a chap here that she's supposed to be seeing?"

I could hear the muffled sound of a man's voice at the other end, then there was a silence before he spoke again.

"Cheers Pete. I will get him to wait down here."

Sergeant McDonald put the phone down carefully and then looked up.

"She will be down in a few minutes sir. Would you like to take a seat?"

I thanked the Sergeant and sat down on one of the hard plastic chairs on the opposite wall. The reception areas of police stations had never been the most luxurious of places. The less there was to damage the better, I guess.

A few minutes turned into thirty, but eventually the red door at the side of the reception desk swung open and in walked a tall woman, late thirties, longish brown hair, with a bright smile. The way she bounced into the space indicated an athletic nature, perhaps someone who enjoyed outdoor sports.

She came directly over to me and held out her hand, and despite the pain in my right knee, I got to my feet and accepted the greeting.

"Good morning, Mr Hunter. Please to meet you. Sorry to have kept you waiting, but I had a meeting to attend about your friend, Mr Jenson."

"That's no problem, inspector. I know how busy it can get in your line of work. I just wanted to find out any more details about what happened, he was a good friend of mine."

"Ok, Mr Hunter. Well, if you come with me, we can jump into one of the interview rooms and we can have a chat."

I knew exactly what that meant, *'let's see if this guy had anything to do with it. Does he have an alibi, was he involved?'*

"That's great, thanks inspector. More than happy to help."

She ushered me down a long corridor. It had that sweaty, perhaps fearful smell left by people who might well have been in a lot of trouble and knew it. It was a bland and neutral place, lights regularly spaced, numbered doors with red and green lights above.

We stopped at number five. She turned the thumb lock on the door, opened it and showed me inside. I sat down on another hard plastic chair. There was the usual recording equipment on the desk and a camera in the corner. It felt like old times.

"Now, Mr Hunter, what do you know about Mr Jenson, his movements, friends, enemies etc?"

She smiled a well-rehearsed smile, one that she had used a million times before - friendly without being personal.

"Before we begin, DI Smith, I spent twenty-five years in the Met Police. I had attained the rank of Detective Chief Inspector, so please feel free to check that out. Now, I don't suppose you believe a word of that, but it's true and I know exactly how this interview is going to pan out, so let's get to the point.

Mr Jenson, or Jenks as he preferred, was a friend of mine and helped me in some of my investigations. I know he was a petty criminal, and he had a considerable record, but he had an uncanny knack of finding stuff out. So, I used him and occasionally paid him. I rang him yesterday to have a chat, no more than that, to see if he had anything interesting to tell me. I know you are going to ask me about my whereabouts, so if you check the till receipts and the CCTV cameras of the Hesketh Arms in Churchtown, you will find my credit card was used to pay for some drinks on the evening in question. I can also give the names of credible witnesses who I had meetings with during the afternoon."

She smiled, this time a somewhat more genuine effort, and then she laughed, looking down at the desk.

"OK, Mr Hunter. I can see you know the drill, so let's get to the point. I think you might have guessed what happened to your friend by now. So why was he killed and by whom? That's what we need to find out."

"If I knew that DI Smith, I might still have my friend with me. I don't have a clue. He was not a man to make enemies. He was just a low life who existed in the margins, under the radar, almost being straight but not quite a real criminal, if you know what I mean?

He was asking around for me. See if there was any information on a missing girl, Gwen Walker. Her mum Kim Walker got in touch, said that she wanted some extra work doing on the missing person's case. It felt a bit odd really. I just got this gut feeling that all wasn't as it should be. I told her to get in touch with you guys, but she said she had, but there was something else to this case and she couldn't tell me what.

I tried my best to find out, but she was absolutely panic stricken and wouldn't tell me a thing other than, Gwen was taken."

"She was taken? How did she know that?"

"That's what I asked her, but she was adamant that she has been taken, no other scenario was even in play. So, I sent my friend Jenks off to see if there was any word on the street. Taken could also mean kidnapped, it could mean debt, bad deal gone wrong, it's serious I am sure of that. I got a text from Jenks saying that he had some important information, so I phoned him, that's when you picked the phone up.

It's entirely possible that Jenks paid for that information with his life DI Smith. I know there could, and probably are, another dozen reasons why someone bumped him off, but it's possible."

"OK, Mr Hunter. I need to speak to the MISPER Team. See where they have got to with the investigation."

"Listen, DI Smith, let's not get too excited about all of this. There is probably nothing in it, but if there is, and she has been kidnapped, then her life may well be at risk. I also promised Mrs Walker my absolute discretion, but given Jenk's murder, I think things have gone up another level."

"I agree, Mr Hunter. Have you got any contact details? I will keep you informed and don't worry, we will treat this with the greatest of discretion and tact."

"This is my card. Better use the mobile number. Oh, and another thing, did you recover Jenk's mobile? There might be a bit of info on there for me?"

"Sorry, Mr Hunter. We have searched the place thoroughly, no mobile. I thought it strange given his drug dealing, but there isn't one there. There are other things missing - laptop, and his car. Seems that someone wanted to make sure they had whatever they had come looking for. It looked like someone has done a very thorough job or has employed someone to do the same. If this was a drug deal gone wrong, then why take his belongings? What use could a mobile phone be do a degenerate drug dealer? Why take his car? If it was worth £50, they would be lucky?"

"Listen, DI Smith, I am going to make my way to the office. If you have finished with me? I need to think about this and try to figure out exactly why this happened to Jenks. You have my contact details, so please get in touch anytime you want and please keep me updated on the case. Also, please ask you colleagues in the MISPER Team to tread softly. I did promise Mrs Walker discretion. She is more than worried, she is frightened!"

"I will, Mr Hunter. I will need to speak to you again, and if you come up with anything on this case you have to pass that on. Do I make myself clear?"

"Crystal, DI Smith. Don't worry."

DI Smith escorted me out of the station and back onto Albert Street. The day had turned into a muggy affair. Gathering grey clouds suggested a storm in the making, perhaps indicative of my life in general. It took a few minutes to reach the carpark at the back of Wayfarers Arcade. I flashed my contract pass and entered.

I sat in the car as the first drops of rain began to patter onto the roof. I had been thinking about the case of the missing girl on the way to the office. The more I mulled the whole thing over, the more I began to think the murder of Jenks had something to do with it. The problem was, whatever he found out was now lost forever. His mobile phone and his laptop were gone. I guess they would have been smashed by now and thrown into the local canal.

I jumped out of the car and made the run towards the main building. The rain was becoming more persistent. I pushed the key into the office door lock and it turned clicking as it did so. As I pushed the door open, I was greeted by that familiar smell of cigarettes. Goodness only knows why. The door slammed shut behind me, "damn I didn't get any milk. I guess it's black coffee again."

I gave a cursory glance over to the phone on my desk. I didn't expect any messages as business had been decidedly bad of late. Well, that was before the last 24 hours! I saw the little red-light flashing. I almost ignored it as first, "it's probably the Inland Revenue again, wanting their 3k in tax that I didn't have."

I filled the kettle and clicked it on. One coffee and one sugar into a cracked blue mug. I then turned and decided to listen to the answer phone. It was bound to be someone wanting money. Perhaps Fat Tony giving me the final warning about the end of the month.

I sat at my desk, reached forward and pressed the 'REVIEW' button and listened with no great enthusiasm.

YOU HAVE TWO MESSAGES AND NO SAVED MESSAGES.
PRESS STAR TO LISTEN TO YOUR FIRST MESSAGE.

FIRST MESSAGE.

"Hello, Mr Hunter. This is Adele. I need to speak to you as soon as possible. Things have taken a turn for the worse. Please call me, I need your help. I think he is going to kill me. Please ring me as soon as you get this message."

SECOND MESSAGE.

"Hi mate! Your best snout Jenks here. Listen, no point in coming around tonight. I am off out. Got a bit of a deal on, you know how it goes. Anyway, about that girl who's gone missing. Sorry I couldn't leave any more information when I texted you, but I had no more credit.

Anyhow, this is some hot news. Don't know if I believe it myself, but it comes from a reliable source, so it's got to be good mate.

The fact of the matter is, she has been taken, kidnapped, bloody cheek of the man. Anyway, it's all about her dad. He owes bundles of cash to a big boss, so they have taken her until he pays them back. Apparently, they have threatened to sell her into the sex trade if he doesn't pay up, and according to what I have been told, they bloody mean it. You have got to sort this out as soon as you can, Lee. These guys are for real. They are callous bastards. Trust me!

Anyway, got a date tonight so speak soon."

There was a click as the phone went dead.

NO MORE MESSAGES.

"Jenks, you bloody idiot! Who the hell are 'they'? Where are they holding the kid and where do I start?"

I couldn't believe what had just happened. Talk about half a job. Great information from Jenks, but what the hell did it mean? The kettle clicked off behind me, without thinking I got up, poured the boiling water and stirred the cup. I perched myself on the edge of the worktop and scratched my head as I gazed at the steam whirling up from the cracked mug in my right hand.

I wasn't sure if this was a step forward or no step at all. At least I knew she has been taken and why. I had to contact Mrs Walker and give her the news. Somehow, I knew she was already aware of the details. Thing was, what else did she know?

I sat back down at my desk and readied myself for the conversation with Mrs Walker. As soon as I could find her number. Before I could dial there was a knock at the door. It wasn't just a tap. It was more like a blow.

"Bloody hell! People actually want to see me! I must have done something right this week, or perhaps something very wrong. Come in, it's not locked!"

The door swung open with some alacrity, and in strode Adele, dressed to the nines, perfect hair and makeup. She slammed the door behind her so hard I thought it would break. She clearly had been crying. She took a huge breath and started to speak.

"That bastard hurt me last night. I had to go to A and E to get it put right. If you don't sort it out now, I will do the job myself. I hate that fuck. He is the lowest of the low and I don't care if they take the cars, jewels and clothes off me, he has to go and now!"

The tirade took me back somewhat. I am used to verbal's during my time in the Met, but not from such a refined and beautiful woman.

"Adele, please take a seat. You need to calm down. You can't just go around killing people. The police don't like it you know, and you end up spending the rest of your life in jail."

"I don't care. I am sick of him! You don't know what it's like. I deserve better than him. Please, Mr Hunter. Get him out of my life and do it now!"

"Listen Adele, I am more than happy to put the frighteners on your husband. I could even organise a lady I know to engineer a compromising situation. You might even be able to divorce him and take all his money, but I am not an assassin. You have got the wrong guy."

"I have got the right man, Mr Hunter. I have got you. A down on his luck, bankrupt PI, with debts all over town. Don't underestimate me, I have done my homework. I know about you, your past, your debts. You need my money, you need this job otherwise you will end up just as dead as I want my husband."

How the hell did she know all of that? A lucky guess perhaps? Maybe a good lawyer could find out much of it. She was either a very clever woman or knew someone with insider knowledge on me and my situation. Maybe she was both, but I had to admit, she was spot on.

"Look, give me a few days to come up with a plan. You said Saturday. How about we meet in the Great Himalayas restaurant on Lord Street, Saturday night, say about 8pm? I am sure I can come up with a plan to get rid of him that won't involve both of us spending the next twenty years in Strangeways sowing mailbags. Just give me a chance. I will get the job done Adele, trust me."

"OK, Mr Hunter. You have until 8pm on Saturday. But let me say this, if there is any chance that the bastard could come back to get me, then the deal is off. If he can kill me, he will, Mr Hunter. He does not suffer from the same moral issues as you do. Also, if he finds out you had a hand in it, he will kill you as well, and I don't use those words loosely. When I say kill, I mean guaranteed death, not a kicking behind the local bar!"

The look on her face confirmed what she had just said. Irrespective of what the end game was with her husband, if this went wrong, things were going to get ugly. I had to come up with a plan and it had to be good. I either had to convince Adele to leave him and seek out a better life or I would have to kill him. Neither alternative seemed either plausible or possible. What the hell was I going to do?

"Right, Adele. We will meet Saturday. I will have a solution for you, so don't be late."

She didn't reply. She just turned and stormed out of the office, slamming the door behind her. The smell of her perfume wafted back towards me as the door crashed into the frame. She might have been a beautiful woman, but she was not someone to be trifled with. Why oh why didn't I just say no and walk away sooner?

Anyway, Saturday was a while away yet. First things first, I needed to have a chat with Mrs Walker. I had some very searching questions to ask, and I had to be discreet. I couldn't really tell her that the man who found this information paid for it with his life. To be honest, I wasn't quite sure what I was going to say, but I picked up the phone and dialled the number.

"Hello, Walker residence."

At least it was Mrs Walker. Her voice sounded broken and rough. She had clearly been crying. I didn't blame her of course. I had dealt with dozens of such cases, but it never got any easier. I had two daughters of my own and the inevitable comparisons would flash through my mind.

"Mrs Walker, it's Lee Hunter here. I have some information regarding your daughter, and I need to ask some more questions. It's not a good idea to do this kind of thing over the phone. I wonder if we could meet somewhere in private for a chat?"

There was one of those prolonged and awkward silences over the phone. I was just about to ask again when...

"You can come to our house if you like, Mr Hunter. It's as good a place as any, and at least we can talk in private."

"That's great, Mrs Walker. I will be there in about thirty minutes, if that's ok?"

"I will be here Mr Hunter, goodbye."

The phone clicked and went dead. That was a bit odd though. I said I had some more information and she didn't even ask what it was. If someone had said that about my missing family member, I would want to know what information you had? It kind of confirmed what I already knew. She was fully aware of what had happened to her daughter and she just wanted me to find out why someone had taken her.

I launched myself out of the office and onto Lord Street. It was pouring down. Not so bad being under the verandas and the cover of Wayfarers Arcade, but I soon got wet as I exited and ran into the carpark. The car immediately steamed up, and I hit the various demist buttons, pressed start and set off for Stretton Drive and my meeting with Mrs Walker.

An Industrial Estate in Southport.

The place was very cold and foreboding. There was no sound except her breathing. Her hands were tied behind her back. They had been hurting, but now were completely numb. Her back ached remorselessly. The pounding of the muscles was unbearable as the wooded chair pushed into her flesh.

The blindfold had slipped somewhat allowing at least some light to enter. She was completely unaware how long she had been sat here, but thirst and hunger had begun to take its toll.

Someone entered the room. They seemed to be a long way off. A door closed behind them. Their steps were slow and measured. Feet crunched on the floor to the sound of broken glass, dust and emptiness. She began to shake uncontrollably. The taste of vomit filled her mouth as a warm flow ran down her leg and into her trainer.

The person got closer and stopped, then moved behind her. She railed against the restrictions holding her, but to no avail. She could hear the breathing as the person got closer, then something pulling at her bonds. Perhaps loosening them. Her arms fell by her side, but the pain in her hands resumed with a horrific pounding.

"Why don't you take that blindfold off Gwen? There's nothing stopping you now. You are free."

She didn't move, couldn't. Her body was wrecked with pain from the result of sitting tied to a chair.

"Come, let me do it for you. You must be frightened, Gwen, but there is no need. Some of these guys have been neglectful. They forget how frightening it must be for you."

She welcomed the blindfold being removed even though the light dazzled her eyes. Gwen looked around. The area looked like an abandoned warehouse or an industrial unit. It was completely empty. The floor was a dusty grey concrete, as were the walls. There didn't seem to be any openings in the walls. The only light being provided by roof windows running high up on either side of the building.

She could sense him lurking behind. She craned her neck around to try and catch a glimpse. Standing just behind her right shoulder was a man, perhaps in his sixties, with shoulder length grey hair. He had a scruffy appearance, unshaven, a grubby blue fleece and jeans. He wasn't much taller than she was. He was scrawny, with a drawn face and sunken blue eyes.

"So, Gwen, I bet you are feeling a little better now those ropes are off. Just try and relax and this will be over before you know it."

He moved around in front of her. He had a large bottle of water in one hand and a packet of supermarket sandwiches in the other.

"I am going to leave these here. Try and eat something or at least drink the water. There is a toilet in that room, over in the corner. I will be back in a couple of hours. I have a few questions I need to ask, but don't worry, nothing too serious."

Without saying another word, he turned and walked briskly towards the door from which he came. He exited, locking it behind him and the place was quiet again. The gloom and terror returned, settling like winter snow.

Stretton Drive. The Walker Residence.
Saturday AM.

I hated calling on people in their own homes. I don't know why. It just seemed a little too personal somehow? Anyway, I was here now and I needed to clear a few things up with Mrs Walker - namely why her daughter 'had' gone missing? It was time for the truth. A good friend of mine may have paid the ultimate price for poking around in this sorry little tale, so I owed it to him to get to the bottom of things.

I rang the bell for the second time. There was a suggestion of a chime from inside the house. I stood back to see if anyone was upstairs, but nothing. Just another fine semi in a nice part of Southport. I looked down the side. There was no garage, just a drive and then the side entrance. Maybe I should take a walk around the back. Perhaps she is in the garden? I was just about to sally fourth when I heard the front door opening.

"Hello? Is there anyone there?"

"Sorry, Mrs Walker. I am here. Just about to go around the back."

"Come in, Mr Hunter. How can I help?"

I followed her into the kitchen. Blue fronted units and a huge glass window overlooking a long garden. I wish my scummy flat looked this good.

"Grab a seat, Mr Hunter. I will put the kettle on."

"Call me Lee, Mrs Walker. I prefer a degree of informality. In any case, Lee is considerable shorter the Mr Hunter."

"Only if you call me Kim. Now, how do you take your coffee?"

"Thanks, Kim. Black, one sugar."

"There you go, Lee. Now, how can I help?"

"There is no easy way of saying this Kim, so I will come straight to the point. I know your daughter was kidnapped. I think this was due to debts accrued by your husband. You should have told me earlier Kim. Why didn't you?"

She looked at me with daggers in her eyes. There was a certain anger in her eyes, a visceral flash of rage. She had been found out and didn't expect it. Someone else knew her story, knew the lies she had been telling and she didn't like it.

"Sorry Lee, I am not sure what you mean. Kidnapped, debts?"

"Listen Kim, I spent a quarter of a century in the police force. I completed many a long year in the MISPER Team, so please don't try and pull the wool over my eyes. I have seen every possible situation, heard every conceivable story. Your daughter's life is at risk...right now, today. If you don't start telling me the truth, I will walk away and anything that happens to her will be your fault. I have seen situations like this and they never ever end well. There is a very good chance that she will die if you don't start being straight with me."

There was a long silence. She turned around and looked out of the window. I couldn't tell what her exact reaction had been, but it had better be the one I wanted. There was no point in me continuing in the way she wanted - just kicking the dust around to see what, if anything, came up. I needed the truth so I could focus all my efforts in getting her daughter back before it was too late. The problem was, in my inner mind, I believed it was already too late!

Eventually she turned back to look me. It was clear from her face that she was very angry indeed. I expected to be thrown out at any minute, but she was the boss though. It was all up to her, including saving the life of her daughter.

"Right, Mr Hunter. You may be right about her being kidnapped, but I don't know why? As for my husband, he has also gone missing. I have not seen or heard from him since Sunday night. As for the debts, I know nothing about them. I just want my daughter back and I want her back now!"

"Then you are going to have to level with me, and please remember I have spent all of my working life listening to people who are trying to spin me a line. I can see right through them like I can see right through you. You knew what had happened to your daughter, so why didn't you tell me? And please don't suggest that you didn't know anything about your husband, or his present whereabouts."

"Please, Mr Hunter, Lee. I am desperate, you have to help me."

"Then you need to tell me all that you know. I must know everything or I won't be able to help you. Make no mistake about this Kim. If I find out that you aren't telling me the truth, I will drop this case with immediate effect and any chance of finding your daughter will simply disappear!"

She stared at me for a moment or two, weighing up the consequences of telling me everything or me walking out of her life for ever.

"OK, Lee. This is everything I know, and I mean everything. Tuesday after school my daughter went missing. That night I phoned the police who put a plan into action, but of course, nothing has been resolved. It's now Saturday morning and I am desperate, Lee.

I have not seen my husband since last weekend. He went out for a drink on Sunday night and I haven't seen him since. I have rung and texted him, but nothing. To be honest, there isn't anything strange about that. He often goes missing for days on end, but he says it's just business. I don't ask anything more. I have learnt to keep my thoughts to myself regarding his business and private life."

"Why do you say that, Kim? Learnt to keep your thoughts to yourself?"

"He doesn't seem to have any kind of regular work. He spends hours on his phone, days on end in his home office, never puts a suit on and rarely goes out during the day. He often disappears for a long weekend though, or several days in the week. Don't get me wrong, we are never short of money. Always lots of cash in the joint account. He loves buying me nice things to wear, latest fashions for Gwen, best food for the freezer, expensive holidays every year. I am always well taken care of, but I have long since given up trying to find out what it is that he does for a living. He just says, *'leave it up to me darling. I am the man and it's my duty to provide'*. If I push him any further, he gets angry and just turns away."

"Do you think his work has anything to do with Gwen disappearing?"

"You tell me, Lee. I can't say one way or another. You spoke about debt. Well, there is currently 15k in the savings account and a further 3k in the current account. We are not short of money, never have been."

I didn't want to alarm her but some of the amounts of money I have come across in the Met were staggering. Plenty of these big-time criminals would have 15k in their wallets! I have been there on raids when we seized hundreds of thousands of pounds in cash. If her husband was in debt to a big-time criminal gang, the money in their savings account would probably be the equivalent to the £115-67 that I had in my account!

"Can we therefore assume that the disappearance of your husband is linked to that of your daughter?"

"I don't know, Lee. He didn't seem unduly worried about anything. Things seemed somewhat normal, but the obvious conclusion is yes, it is."

"Right, so who is he involved with? Unless we know that we might never sort this out."

"Lee, I don't know who he is involved with. I have never known that. That's what I hoped you could find out. He has never disclosed anything about his business dealings and there is never anything of the bank statements other than the amounts being paid in. Trust me, I have tried to find out about things all of our entire married life, but whatever he does is well hidden Lee. I know nothing, nothing at all."

"OK, Kim, leave this with me. This is clearly not the normal MISPER case as the regular rules don't apply. Probably your daughter is being held somewhere and at this present time is relatively safe and well. It's important that you contact me if you find out anything more or if they contact you.

You must always keep the local cops informed. Don't leave them out of the loop on this. They will have contacts and intelligence they can use.

Whilst these people won't want to harm your daughter, she is the only thing they have that will resolve whatever is troubling them. But there is a time limit on this.

We need to find her, but we also need to find your husband. He has the key to this and only he knows how to unlock the situation. Have you got a holiday home, caravan, boat somewhere where he might have gone?"

"No, I have tried to think of where he might be hiding, but nothing has come to mind."

"I am sorry to ask this Kim, but does he have anyone who might be willing to put him up for a while? Perhaps a lady friend?"

"Who knows Lee? As I said he disappears from time to time. The thought has occurred to me but if that's the case, I don't know who she might be."

At this point she dissolved into tears. It was the first time she had showed any weakness or emotion other than fear. She gripped onto the kitchen worktop with all the strength she had. At any moment, she looked like she could fall off the tall stool she was sitting on.

I stood up and walked over to her. She wrapped her arms around me, sobbing as she buried her head in my chest.

"Lee, you have to find her. She is my beautiful Gwen. She is my life. Please sort this out."

I held onto her tightly. The problem was, I had no idea where to start. Her husband could be anywhere. It wasn't beyond the bounds of possibility that he was already dead. As for her daughter, goodness only knows where she was, perhaps Jenks was on to something, but he was dead.

One thing was certain - this was a very serious situation. Jenks had been murdered, her daughter had been taken, and her husband was, well goodness knows where?

An Industrial Estate in Southport.

The key clunked into the lock and she stood up and ran to the far side of the unit, shaking uncontrollably. As the door opened, she saw the grey-haired skinny man has returned. He looked at her and smiled and then turned and locked the door behind him.

"Gwen, sorry I have been so long. Is there anything I can get you? I see you have drunk some of the water, but you must try and eat. Keep your strength up dear."

She pushed herself into the corner, as far away as possible from this man, further into the darkness. She was shaking violently. She was trapped, unable to flee or summon help.

He advanced towards her and stopped short of the wooden chair in the middle of the room. The light from the glazed panels in the roof illuminated him, casting shadows down his angular face, making his eyes appear even more sunken than before.

"Come on, Gwen. I won't hurt you. Come over here so we can have a chat. I have a couple of mars bars here. Look, I will pop them on the chair. You can eat them a bit later if you like."

He pulled the two chocolate bars from his jeans pocket and dropped them on the chair in front of him. One of them bounced onto the floor, kicking up a puff of dust as it hit the concrete.

"Listen, sweetheart. I need to ask you a couple of questions and you need to answer me. The thing is, if I don't get the answers from you, some more men, very nasty men, will come in here to ask you the same questions and they won't be as nice as me. So, come over here and listen to what I have to say."

She wanted to move and comply with the instructions she was given, but she couldn't. An invisible force seemed to be holding her in place, keeping her tied into the corner.

To her horror, he started to walk towards her. Slowly at first, but then quicker as he got closer. He had a sickly smile on his face. She could see his rotten teeth, yellow and brown. He held out a hand, fingers stained with nicotine, fingernails grubby and long.

It wasn't long before he was standing in front of her. The smell of his rotten breath made her feel sick. His dirty appearance disgusted and repulsed every fibre of her soul.

"Now, Gwen. You are such a pretty girl. Look at you. Lovely auburn hair, pretty blue eyes. I love your sweater. Red is my favourite colour, and those jeans, they really look great on you. It would be a shame if these nasty men came in here and hit you. I would hate to think that was happening. All you need to do is answer my questions. How about it, Gwen? What do you say?"

She wrapped her arms around herself as tightly as she could. She was a strong girl. Her father had taught her to be resilient, face danger and not back down.

"What do you want?"

"That's nice, Gwen. At least you are speaking. All I need to know is where your father is? You see, he seems to have gone missing and he has something that belongs to my boss, and he wants it back."

"I don't know what you mean, missing?"

"Gwen, he won't answer his phone or anything. Where do you think he might have gone? Is he hiding somewhere you know? Perhaps a secret place he might go?"

"I have no idea what you are talking about. He must be at home. Go and ask my mum. Now let me go! I need to go home!"

"Sorry, my dear. I need you to answer me. You must know where he is. You must at least have an idea? If you can't help us, we will keep you here until he gives my boss what he wants. Look I have your mobile here. Why don't you ring him and ask him where he is? Ask him to come here perhaps?"

He pushed the Apple iPhone 12 towards her, "Go on, Gwen. Give him a call."

She snatched the phone, entered the pin code and selected her father from the favourites list. The phone clicked and started to ring. It rang for several minutes, but there was no answer.

"That's a shame, Gwen. Why don't you try and send him a text? Just say that you have been taken and he needs to contact the syndicate as soon as possible."

She did as she had been asked. The text message disappeared. The man took the phone back and put it into his pocket.

"Well done, Gwen. Now, I must report back to my boss. I will remember to tell him that you have been really helpful. Now don't forget your mars bars. I will be back soon. This will be over shortly, I am sure. See you later, sweetheart."

He turned and left the space, locking the door behind him.

My Grubby Flat.
Saturday PM.

I sat on the sofa, holding the coffee mug in the palms of my hands. My head spinning with the problems facing me. I had Adele wanting me to kill her husband, Fat Tony wanting to kill me, a missing father and daughter, and to be honest, I haven't got a clue what to do about any of it.

Right, get a grip! Mrs Walker can wait until later. First, I must deal with Adele. I was supposed to be meeting her tonight, with a plan! Well, that's going to be a miss then, and I dare say she won't give me the 30k because she feels sorry for me!

I am just going to have to say I can't help. I am not a contract killer, just an ex-cop, so get used to it. The problem was, I couldn't ignore the idea of all that money slipping through my fingers. In fact, last night I had a dream about it blowing away in the wind and in the distance, Fat Tony standing laughing at me. Not nice.

I was just starting to contemplate the idea of throwing myself out of my flat window when the phone rang. I looked down at the table in front of me. It sat vibrating and ringing, slowly pirouetting clockwise as it did so. Should I pick it up or just leave it? Throwing myself out of the flat window did seem like a good idea, but being on the ground floor, it probably wouldn't help.

Right, be professional and answer the phone. You volunteered for this job, so get on with it. I was just in the action of leaning forward to answer the damn thing when the doorbell rang. I sat back in astonishment. A couple of days ago, no one wanted to talk to me and now look - it was like being a major celeb on Oscar night!

I decided to answer the door. It was unlikely to be either Adele, Mrs or Mr Walker or their errant daughter. Better this way. Perhaps a brief distraction from my throbbing head, even if it was someone who wanted to enlighten me in the glories of the Lord. As I stood up, the phone stopped ringing, "never mind, they will leave me a message, I am sure."

I looked through the peep hole in the front door. To my amazement, it was the woman from next door. I wondered what she wanted from me? Kill her ex? A drug deal gone wrong? International terrorists trying to kidnap her? Perhaps, it was something mundane like, "Can I borrow some sugar?" Somehow, I doubted it. The way my life was going now, it was bound to be something major. I opened the door and tried not to look surprised, be cool, smile and be hospitable.

"Hello, everything alright?"

"It is. I saw you the other day and felt bad that I didn't say hello, and just walked away. I was always taught to be respectful and pleasant. It wasn't like me and it's about time that we got to meet. My name is Ruth, Ruth Davenport."

She held out her hand. I looked down and accepted the gesture. Her hand felt small in mine. It was then that I realised I had never really looked at her properly. She was about 50, blonde hair, about 5 foot 4ish, blue/grey eyes, nice figure, and a white, friendly smile.

"Nice to meet you, Ruth. My name is Lee Hunter. Fancy a coffee? I was just about to make one?"

That was a lie and if she did come in, she would see my still hot mug sitting on the table.

"Erm, well why not? Nice way to meet your neighbours, I guess."

I ushered her into the flat and closed the door. I caught sight of another one of those BMW X6's just leaving the carpark. Maybe I won't buy one. They are getting a touch too common, if you ask me. Anyway, I followed her into the living room and quickly picked up the still hot cup and whisked it off into the kitchen.

"How do you take it, Ruth?"

"Oh, white, one sugar is good for me."

"How long have you lived here?"

I caught a glimpse in the corner of my eye as she joined me in the kitchen.

"About four years now. You haven't been here that long though."

"No, just a month or so. My last place went on the market, so I had to vacate."

I poured the hot water into the chipped mugs and returned to the living room, sat down and began to chat. It was lovely to talk to someone who didn't want something doing for them, whose husband or wife wasn't having an affair, didn't want someone monitoring, taking drugs or anything else vaguely detective like.

We sat in my not so glamourous living room and smiled at each other. Two lonely people who just wanted to reach out. The time seemed to fly by. We both had a lot in common - divorce, children about the same age - hers were living with her most of the time.

The evening blended into one long chapter of laughs, silly stories, and chat. It was so nice to talk to someone. I mean really talk like two people who were interested in one another's story. I can't remember the last time I just chatted to another human being. It's odd how you remember enjoying some things, especially when you are reminded how long it was since you experienced them last. Time just melted away. I didn't bother looking at the clock. It didn't seem relevant. It could have been 10pm or 5am. It wasn't important.

Anyway, she went back to her place and returned with a bottle of red. That quickly disappeared, so we launched into my vodka and then the remains of a bottle of gin. I can't remember much after that.

My Grubby Flat.
Sunday AM.

I woke Sunday morning feeling very ill indeed. I had managed to put myself to bed, I think, which was a bonus. I can't begin to explain the taste in my mouth and the pain in my head, but I guess I shouldn't complain, it was self-inflicted! I laid there for some considerable time wishing I was dead and promising myself never to drink again...some hope!

There was however a little nagging feeling in my head. Occasionally you get that feeling something is missing. I should have done something, but what? I couldn't focus my damaged brain on exactly what it was. Perhaps something about last night? No, that wasn't it. I assured myself that nothing happened that I might later regret.

Then it hit me...shit on a stick! I agreed to meet Adele last night, in the fancy restaurant in town. We were due to have a meal and discuss what to do next. It was going to be my big chance to say 'no'. I wasn't going to kill her husband. Instead, I got very drunk with the woman from next door. Not very professional Lee, but I did enjoy it, I think.

Damn it to hell! Well, that's blown any chance of paying off Fat Tony. Perhaps it wasn't a bad thing, I guess. At least I won't get drawn into some sordid murder plot, like a cheap novel and end up doing life and all for 30k. Maybe Ruth had done me a big favour by calling around yesterday. I needed to thank her for that.

I really needed to contact Adele though. I might be strangely pleased on how I missed out on the job, but my professional nature required me to give an apology. I sat up in bed. The room didn't spin, well not very much. Still naked, I dragged my sorry ass out and into the living room. There still sat on the table was my mobile. The very same phone that did a pirouette last night as it rang.

I picked it up, tried to focus on the screen as I put in my security code. The screen had a message and screwing my eyes up, I tried to read the message.

YOU HAVE ONE MISSSED CALL AND ONE NEW MESSAGE.

FIRST MISSED CALL – Adele, yesterday at 17.06.
ONE NEW MESSAGE, LEFT ON SATURDAY AT 17.07. PRESS 3 TO LISTEN.

I thought about that for a minute, 17.06. Odd that she hadn't rung me during the evening demanding '*where the bloody hell are you?*' Perhaps she had given up waiting and just went home. With a bit of luck, she will have become totally exasperated by me and switched to someone else. Now that would be nice. Anyway, I pressed three and sat on the settee to listen to the message.

"Hello, Mr Hunter. It's Adele here. Sorry, but I can't make tonight at the Great Himalayas restaurant. I forgot about a prior engagement. I hate to let folk down, but can't be helped. Anyway, let's meet today. Say lunch in the Bold Arms? It's opposite the Hesketh pub. I have something for you and I think you are going to like it. Anyway, must rush. See you later."

As the announcement reminded me that '*you have no more messages and no saved messages*' my heart sank.

"Damn it, I thought I had got away with that. I imagined her ringing another private detective and trotting out her sad story, trying to get him to pull the trigger on her husband. Now I will have to meet her and all this will start again, but at least I will get the chance to tell her, once and for all, that I won't be doing what she asked. So much for being happy, that will teach me, "you just aren't meant to be happy, Hunter. Accept it and get on with your life."

It was at that precise moment that I heard a noise behind me. I jumped up to see what the hell it was. I had forgotten that I had just jumped out of bed and, of course, in my state of complete undress. In any case, who the bloody hell was in my flat on a Sunday morning?

"Is that your police truncheon or are you just pleased to see me?"

I felt my face turn beetroot red. I looked down at the offending article. I couldn't think of what to do or say.

"Do you always talk to yourself, naked on the settee on a Sunday morning Lee? I don't suppose it's doing anyone any harm. Odd thing though. I must say that I could think of better things to do this time in the morning...certainly on a Sunday."

To my absolute horror, there stood Ruth. Fully dressed, hair a little unkempt, but looking as lovely as she had done the night before. For just one moment, I wanted to walk over and hold her, but I guessed the ensuing charges of sexual assault would not look good on my record.

"Erm, yes, erm sorry Ruth. I will go and put some clothes on."

I rushed past her and into my bedroom, trying to cover myself up as best I could. What the hell was she doing here? What had happened last night?

Once dressed in a pair of jeans and an old T-shirt, I forced myself to go back into the living room. I so much wanted to hide in the bedroom, but that was never going to work. With a deep breath and trying to look relaxed and chilled, I opened the door and walked back into the room. She stood there with a huge smile on her face, shaking her head and giggling.

"I have to say Lee, rather impressive, if somewhat of a surprise. Hey, I am fifty something years old and you are not the first naked man I have seen. So, no problems. I should have warned you first. I guess you are just used to living alone."

She laughed again as she stared down at my still bulging crotch.

"I can't remember what happened last night Ruth. I assumed you went home?"

"Yeah, that was the plan, until we decided to get some sleep at 4am and I realised that my keys were in my bag, which I had left on the kitchen top when I went for the bottle of red. Anyway, you said I could stay in the spare room, which I did. Now that my eldest is back, I can get into my flat again. Don't worry, Lee. You were a perfect gentleman. So, until next time."

With that she turned and with a great big smile left my place, closing the front door behind her. I didn't want her to go. I half reached out, but she was gone. I hoped it wasn't the last time she called in. Perhaps next time I would remember that I wasn't alone when I got up in the morning.

Now all I had to do was make up some cock and bull story for Adele as to why I would be turning down 30k. This wasn't going to be easy. I could almost hear her screaming at me, but there was no way I was going to be her hitman, not a chance.

The Bold Arms, Churchtown.
Sunday Lunchtime.

The carpark was already full at the back of the pub, so I ended up parking opposite Saint Cuthbert's Church and walking across the road. It is a square, with the church on one side and the Bold Arms and the Hesketh pub on two of the others. The fourth side carried the road into Southport from Crossens and Banks. It meandered past the Botanic Gardens, which is a lovely place for a stroll on a sunny afternoon.

I could see her fancy Maserati parked to the side of the Bold Arms. She was waiting inside. I looked up at the sky and for once it was a clear blue, no rain for the short time I thought. That made a change.

As I walked down the pavement towards the driver's door, it reminded me of my time as a traffic cop, stopping speeding or pissed motorists on the streets around London. Those days where well behind me now. I kind of missed them I guess, as well as the camaraderie and great friends I made. I wondered what they were all doing now. Not walking up behind a stunning woman called Adele, sitting in a bright red Maserati, I bet. I saw her glance in the rear mirror as I approached. She slowly opened the door and slid out.

Those long legs and sexy ankles came first, sporting some very expensive looking heels. She took her time, being playful with my desires perhaps or just making sure her image, like her perfume lingered in my consciousness. Her dress rode up just enough to expose her knee. Nothing crass or vulgar, but enough to tease. It made me wonder about her underwear. It's colour and material, the way it must be caressing her perfect curves. Next that flawless body slithered out, long hair blowing in the wind, she was a picture of perfection, dressed in very expensive clothes.

She slowly turned to look at me, a gentle and inviting smile. She was way out of my league. Truly a woman who could have any man she wanted. The thought did strike me as to why she didn't just leave her husband and go and find the next millionaire? The circles she must be moving around in didn't include smelly little Herbert's like me. So why kill him? Why not just find the nearest stockbroker, surgeon or pilot in her address book? There was no doubt about her ability to attract any man she wanted, so why not do that and leave him far behind, and not risk spending the next twenty years in jail?

"Hello, Mr Hunter. I am so sorry about last night. You must have been very annoyed when I phoned."

I laughed inside. Little did she know that I had completely forgotten about the whole thing, especially when Ruth's red wine started to take effect.

"That's OK, Adele. These things happen you know. I settled down and watched the football. No problem."

She opened her bag and fumbled inside before bringing out a white envelope.

"This is for you, Mr Hunter. It's a little cash to help you start with your task. I didn't want to hand it over in the pub. You never know who's watching."

She walked straight up to me and pushed the envelope into my hand. This was going a bit too far. I was just about to turn her down, accepting money was not something I had anticipated doing. I looked around to see that no one had just witnessed what had happened. That was at least a good start.

"Listen Adele, I can't accept this. I need to discuss a few things with you first."

She was just about to reply when her phone started to ring. She plucked it out of her bag, thumbed in the code and put it to her ear. She flicked her hair to one side and turned to face away from me. I couldn't help listening to what she was saying. I guess it's the ex-cop in me.

"What do you mean? He paid that back last week so that bill is settled. No, I can't come over now I am busy. What? No, you can't just ask for more. Look, are you in the office now? Right, well, I will be there in fifteen. We can go for a drink and talk about this."

She turned back to face me. Clearly very annoyed at what had just happened.

"Look Lee, I have to go and sort this out. It looks like we will never actually sit down and eat anything together. I am so sorry. I hate letting people down, it's not what I do. I will ring you tonight and we will sort something out. We can go to a very intimate Italian I know. Very expensive, but extremely discreet. You will like it there."

Without another word, she turned around, walked off to her Maserati and slid back into the driver's seat, leaving me standing outside the pub like a jilted lover. My mind contained flashing images of quiet corners in the Italian restaurant, holding hands and flirting with this goddess and talking the night away. Of course, that was just my sick mind fantasising about an evening with the stunning Adele. Some hope! As my attention returned to some state of normality, I realised I was still holding the white envelope, containing, well goodness knows how much?

I quietly looked inside. It was full of fifty-pound notes. At a guess, I would say about a grand at least and probably a lot more! Now what am I going to do? I needed to give this lot back to her. I ran to the side of the car and knocked on the window. It silently slid down and she looked somewhat bemused, perhaps even shocked as I pushed the envelope back into the car.

"I can't accept this, Adele. I won't be killing anyone. Let's make a date and talk about what I can do, ring me tonight."

She didn't reply. She looked straight ahead as the car a roared off, turning right by the Bold Arms.

Right - a pint and a bite to eat in the pub and start to plan what I am going to say when she finally rings me. This crazy situation was already out of hand. Tonight, I will be putting a stop to it, once and for all.

I sat down at a table in front of the windows overlooking Botanic Road. A very pleasant and historic part of town. My cheeseburger with chips and pint of beer sat on the table in front of me. I was just about to tuck in when my phone buzzed in my pocket.

TEXT FROM – Ruth.
HI LEE, IT'S RUTH HERE. IF YOU ARE WONDERING HOW I GOT YOUR NUMBER, I THINK WE SWAPPED THEM LAST NIGHT, BUT I WAS SO DRUNK I CAN'T REMEMBER DOING IT LOL.

I REALLY ENJOYED LAST NIGHT. IF YOU FANCY A REMATCH, GET BACK TO
ME. XX

I stared at the message for several moments. It was fun last night. Well, I think it was, until this morning that is! I slipped the phone back into my pocket and tucked into my lunch. The thought of another evening with Ruth was very appealing, I must admit. I didn't want to make a mess of it and knowing my life, that was very likely to happen. I would reply in due course, but when things had settled down with Adele. Ruth deserved that much at least.

An Industrial Estate in Southport.

The bag was pulled down over her head. There was no way she was going to see out of this. She could feel it drawing tight around her neck and it gave her a terrifying jolt as it constricted about her throat. She panicked, trying to push those people away, kicking out, more in fear than in anger. She screamed, twisted from left to right, but the men holding her would not be shaken loose.

Someone grabbed her hands and yanked them behind her back. There was a searing pain as her shoulders were pulled behind her in an unnatural movement. Her head was pushed forward and she could feel the sharp plastic of the cable ties cut into her wrists. There was a familiar voice somewhere in the darkness. It was the smelly grey-haired man and his hissing speech reeked of rotten teeth and bad breath.

"Listen you lot! The boss didn't want her harmed. Well, not yet. If she dies, so do we. Let's not kill her until he tells us to, hey!"

She felt the clamour behind her ease slightly, but then she was pulled up to her feet and marched off in the direction of the door.

"Don't start telling us what to do, you little shit. I don't care what happens to her and neither does the boss, so wind your fucking neck in, right!"

"Don't say I didn't warn you lot. Let's not break any bones yet. That's all I am saying."

She felt herself stumble once or twice, and the intense pain in her shoulders as she was pulled back upright. She was being thrown about and being handled like a cheap toy. She couldn't breathe properly, gain her balance or establish her steadiness.

"Try walking, you stupid bitch!"

There was a slap to the back of her head. Flashing lights danced around in her eyes and she stumbled again. This time there was no rescue. She fell to the floor, hit her head and the world went quiet.

"Now look what you goons have done! I hope she's OK. Get her in the van and over to the other site and lock her up in that bloody container."

"Yes, and how long do you think she is going to survive in there? The last victim we locked up lasted 48 hours. She will be dead by Wednesday. Suffocating and crying in the darkness. So go and fuck yourself! As I said, the boss doesn't give a toss about her, just what he is owed."

"I don't care about that. I just want to tell the boss she is alive and we put her in the steel container. What the fuck he does with her after that is up to him, capeesh?"

My Grubby Flat, Again!
Sunday PM.

To be honest, I was absolutely knackered. Last night had wrecked me, and the couple of pints and that burger in the Bold Arms had finished me off. I had decided to go home and have a nice afternoon nap.

I was just drifting off nicely to that warm place just before your brain shuts down completely. It was comfortable in my bed. I had the pillows just as I liked them. A couple of hours should do it. Might meet up with Ruth tonight, I might get lucky, but knowing me, probably not.

The dream started well enough. I was walking down Lord Street towards a crowd of people. They seemed to want to give me lots of money. I quite enjoyed that feeling. All my money woes disappearing in a flash. Trouble was, before they handed me anything, I was being dragged back to reality by the phone ringing and buzzing on the bedside table. I had two choices, ignore it and go back to my dream, or spend the next hour awake and wondering who it was. I decided to answer it. Perhaps if I could stall them, I might be able to do both and go back to sleep again. Fat chance of that!

I didn't bother looking at the caller ID. I was way too sleepy for that.

"Hello, Lee Hunter."

"Lee, it's Kim. Kim Walker. My goodness, please I need your help! Please Mr Hunter!"

The obvious terror in her voice immediately sprung me back into consciousness.

"Slow down Kim! What on earth is the matter?"

"I've got a text, Lee. It's about my daughter. They are going to kill her. She will be dead by Wednesday, Lee. You have got to find her, please!"

The confusion in my mind was overwhelming. Was this another dream? Was I still asleep or had she just said they were going to kill her daughter? I sat bolt upright in bed and looked at the phone.

CALLER ID – Kim Walker. 1:06 seconds.

No, this wasn't a dream. I was wide awake. I had to think, stay calm, be positive, assess the situation and act accordingly.

"Kim, let's take this from the top. What exactly has happened? Take your time and don't leave anything out."

"Lee, they've sent me a text. I will read it. It says..."

'WE HAVE YOUR DAUGHTER. SHE WILL BE DEAD BY WEDNESDAY IF YOUR HUSBAND DOESN'T COME AND SEE US. HE KNOWS WHO WE ARE AND WHY HE HAS TO COME. TELL HIM HE HAS TO SEE THE BOSS OR YOUR DAUGHTER DIES.'

I had to admit this was bloody serious, but I had to stay as calm as I could. Me panicking wasn't going to help the situation.

"Kim, I am on my way. I assume you are in Stretton Drive? I will be there in half an hour. Don't do anything or call anyone until I get there. Do I make myself clear?"

"I will be here, Lee. Please hurry!"

I had a quick wash, threw on some clothes and stormed out of the flat. What on earth was I expecting to do about any of this was beyond me. The only person who knew anything was Jenks and he was dead. The police weren't aware of the kidnap angle and now the girl would be dead in 48 hours. Damn it! I should have picked an easier way to make a living.

The drive over to her house was not an enjoyable one. What the hell was I supposed to do? I could think of just one thing. The problem was, I might end up like Jenks and that really didn't appeal to me.

Murder Squad Office. Southport Police Station.
Sunday Evening.

The phone rang several times before DC Evans finally reached for the receiver. It was Sunday evening and his mates were out on a stag night, but Detective Inspector Deborah Smith wouldn't give him the night off. He was not a happy teddy to say the least. He wondered if he should just let it ring. After all, what the hell was going to happen at this time in the evening? In any case, it was bound to be his mates taking the piss, all out having a good time!

Reluctantly he decided to answer. It could be his boss DI Smith checking up on him, making sure he was still at work. To be honest, he didn't want to get on the wrong side of his boss. She was a formidable woman and someone you wouldn't want to anger, especially as a newly promoted detective constable.

"DC Evans, how can I help?"

"Hi Mike, it's Steve here. I am out with a couple of patrols. They were called to a house in Hillside. The cleaner just arrived for work and, sorry mate, but there's a dead man here. I don't want to spoil your Sunday evening eating your Chinese take-out in the office, but the three bullet holes in his head might just indicate a murder! The last time I checked, that's your department mate. Nothing to do with me. So, get your arse down here as soon as!"

There was a momentary silence as the news filtered through DC Mike Evans head. He had to engage his professional brain and switch off the slightly angry young guy at work whilst his mates were enjoying themselves. This was the beginning of his first case and he didn't want to screw it up. He took a deep breath, focused his mind and began.

"Three bullet holes...that rules out suicide I guess."

"More than likely Mike. Unless he is a very quick shot, you dumb fuck!"

He could hear his friend and colleagues laughing at the other end of the phone.

"Look Mike, I am getting the PCs to secure the scene. Do you want me to call the SOCO's in or do you want to? It's a bloody mess here. Footprints, a smashed mobile, spent cartridges, bloody prints everywhere. Just to help you out mate, it needs securing and securing now. You should be calling in the Crime Scene Officers, but I am more than happy to make the call."

"No Steve, you call them in. I am on my way. I will buzz DI Smith. She can meet us there. What's the address mate?"

"3 Claridge Road. It's opposite the golf club. Bloody great big place. Quadruple garage, swimming pool, garden the size of three football pitches, Rolls Royce parked in the drive, the bloody lot! How the hell people manage to pay for all of this escapes me. Must be worth millions."

"Sit tight, Steve. We are on our way mate. Just don't touch anything! I am phoning the boss now."

Detective Inspector Deborah Smith was relaxing in the bath when her work mobile started to ring. With an air of exasperation and a considerable amount of irritation she reached down and put the wine glass on the floor next to the bath.

"Bloody, bloody hell! Just when you start to relax. What does that stupid DC Evans want now? He'd better not be asking to slip off early. He's going to get an earful from me if he does!"

"DI Smith here. What's up Mike? This better be good, that's all I can say."

"Sorry boss, but there's been a shooting. It's a mess, so I think you should be there. Hillside, opposite the golf club."

"Damn it, Mike! Why on my day off? Couldn't they wait until tomorrow to begin slaughtering each other? Ok, text me the address and I will be there in an hour or so. Have you called the crime scene people?"

"They are on their way boss. I am leaving now. I will see you there."

The phone went dead. DI Smith gazed down the bath towards the tap end.

"Sorry Marcus, it's work. I need to go. I don't suppose I will be back this side of dawn, so see yourself out and don't forget to empty the bath."

DI Smith slammed the front door behind her. The night was damp with the first of the forecasted rain beginning to fall. Still cursing and biting her lip in frustration, she pulled up the collar of her coat in a vain attempt at keeping out the cold and wet. Her old blue Ford Escort was way beyond its best. In fact, it was a miracle it worked at all. As she wound down the window to help clear the windscreen, the smell of the bubble bath on her wafted around the car. She smiled as she remembered the look on Marcus's face when she told him she would have to go. He was a good guy, one of the few. She hated letting him down. She resented the job intruding into her life the way that it did, but it was more than a profession for her. It was a passion.

Eventually she turned into the drive of 3 Claridge Road, Hillside. The car jolted to a stop, a couple of feet behind the silver Rolls Royce parked in the driveway. She made absolutely sure she stopped well before making contact. Her boss would not have appreciated a bill for rear ending a one-hundred-and-sixty-thousand-pound car.

The light had long since faded, but the first of the SOCO's had arrived and a couple of lights had been erected at the front of the house. It cast an oddly yellow hue, illuminating the house, casting shadows upwards like manic fingers pointing towards the night sky. DC Evans came walking from the front of the property. The size and grandeur of the double oak doors and brass fittings impressed him. This was a million-pound house and it looked every bit of it.

She was hardly out of the car when DC Evans jogged up next to her, clearing the driving drizzle from his eyes.

"Evening boss. It's a mess in there! Blood everywhere, broken furniture, empty bullet casings, the lot."

"What killed him?"

"Three shots to the head, blown the back of his scull away. We are assuming it's the man of the house in there. Could be an intruder though."

"Who found him?"

"The cleaner. She was asked to come in this evening. There was supposed to be a party tomorrow afternoon, so they wanted the place looking spick and span. Apparently, not sure who called her - said she would pay double money. Nothing new in that, she often got a late call to come over and clean the place ready for a last-minute bash."

"Where is she now?"

"She's in the SOCO's van - absolutely distraught boss. Not surprised to be honest. Whoever it is in there, it's an awful sight. Turned my stomach for sure. I said I would call an ambulance for her, but she refused. Her husband is on the way. Told her we will need a statement before she goes anywhere though. She seems OK with that."

"Thanks Mike. Keep things moving in there. I am going to have a word with the cleaner. I will be with you in a minute or two."

DI Smith stood in front of the house. Despite the activity of the SOCO's and police, it looked strangely normal concealing the horrors within. She had attended several serious crime scenes during her career and this kind of event was almost always perpetrated by someone known to the victim. Consequently, if this was the man of the house, there was only one person in the forefront of DI Smith's mind at this present time - that was the victim's wife!

The blue flashing lights of the SOCO's van were mildly annoying - casting shadows over the lawn area to the front of the house and reflecting amongst the rain droplets falling around and about. The rear of the van was open. In it sat a woman, possibly 70 years old, small in stature, grey hair. She had that blank staring expression of someone who was in shock. She needed help and the paramedics were going to be called whether she liked it or not. She walked up to the rear of the van, maintaining a calm and professional manner.

"Hi, my name is Detective Inspector Deborah Smith, but you can call me Deborah. I am in charge of this incident. I guess you are feeling very upset right now. I have taken the liberty of calling the paramedics. I really think you should see them. My boss is aware of the incident, but it's now my case, so I would like to have a chat with you if that's OK?"

The woman slowly turned to look at Deborah, but it was clear that emotionally she wasn't there. Her traumatized brain had partly shut down.

"What's your name? You can call me Deborah or Debs if it's easier. Everybody else does."

The lady was shaking, wringing her hands together, rocking slightly front to back.

"Sandra...my name is Sandra Summers."

"Hi Sandra. Now I know you've refused any medical help, but I really think someone should give you the once over. I will stay with you, don't worry. It's just the paramedics. We need to make sure you are OK? What do you say?"

Sandra continued to stare out of the back and into the darkness. She showed no outward emotion, just an empty blankness, a detached visage.

"If that's what you want, Deborah."

"No Sandra, it's for the best. You have been through a terrible ordeal. We need to get you checked out. It won't take a minute and your husband is on the way. It's OK, don't worry. If you prefer, he can stay with you when the paramedics arrive. They are very professional, you know."

"OK, so long as you stay with me until my husband arrives. I feel sick and frightened. It was so shocking to see him like that."

"I will Sandra, I promise. Before they arrive, can I ask, who asked you to come into work today?"

"Oh, it was Mrs Barnes. She insisted that I come in."

"That's great Sandra. I am so sorry to ask, but can I assume that's Mr Barnes in there?"

"Yes, it is. Lovely man, or at least he was."

With that, she burst into tears. DI Smith took the opportunity to wrap a comforting arm around the distraught Sandra Summers. Shock was a terrible thing and could even be a killer. She had to be very aware of that, but she needed as much information as possible whilst it was fresh in Sandra's mind. DI Smith continued to speak in a soft and sympathetic way, just as she had been trained to do in this kind of situation.

"Sandra, you said you had been called in to do some cleaning prior to a party tomorrow. Can you remember who it was who called you in and when that was?"

Sandra Summers looked down at her trembling hands, tears rolling down her face. The tiny droplets splashed onto her fingers as they twitched and writhed together. DI Smith wasn't certain there would be an answer, but she had to try. The first hour after such an incident was very important. Any witnesses must be questions whilst memories were still fresh and not tainted by time.

Sandra Summers took a deep breath and tried to compose herself before answering, "It was Mrs Barnes."

"You said it was Mrs Barnes who called you in. To be clear, Sandra, that's the wife of the man lying dead in there. It was his wife who called you in?"

"Yes, it was early this morning. She asked me to come in for a couple of hours this evening - said she needed the place tidying up for a party tomorrow."

"Did she say anything else, Sandra? Did she mention her husband when she spoke to you?"

"No, she just said to get here about 5pm and her husband would let me in. I thought that a bit odd as I have a key, but I didn't think any more of it. I arrived at about half past four. I checked my watch before my husband dropped me off. I like to be on time you see. The front door was already open, so I walked in and into the main living room and that's where I found him."

Sandra broke down once more, sobbing uncontrollably and DI Smith pulled her close.

"It's OK, Sandra. I can't begin to imagine how you feel, but I am here now. I will make sure you are taken care of. You are safe, don't worry."

"Thanks, Deborah. Do you think they will try to kill me? Do you think I am safe?"

"You are perfectly safe, Sandra. I promise you. This has nothing to do with you. It's more than likely a family matter. I am an expert in these things. It's probably someone close to Mr Barnes - someone who knows him very well. This will be a domestic confrontation, so there is no need to worry at all."

"What? A member of Mr Barnes family did this? That's terrible, Deborah. Mind you, in all the time I have known the Barnes's, I have hardly ever heard of them speak of family members. They don't have any children. I have never seen any parents. I know he has a brother in New Zealand - something to do with engineering, I think? The only family I have ever seen here is Mr and Mrs Barnes. That's about it. They don't even have a lot of friends. Mr Barnes spends much of his time away - certainly most weekdays."

"Do you know what he does and Mrs Barnes for that matter?"

"She doesn't work. She is a lot younger than he is. She just does lunch with her friends, buys expensive clothes and goes to the gym. Mr Barnes has a private healthcare business, small private hospitals, care homes for the rich. They are all over the country. He is a very successful man, you know."

"When was the last time you saw them?"

"I saw Mr Barnes on Friday, when he came home from work. He seemed very happy. He was looking forward to a golf tournament this weekend. He so loved playing golf. His wife popped in and then left. Not sure where she went. That was the last time I saw her. Adele seems to come and go as she pleases. Not sure what she does most of the time."

"Oh, Adele. That's the name of his wife is it, Sandra?"

"Yes, Adele Barnes. She drives a very expensive car. My husband would love one. He says it's a Maserati Ghibili Tofeo. It's bright red with a cream leather interior. It does look nice. She drives it about like it's a race car."

"I don't suppose you know the registration, do you Sandra?"

"Well, it's kind of like her name, something like ADE then with some numbers, I think. I am not an expert on car things. I hate the cost of them and all the pollution they cause."

"That's really helpful, Sandra. I am sure we will find her soon and break the news about her husband. You have been so helpful, and if I am not mistaken, here are the paramedics. I will leave you in their capable hands and I will catch up with you soon, I promise. This is my card. If you ever fancy a chat, just give me a call, and don't worry, this incident has nothing to do with you."

DI Deborah Smith walked back towards the house. The Crime Scene people were carefully moving around in their white disposable suits, taking photos, protecting the scene and erecting screens to deter onlookers from the road. A familiar face appeared from within the house and moved directly towards DI Smith. It was the Senior SOCO, a lifelong friend of Deborah's, and one very much respected by everyone in the force.

"Well Kaye Marie, fancy seeing you here. You get to all the best places."

The two women laughed, "Only by invitation, Debs. It's a bloody awful mess in there. Just as I like it. Nothing like a horrifying murder scene on a Sunday night to finish off the weekend on a high note."

They laughed again. In their line of work, a rather twisted sense of humour sometimes helped, especially in the face of such horror that lay inside the house. It was their way of disguising the distresses of their professions, protecting themselves from the trauma and shock.

"So, what have we got then, Kaye? Apart from a dead man with half a head and blood everywhere?"

"Nothing much at this time. The first sweep hasn't turned up any weapon yet, so you need to organise a search of the surrounding area. I would suggest a medium calibre gun, perhaps a 9mm. The shots must have been delivered very rapidly, so that might suggest a semi-automatic pistol rather that a revolver. Also, some superficial burns would also suggest a point-blank shooting, or should I say, execution!

Not sure of the identity of the deceased, but a couple of photos would suggest it's the occupier - a Mr Francis Jackson Barnes. It's certainly murder. No way did he do this to himself.

His wallet is on the hall table containing over three hundred pounds in cash. Some jewellery upstairs, a very expensive Rolex watch on the deceased and the keys to his Roller, so that might rule out robbery? This looks like a murder for revenge, possibly a contract killing, something along those lines but I will keep you posted."

"Thanks Kaye. I need to find his wife, Adele Barnes. I have a make on her car, so I don't think it will take long. Keep me posted. This is a high profile killing. Not many millionaires get shot in the head three times in this town! The press is going to be all over it, as will the top brass at HQ, so we need to get some answers and quickly."

"Will do, Debs. Oh yes forgot. Just by the body was a business card. Looks like it might have fallen out of someone's pocket. I have it here in this evidence bag. Might be significant. Odd that it lay just by the deceased. Could be the calling card of the killer perhaps, or just a coincidence?

LEE HUNTER.
PRIVATE DETECTIVE.
All types of investigations undertaken.
By the hour, day or contract work.
Absolute discretion assured.
Full references available.
Contact 011743 65994, 24 hours a day.

Stretton Drive. The Walker Residence.
Sunday Night.

Kim Walker was shaking uncontrollably as she opened the door. I felt desperately sorry for her. Gwen had gone missing and would be dead in a couple of days if we couldn't do anything to stop it. Her husband was – well, nowhere to be seen and she felt utterly helpless and none of this was her fault!

Her face was an image of stress and fear - little colour, black bags under her eyes, makeup streaked down her cheeks due to of hours of crying. She opened her arms and fell towards me. I caught her and held on as tightly as I could. Her sobbing made my whole body shake.

"Let's get you inside, Kim. I will make us a drink. Let's see if we can get this thing sorted and your daughter back safely."

She seemed to be a woman lost - utterly destroyed by the events of the past few days. I wondered if things would ever return to normal for her or was this was just the beginning of a life of sorrow, bereavement and torment. I sat her down on the settee in the front room, clicked on the kettle and made two coffees. I dispensed a double scotch into each blue mug. I didn't really think it would help, but I couldn't think of anything else to do.

She took a gulp of the coffee and her eyes lit up at the unexpected experience.

"Where the hell did you get the scotch, Lee? My husband won't have alcohol in the house."

"I brought it with me, Kim. Just a bit of experience on my part. Situations like this need a little help from time to time."

"Oh, so you have been involved in kidnappings before?"

"In my time as a cop, it's never an easy thing to manage, but I am here and I will certainly do everything I can to sort this out, Kim."

Her face relaxed noticeably. I wasn't sure if it was the whiskey or what I had just said. The problem was, I didn't have a clue on what to do next, not anything that might really help that is. She had that look on her face of expectancy. She sat forward on the settee, as if she really wanted me to say something - anything that might make her feel better.

"You said you had an idea, Lee. Something that might help. What are you thinking?"

"OK, we need to make contact with the gang. It's imperative that we convince them that your husband has completely disappeared. That you know nothing of his whereabouts and can't contact him. We could try to do this via text, but I really think it would be better seeing them in person.

I am going to try and set up a meeting with them, try to explain what's happened and the position you are in. I am reasonably certain this won't gain the release of your daughter, but maybe, just maybe they will let her live until we can find him. It will buy us some time, maybe the police will find her, perhaps they will get bored and let her go, let's hope.

It's not much Kim, but it's all we have. I don't really think they want to do any harm to Gwen. I am sure of that. In any case, if anything does happen to her, they will have lost the only bargaining chip they have and that would be a disaster for them.

I guess if I can convince them that I will find your husband, and if necessary, deliver him in a swap for Gwen, they might just take the bait. Once I have found your husband and that part of the plan is done, we can then hand the investigation to the police and let them take over, controlling the swap and bringing your daughter and husband in safely. The question you have to answer, Kim, is if this all goes terribly wrong, are you prepared to swap your husband for Gwen and never see him again?"

She looked perplexed, at odds, with what I had just said. There was no doubt in my mind that Gwen was her priority, but if this went wrong, would she be willing to potentially sacrifice her husband?

The silence seemed to last for an age. She sat motionless, staring into her coffee. I was at the point where I needed to ask her directly what her thoughts were, but she looked up and drew a big breath.

"Listen, Lee. You need to do whatever it takes to get Gwen back. I don't care what it takes or who loses out, she must come back safely. My husband is the instigator of this. It's his fault Gwen has gone missing. If that costs him his life then so be it!"

Those last four words were spat out with a perceivable venom. It was clear to me what had to be done and who might end up being sacrificed in the end.

"Right, Kim. Let's have a look at that text you received. With a bit of luck, they will be waiting for a reply."

With shaking hands, she handed me her mobile. We scrolled down to the message and pressed reply.

MY NAME IS LEE HUNTER. I AM A PRIVATE DETECTIVE. IF YOU WANT TO CHECK ME OUT, I AM ON THE INTERNET AND MY OFFICES ARE ABOVE THE TAXI FIRM ON LORD STREET.
MRS WALKER HAS NO IDEA OF THE WHEREABOUTS OF HER HUSBAND AND THEREFORE CANNOT CONTACT HIM. CONSEQUENTLY, YOU WILL NEVER BE ABLE TO RECLAIM WHATEVER IT IS THAT BELONGS TO YOU.
I WOULD LIKE TO MEET WITH YOURSELVES AND DISCUSS A PLAN TO FIND AND DELIVER HIM TO YOU. THIS IS SOMETHING I CAN DO ON YOUR BEHALF, ITS PART OF THE WORK I NORMALLY UNDERTAKE. I HAVE CONTACTS AND INFORMANTS THAT WILL BE ABLE TO HELP FIND HIM.
IF YOU CALL OFF YOUR THREATS TO GWEN AND KEEP HER SAFE, I WILL GUARANTEE THE DELIVERY OF MR WALKER INTO YOUR HANDS. NO QUESTIONS ASKED AND NO POLICE!
I AWAIT YOUR REPLY. PLEASE USE MY WORK MOBILE 011743 65994, NOT THE NUMBER FOR MRS WALKER.

I pressed send and sat back. I didn't expect a reply any time soon. To be honest, I didn't have a clue what I was going to do even if they did reply! So, I made my way into the kitchen and made another coffee with a shot of whiskey or perhaps two.

The Murder Scene.
3 Claridge Road, Hillside.
Sunday Night.

The night had closed in, surrounding 3 Claridge road in a dark blanket, covering the evil crimes within. The constant hum of the Hyundai generators was the only sound. The lights that they powered shone onto the house and illuminated the surrounding trees and landscape. Despite the activity in and outside the murder scene, there was little conversation or discourse of any kind. The team of crime and forensic investigators were busy in their allocated tasks. Obsessive attention to detail and an absolute desire to get at the facts drove them on in a relentless quest for the truth.

A fine drizzle had established itself, the kind that soaked everything it touched. The warmth of the day had now been overtaken by a chill and clawing humidity. Kaye had marshalled her technicians - each detailed to gather evidence of all kinds. It was the beginning of the case, a case of murder. This was the kind of investigation she and her team were trained for - the dead had a voice, a right to justice and they would provide that for them.

DI Deborah Smith had been on the phone to her boss. He would meet her in the morning. In the meantime, it was her case and she was the investigating officer. With her coat wrapped closely around her, she slid out of the old blue Ford escort and scampered towards the door of the house.

"Kaye! Oi! What's going on in there? I need to come in. The powers that be want an update."

Kaye Marie turned to face Deborah. She had the appearance of a woman absolutely involved in her job. There was no room for complacency or lack of effort. A man was lying dead in his own home and they had to find the murderer.

"Hi Debs! Sorry, I just have a lot to organize. Get your gear on and follow me. Stay on the foot pads. We don't want to contaminate anything in here."

The inside of the house was now the domain of the Scenes of Crime people. It has been owned by them and would not be handed over to any other agency or persons until they have collected all the evidence they needed - no matter how long it took.

Deborah pulled on her protective gear - over boots, white coverall, face mask, hairnet and gloves. After being checked in, she followed Kaye into the main living room. Despite her experience in the police and the murder squad, there was always a moment of apprehension as she entered the scene of a murder. The smell of blood, the unique atmosphere surrounding the violence that has been committed was always palpable.

Walking on the square footplates that have been put on the floor to limit contamination and restrict the avenues of movement, she eventually reached the murder scene. The room itself had been brightly lit. Men and women in white suits were busy at work. Some were taking photographs, others collecting samples, one was marking the places where evidence has been removed.

The whole scene was one of enterprise, but also carnage, blood and death. The deceased lay on the plush carpet. He was on his back, arms outstretched. There were three holes in his head - two to the forehead and one just above his mouth. It was clear, even from where Deborah was standing, that the man's head has been blown apart by the force of the bullets. His life blood and brains lay splattered all over the far wall. He lay staring up at the ceiling. The last thing that those eyes witnessed was the person who ended his life. Now they were cold and lifeless, clouded by death, dry and distant.

His mouth, gaped open, as if shouting, but no noise came forth. He lay in a sticky dark red pool, mixed with grey matter, bone and gore. Whoever had done this clearly intended to kill. They had put the gun to this man's head and watched as his head disintegrated. This was not the act of a jealous lover or a casual burglar - this was the work of a cold-blooded killer. Someone who clearly enjoyed their work.

"So, what's the thinking so far, Kaye?"

"Well apart from the obvious, the only thing of note was that business card found just over there, by his right hand. Not sure if he dropped it when he was shot or it was dropped by someone. The bullets were as I expected - three 9mm. We have recovered all three, or the remains of them. They will go to the ballistics lab tonight.

Nothing much else currently. We are doing the usual evidence gathering, swabs for DNA, fibres, etc. Other than that, nothing to add. No sign of the gun. You need to organise that. Oh yes, the CCTV."

"What about the CCTV?"

"Bad news, I am afraid. There are cameras around the property. One of the first things my techs looked at, but the system is offline. Whoever did this knew what they were doing Debs - switched it off and deleted everything before they left. We will take the recording unit and double check, but my guys are really good at this kind of stuff and they don't think there is anything left to look at."

"Fuck it! That's going to slow this down. I was hoping we could see who did this. Not so lucky, eh?"

"No Debs, but we will get the stuff back to the lab and see what we can do. You never know...fingers crossed."

"We need to find his wife and that detective. The one on the business card. Seems odd that his card is right in the middle of the murder scene. It's a bit clumsy for a man who found and then deleted the CCTV recordings? Mind you, perhaps there was a bit of panic. Maybe he was disturbed, who knows? I will get Mike Evans to track him down and bring him in. We need to have a chat with this Lee Hunter."

Just then Deborah's phone began to ring. Waving goodbye to Kaye, she carefully removed it from her pocket as she exited the house.

"DI Smith, can I help?"

"Yes Inspector, this is Detective Chief Superintendent Martin Kiff here. I am aware that you are heading up a murder involving a Mr Francis Jackson Barnes. I need to make myself clear, Inspector, I want this case resolved as soon as possible. Mr Barnes is a well-known man in the community. I would like to think we can bring the person or persons responsible for this terrible crime in with the greatest rapidity.

I am sure you won't leave any stone unturned or spare any amount of resource when dealing with this case. You have my absolute support and authority to get this crime solved and to use whatever you need to do it."

"Yes, sir. Thank you for your support. How far can I go with using your name to acquire extra resources?"

"You can have what you want, when you want it - no matter the cost. If you have any problems, just give me a ring, Inspector, and I will bang heads together. Get this job done and tucked away, and you can expect a significant amount of reciprocity from me when it comes to your next promotion board. Do I make myself clear, Inspector?"

"Oh, perfectly clear, sir, and thanks again. I will ensure we get of man."

"Well done, Inspector. Now sort this out. I know you won't let me down, will you?"

With that the line went dead. Deborah stood in the blowing drizzle double checking with herself that she had just had that conversation. It was nice to receive the support of a very senior officer in her force, but the underlying threat of what will happen if she didn't 'get it done' was clear to see. She had been involved in 'get it done quickly' investigations like this before. Not as the investigating officer, but as one of the team. The pressure from the top was relentless, and on more than one occasion, it hadn't ended well. One sad example was her friend Inspector Mark Simmonds. He couldn't close the case - couldn't find that vital piece of evidence and so the perpetrators got off scot free. Mark Simmonds had a nervous breakdown, eventually lost his job and everything that he cared for - and all because he couldn't 'get it done'!

She was still contemplating what had just happened when she became aware of someone moving towards her from the house. He was tall, a little over six feet, well built, a shock of ginger hair and bright blue eyes. It was Detective Constable Mike Evans.

"Boss, Kaye said you wanted a word?"

"Yes Mike. I have a job for you. You need to go and find his wife. Shouldn't be too hard, not with her car and lifestyle. Listen, there is pressure building from above on this, so don't mess it up. I want her in interview room 1 tonight. Do I make myself clear? Go and have a word with the cleaner before the paramedics take her away. She has some info about this lady, including her car reg and make."

"I will get on it straight away."

"I am going to get the uniforms to pick up a certain Lee Hunter - the private detective. They found his business card in there, probably making him the number one suspect right now. To be honest though Mike, it seems a bit contrived. Doesn't feel quite right, but if you get Mrs Adele Barnes and the uniforms bring in this Lee Hunter, we should have the murderer. All we need to do then, is to find out which one of them did it."

Back to My Place.
Sunday Evening.

As I suspected, there was no immediate reply from the gang. This kind of offer would inevitably be discussed perhaps between several parties. I was relying on the fact that Gwen was their one and only bargaining chip. If she died, they would have nothing.

It was a big risk. They might just kill her anyway once they have her father, or kill me for even volunteering such a plan.

What would happen if I couldn't find her dad? I hated to think. To be honest, it wasn't really a plan at all, it was more of a hit and hope. I couldn't think of anything else - perhaps there was nothing else. No other way of securing the life of this young girl. The absolute truth is, if Kim hasn't got a clue where her husband was, how the hell was I supposed to find him?

Anyway, it was a start. Let's see if they get back to me first. There was no guarantee of that. If I could only find out what it was the gang was looking for, that would help. Once I had established the facts surrounding the case, I might get some idea about why he had absconded?

Right, wait for that call - stay sharp Lee and don't fuck this up. Gwen's life depends on me. Let's get this one right. OK, what else has happened today? Oh yes, there was the text from Ruth this lunch time. I had forgotten about that. She wanted a re-match. I don't think I could manage that, but she might appreciate a curry and a glass of red. I stopped the car, got out my phone and scrolled through the texts until I finally reached the one from Ruth. I typed my message and pressed send.

HI RUTH.
SORRY I HAVEN'T GOT BACK TO YOU BUT IT'S BEEN A DAMN BUSY DAY.
HOW ABOUT I GRAB A TAKEAWAY ON THE WAY HOME AND A BOTTLE OF
RED?
LEE XX

Right, done. Let's see if she gets back to me. I dropped the mobile into the drink's container on the dashboard and continued to drive home. The night was turning into an absolute stinker. The drizzle turned into a heavy rain and a gale was starting to blow off the Irish sea. I didn't like this kind of a night. It made the windows in my flat rattle and kept me awake.

I needed some company to keep my mind off the incessant noise, and to be honest, someone to talk to, enjoy the evening with and escape to a different place with. There were often times in my line of work where nothing much happened. Watching for that cheating husband or wife might involve sitting in a car or outside a restaurant for hours. There was always too much time to think, and in my case, feel lonely.

It has been over two years since my marriage ended, and if I was honest, it was over several years before that when I was all but divorced. That was my fault of course. Long days at work and too many nights down the pub. The inevitable happened and we went our separate ways. And here I am, a lonely man wishing he had done things differently.

The irony is, I have left the police, I don't drink, well, not all the time and I am still as lonely as I was back then. I often wondered if everyone is like me - standing on an island, looking out to sea.

Odd though, the people I've met often seemed to be happier than I was. The truth was, when I met others at work or down the pub, they just appeared to be happy. In reality, they were like me - standing alone on their own little islands, wishing things were different. Wanting a special person in their lives, wishing they hadn't married the one they had. I deliberated if anyone was really happy? If they had everything they needed or even knew what that was?

Anyway, I needed to cheer up. The probability was I would be dead by the end of the month. Either Fat Tony would fillet me for not paying back my debts, or the gang, who had Gwen, would kill me just for the fun of it. So, it was full speed ahead with *operation fun and frolics'*, and it started now.

I was about halfway home when my phone buzzed. I decided to be a law-abiding citizen and pulled over to read the message. In reality, it was nothing to do with obeying the law, I needed to put my reading specs on and they were in the glove compartment!

YOU HAVE A TEXT FROM – Ruth.

HI LEE, YEAH THAT'S SOUNDS A GREAT IDEA. ANYHTING INDIAN IS GOOD.
NOT TOO HOT THOUGH!!!!!
MY PLACE TONIGHT. THE HEATING IS ON AND THE RED WINE IS CHILLING
IN THE FRIDGE. WHAT TIME? XX

Now things were certainly looking up. Perhaps my luck has changed for once. An evening with Ruth was just what the doctor ordered. It was *'operation fun and frolics'* part one and here we go! So, the Taj Mahal restaurant for the takeaway, a shower at home, off to Ruth's, and by the sounds of things, I didn't even have to buy the wine. Right, text her back and let's get going.

HI RUTH.
I NEED A SHOWER. I WILL THEN POP OUT TO THE TAJ, SHOULD BE AT
YOUR PLACE IN ABOUT AN HOUR IF THATS OK?
LEE XX

YOU HAVE A TEXT FROM – Ruth.
PERFECT, CAN'T WAIT, SEE YOU AT ABOUT 8.
RUTH XX

I started the car and began the drive home. I felt unusually happy. Perhaps for the first time in months, even years. I turned the radio up full - *Rossana* by Toto blasted out and I sang at the top of my voice. Goodness knows what it sounded like, but it made me feel good.

I have not felt this good for, well, I can't remember when? That surge of dopamine coursing through my body sure felt good. And the evening to come might just exercise the neglected pleasure receptors in my brain a little bit more. Anyway, shower, best clothes, aftershave, off to the Taj and back to Ruth's.

The plan seemed perfect. That was until I turned the corner into the carpark at the back of my flat. I couldn't believe what I saw - a Ford Mondeo, complete with yellow and blue checks down the side and blue flashing lights.

That's just what I needed. Two uniforms with nothing better to do on a rainy Sunday night. What the hell did they want? It must be something to do with Gwen. I wondered if they had managed to find her. A surge of panic rushed through me. Perhaps they have and she is dead?

With my nerves jangling away, I walked towards my flat. But by the time I reached the door, the two uniformed officers were standing right behind me. I turned - that look on their faces I had seen before - it meant business. Whatever they wanted wasn't anything to do with the weather.

"Mr Lee Hunter?"

"That's me, Constable. How can I help?"

"I wonder if you could accompany us to the police station. Colleagues would like to talk to you regarding a recent incident."

I looked at the young man. He reminded me of myself, many years ago, in uniform full of my own piss and importance.

"I don't suppose this is optional? I do have an important date tonight?"

"It's not, sir, but I am sure it won't take long. Please come with us."

With that the two young men flanked me and walked me to the rear of the car. Seemed a lot of fuss just so some detective could talk to me about Gwen. They could have done that by phone or asked me to attend the following morning. She must be dead. I wondered if they have found her body dumped on the beach or in the canal?

Before I could think, I was in the back of the car, door locked and we were on our way.

"What's this all about, Constable? Have they found Gwen?"

"Gwen, sir? Who is Gwen?"

"The girl who's missing. I assume you have found her?"

"Sorry sir. I am not sure what you are referring to. A missing girl?"

"Yes, Gwen Walker - sixteen, abducted from outside of her school."

"No sir, I am not familiar with that case. I am sure it will all be explained to you when you get to the station."

Now I was worried. I wasn't particularly concerned about him not being explicit, that was just standard procedure, but denying any knowledge? So, if it wasn't Gwen, what the hell was it? The rest of the journey was completed in silence. I was worried, the two up front knew it and they liked it that way.

Interview room four in Southport Police Station was a hot and stuffy room. It had an aroma about it - fear, anger, perhaps even regret. The air conditioning hasn't been working for some considerable time, and with no windows or ventilation, it was not the nicest place to be.

I was told that someone would be down presently to speak to me. I was still none the wiser as to what that might be about. I wasn't expecting anyone soon. Leaving someone in this kind of place was normal - let them worry perhaps even panic - things might be more productive that way. Unfortunately for them, I was more than wise to that little trick, having employed it dozens of times myself, they were going to have to try harder than that.

So, I sat back and sipped on my, well best description would be brown liquid, well actually, warm brown liquid with no sugar. I looked at my watch - just gone 8.30pm - so I wasn't going to make the date with Ruth. They had locked away my phone so I couldn't contact her. Yet another depressingly disappointing episode in my life. Perhaps I could talk to her, try and convince her that it wasn't my fault and why these things always happen to me.

I was at the point of getting up and trying to leave. My ass was aching sitting on the hard plastic seat and my stomach was rumbling. Just at that moment, the door swung open and in walked a woman with a familiar face.

"Well, DI Smith, as I live and breath, and can I say what an honour it is. Now what brings you down to this squalid little shit hole they call interview room four?"

"Yes, sorry about the surroundings, Mr Hunter. We are due a refurbishment and this is about the best we have."

"OK, Inspector. Let's cut to the chase. What is it this time that I am supposed to have done? I am bored, my backside is aching, I am hungry and you lot have made me miss my date. As you already know, I was a copper for many a long year, so your silly games won't work with me. So be quick and get on with it."

"Yes, quite, Mr Hunter. Now, I have a few questions to ask and I am sure you will be happy to answer them."

"Not so fast Inspector. Let's hear them first and the circumstances surrounding them. I am not answering anything until I know what they relate to and why you have dragged me all the way down here on a horrible Sunday night."

"What do you know about a Mr Francis Jackson Barnes?"

"Sorry Inspector, don't know the man. I assume it is a man?"

"Have you ever been to 3 Claridge Road, Hillside Mr Hunter?"

"Nope."

"You see, there has been an incident and I have some evidence suggesting that you do know Mr Barnes and the address as mentioned."

"Right Inspector, I am getting very bored with this. What's happened? What do you think I am involved in and what's this evidence you have?"

"We will get to that, Mr Hunter, but I need to know your whereabouts this afternoon. Perhaps around midday?"

"Right, it's obvious you think that I am once again involved in some heinous crime, whatever that is. I can assure you that you are wrong!

As for my whereabouts in the afternoon, check the till records at the Bold Arms in Churchtown. I was in there at about noon having lunch. Before that I was at home and I have an independent witness who will verify that. Shame I won't be seeing her later though! After that I went to see a client, a Mrs Kim Walker, at her house in Stretton Drive. Again, I am sure she will confirm our meeting. I left her house, drove home and was picked up by your boys in blue. I had my mobile on all the time, so you should be able to map out my movements using my data and the mobile masts I connected to. I am sure my car tripped many number plate recognition cameras during the day, so go and get your people to check. I can absolutely assure you that I was nowhere near Claridge road, wherever the hell that is?

Now, unless you think I can be in two places at once, you can charge me with whatever it is you think I did, or can I go now?"

"Just wait a minute, Mr Hunter. We need to confirm your whereabouts. I am not inclined to release you just yet. It won't take more than a few minutes and a couple of phone calls to confirm your story. So, just sit tight."

I could have walked away. They haven't arrested me, so I was free to go. I guessed they weren't completely sure about any possible connection I had to the crime, whatever that crime was? So, I decided not to be a complete twat, as I might need them when it came to the potential deal with Gwen's kidnappers. So, discretion being the better part of valour, I gave her the numbers of Ruth and Kim. A quick call to the Bold Arms should sort the rest out.

Of course, the statement - 'It won't take more than a few minutes' - actually turned out to be bloody hours. Still, I was out of that damn stinking place with a promise that I wouldn't go walkabouts, be a good boy and report back when required. At least I had my phone back, enough money for a taxi and it had stopped raining.

This left me with two outstanding priorities – well, if you exclude finding Mr Walker and Gwen. Firstly, I had to find out what was I supposed to have done to a Mr Francis Jackson Barnes at 3 Claridge Road, Hillside. That would have to wait until the morning, and secondly, I needed to phone Ruth. Try to explain what had happened to me and hope beyond hope that she believes me!

I pulled my phone from my pocket, pressed the key on the side and waited for the thing to come to life. Guess what, the battery was completely dead. What a fucking night! Surely nothing else could go wrong, could it?

By the time I found a taxi and got home, it was gone midnight. Ruth's flat was in complete darkness. I stood at the door for a few moments trying to pluck up the courage to knock, but I decided to talk to her in the morning instead. My flat seemed darker than normal. It had been a crap day - the police had hauled me in, Ruth would probably never speak to me again and I had missed a promising evening. Anyway, I plugged my phone in and decided to go to bed. Perhaps tomorrow might be a better day.

I woke with a bit of a start. You know you get that feeling something is not quite right? It was sometime just after dawn, as I lay there for a while trying to work out what it was. Why I have woken up like I had? It was only when I turned over that I realised that my phone was flashing. I reached out and squinted at the screen.

YOU HAVE THREE TEXT MESSAGES FROM – Unknown – Unknown - Ruth

FIRST TEXT MESSAGE @ 17.07 FROM - unknown.
MR HUNTER, I THANK YOU FOR YOUR OFFER TODAY. PLEASE CONTACT ME ON THE NUMBER I SUPPLIED TO MRS WALKER FOR A CHAT.

SECOND TEXT MESSAGE @ 21.15 FROM – unknown.
PERHAPS YOU ARE NO LONGER INTRESTED IN HELPING US WITH OUR PROBLEM MR HUNTER? I WILL THEREFORE BID YOU GOODBYE.

THIRD TEXT MESSAGE @ 22.28 FROM – Ruth.
LEE, WHAT THE HELL IS GOING ON? I HAVE JUST HAD A PHONE CALL FROM THE POLICE ASKING IF I COULD VERIFY YOUR WHEREABOUTS. I WILL WAIT TO HEAR FROM YOU!!!!

I remembered last night hoping that today would be a better day. It clearly wasn't going to be the case! I looked at my watch - it was 06:22. Where the hell do I start? My old boss had a saying in times like these - '*shit happens*'. Well, he was right about that, and it certainly had!

Murder Squad Office. Southport Police Station.
Monday Morning.

It was a clear, but an unseasonably cold start to the day. A crisp, almost autumn like chill greeted Deborah as she exited the warm comfort of her old Ford. It was early spring, but you wouldn't have known it. She wrapped her coat tightly around herself as she walked briskly towards the station's entrance.

She had called into Joyce's coffee shop on her way in to grab her morning coffee and a hot croissant. Her regular 'fruits of the forest' wasn't available, so strawberry jam had to do. She tried to put off opening the plastic top of her black double espresso, but she had nearly fallen asleep twice on the drive in, so it seemed a good idea to ingest a shot of caffeine to wake her up.

She held on tightly to the coffee cup, enjoying the warmth and lift that it gave her. Deborah hadn't left the murder scene until the early hours, getting four hours sleep at best. Today was shaping up to be a long hard slog and the coffee would only help for a few minutes more.

The office was surprisingly busy for a Monday morning. Looking around, it seemed the whole department was in and hard at work. People moving from desk to desk, exchanging information and thoughts. Other furiously tapping on their computers, making notes, using the offender profiling software. One or two were on their mobiles, perhaps chatting to friends or hopefully calling in favours from their informants.

The heating had kicked in and the waft of warm air was welcome, as was the smell of the coffee machine. Deborah walked into her small office, hung her coat up and sat down. Her phone was already flashing - the red light alerting her to a message.

"Don't these people bloody sleep? Please let me sit and gather myself before you start harassing me."

She snatched at the handset and pressed the 'message' button and waited.

"Hello, DI Smith. This is Inspector Watkins from Derbyshire CID. I was given your extension by the desk sargeant. I think you need to know about this. A patrol found a Maserati Ghibili Tofeo with a deceased woman inside. She has been shot three times in the head. The documents in the car identified her as a Mrs Adele Barnes, with an address from your neck of the woods. Probability is she is not known to you guys, but you never know. Give me a ring as soon as you get in. See if this is anything significant your end or not?"

Deborah replaced the cream plastic handset and sat back in her chair, running her fingers through her hair. She blinked and shook her head several times. Was this a dream or had a woman that they had been looking for just fallen into her lap?

"Well, that boils your two suspects down to one - Mr Lee Hunter. I think we need to talk."

She quickly exited her office. She was looking for one person only and he was sitting conveniently in front of his desk, DC Mike Evans. He was deep in thought - half typing and half gazing into thin air. He never seemed to be doing much, but he had a reputation for producing results, even when he had no real right to.

"Mike, get yourself and a couple of uniforms and get over to see Lee Hunter. We need to talk to him, right now."

"What's up Boss?"

"He was one of two suspects in the murder at Hillside. The other one has just been found shot dead in Derbyshire. I think we can assume that rules out this Adele Barnes woman, don't you? I will get the firearms people over to Hunter's place. Follow them in - don't go in first! Do you understand?"

"Yeah, no problems boss. I guess that makes detective Hunter the prime suspect."

"No Mike, it makes him the only suspect. Now go and lift him before he disappears. Make sure you get him and bring him back here. No excuses and no fuck ups! Make sure you have a couple of handy PCs with you. He might prove a bit of a handful. Also, I need to get the firearms squad on alert. If he is our man, then he is clearly armed and very dangerous. No heroics and no risks! They go in and bring him out. You just get him back here, understood?"

DC Mike Evans quickly grabbed his coat and made a speedy exit for the office door. Before it had managed to swing closed, a familiar, if slightly unwelcomed figure slithered through the ever-decreasing gap, DCI Mark Bruno.

He was a man, about six feet two with greasy, unkempt hair and a pocked-marked face. He was well dressed in a dark grey suit. He did have a roguish charm that some women in the station found oddly attractive, despite his hair and cream suede shoes.

Deborah never really understood why some women found him even remotely attractive. He was the worst womaniser in the whole of the Merseyside Police Force. He has been married three times, all of which ended acrimoniously after cheating with other women. Added to this, he had been under investigation for bullying, inappropriate sexual behaviour, harassment and always appeared to be in debt. Odd thing was though, he always got away with any charge or investigation. He was what Deborah called, 'an undesirable'.

The problem was, he is a Detective Chief Inspector, and as such was Deborah's superior officer. He was the kind of guy who understood the rank system and how to use it to get his own way. He had this knack of getting involved in everything, including meetings, policy groups, and sometimes Deborah's investigations. He made her flesh crawl, but so long as he didn't cross the lines. She tried to ignore him the best she could.

He was the boss of Operation Elm Tree, which targeted major fraud and money laundering, related to gangland activity. It was not the most glamourous post, but it was one that carried a high profile and its boss. Chief Inspector Mark Bruno loved the prestige and glory that went with it.

"Well good morning, Deborah. And how was your weekend? Full of fun and frolics, I trust?"

"Listen Bruno, I don't really want to listen to your lascivious rantings at this time on a Monday morning. I have enough to deal with without your libidinous behaviour, now how can I help? I need to make an urgent call to the ARU."

"Sorry, seems like you got out of bed on the wrong side, Deborah. No one to cuddle up to?"

He gave Deborah a long and exaggerated wink, followed by a slimy smile.

"This conversation stops here if you don't mind, sir. Now how can I help?"

"Sorry Deborah, seems like you need a new man in your life. Anyway, on to business. My boys in Operation Elm Tree, or Op ET as we like to call it, had a marker come up this morning on our database. It seems that one of our major persons of interest has been murdered - namely one Francis Jackson Barnes. Any details that you would like to share? We could always make it over lunch if you prefer?"

"Let's make it a coffee in my office and you're making it. The coffee machine is over there."

He gave Deborah another wink, turned and made his way to the coffee machine. Deborah returned to her office with a smile on her face - *"tosser."*

She snatched at the phone once again. She had only a few minutes to make the call to the Armed Response Unit before Bruno returned. She wanted to get that job underway without him knowing, the last thing Deborah wanted was to assist Op ET in any way, shape or form.

"Right Debs, this is yours - white no sugar if memory serves. None of the black stuff around here, eh?"

"I will pretend I didn't hear that, Bruno. I wouldn't hesitate to report you for inappropriate language or behaviour, but to be honest, I am too tired to be bothered. I guess I will get plenty more opportunities soon. Now, what seems to be the problem?"

"No problems Debs. It's just this Francis Jackson Barnes - seems he's as dead as a drowned cat. That's a damn shame to be honest. We were about to close the net on the little shit. Seems we have a problem now as lots of his contacts will be getting away, scot free. That's not good for business. I hate the idea that criminals are not being punished for their behaviour and it looks bad on our statistics. I need access to your files and info on this case, so we get all the twats involved in the fraud they were perpetrating. I think it would be a good idea if I joined you on this case just to make sure you don't miss anything."

Deborah felt a huge wave of anger swelling up inside. She wanted to fire back at DCI Bruno, but he was superior in rank to her and had a very high profile with the powers that ran the whole show. He was a dangerous man to cross and one that would always gain the support of the senior managers in the force. He was a bully, a manipulator and one of those people who always seem to land on their feet, no matter what the situation he found himself in. She had to hold her tongue, wait for the best opportunity to shoot DCI Bruno down, and this wasn't it.

"I see what you are saying, DCI Bruno. Your case must be very important, I am sure, but this is a murder and I run this show. I will keep you informed of what's going on and as for any evidence pertaining to your case, I will gladly hand it over. As for you joining me to head this case up, well, that's not going to happen. This is my case and that's the end of that."

"I hate to throw rank at you Debs, but…."

"Let me stop you there, Bruno. Firstly, rank doesn't come into it. This a murder case and I am the boss. And secondly don't call me Debs."

It was Bruno's turn to feel a surge of anger, but he was way too clever to get into an argument about this.

"Sorry, DI Smith. I need to go and see my boss, see what he says. I am sure he will back me up. I need to get joint control over this. It's very important."

With that, he stood up and without saying another word turned and left her office.

Deborah sat opened mouthed, "did that just happen? Does he really think he's going to take control of my case? Well, he can think again."

Just as Deborah was thinking that today was going downhill at an increasing rate, like a breath of fresh air, a middle-aged woman - short and willowy with auburn hair - burst into Deborah's office. It was Deborah's number two, Detective Sergeant Sharron Shacklady.

'What did that dick want, Deborah? He's a slimy, horrible man. I wish someone would shoot him and give us all a break. Second thoughts, can I shoot him? I am a terrible shot and it might take five or six bullets to eventually kill him."

The two women laughed. Partly out of the humour of Sharron's comment and partly wishing she could carry out her wish.

"Sharron, glad to see you back, had a nice week off?"

"Yeah thanks. Ready to get back into it. Seems we have a high profile one."

"Tell me about it, Sharron. I have had Detective Chief Superintendent Martin Kiff telling me to *'get this done'*, as well as that grease ball chewing my arse, and it's only been twenty-four hours. I can't help thinking this case has more to it than appearances might suggest Sharron. There's something going on. I don't know what it is, but there are some major players getting involved and that makes me feel very nervous indeed."

"Odd. What the hell does DCS Kiff want? He can't be more than five minutes from retirement. Why does he want to get involved?"

"You tell me, Sharron. He has given me full authority to use whatever resources necessary, no expense spared. I have never come across that one before. Now that little weasel Bruno wants to take charge. Someone or some people somewhere are panicking and I don't know why? Just to add a little more spice to the story, I've had a call this morning from Derbyshire CID - the victim's wife has been found shot dead.

This case is getting interesting. I wonder if someone else might drop their oar in, perhaps the Lord bloody Mayor. To be honest, it wouldn't at all surprise me if the Queen herself called me. What the hell is going on Shaz?"

Sharron laughed, "well boss, I am here and ready to go. So, let's get on with it. What's first on the list?"

"Mike Evans has gone with an ARU to pick up our number one suspect. I will ring Derbyshire CID back. You are going to get up to speed with forensics and the provisional crime report on the murder. Oh, and maybe I will get time to drink my coffee? See you in interview four when Mike gets back. So, not much really for a Monday morning!"

DS Sharron Shacklady laughed as she left the office of Deborah's office. Things looked like they were about to get busy, *just how I like it.*

"Hello, Inspector Watkins, Derbyshire CID."

"Hi, this is DI Smith, Merseyside Murder team, just returning your call."

"Ah, great, thanks DI Smith. Yes, we have a murder down here - one of yours I believe. According to our information she is a Mrs Adele Barnes. She lives near to the golf course. I have played there many times. That is certainly an expensive part of town. I guess that explains the Maserati Ghibili Tofeo. Nice car."

"She is most certainly one of ours and to make things worse, her husband was found dead at the weekend in the family home, opposite that golf course you like so much."

"You are joking? What was the MO?"

"He was shot in the head, three times. Bloody awful mess. Blood and brains everywhere."

"Now there's a coincidence. Same thing with Mrs Barnes. Head blown apart by three shots. Made a complete mess of the cream leather interior. Shame, that will never sponge clean."

Deborah knew she shouldn't laugh at his attempt at a sick joke, but it did make her smile.

"Maybe she should have chosen a different colour, red perhaps?"

They both started to laugh although there wasn't anything even slightly funny about the incident.

"Have you got anyone in mind your end, DI Smith?"

"Deborah, please call me Deborah. Yes, we do. Some two-bit local detective. We found his business card near to the deceased. Not sure what the link is yet, but until we have the full crime scene report, he is in the hot seat. I have sent one of my crew with an Armed Response Unit to pick him up. See what he says when we question him."

"Great, well we are doing the forensics this end. There isn't much to examine to be honest, but there was an envelope with fifteen hundred pounds in it. I am having that dusted for prints. I will keep you posted."

"Thanks Inspector Watkins. It's obvious these two murders are connected. There must be something in the house and the car that will point to someone, I am sure."

"Yep, well, I will have something for you this PM Deborah, so standby."

She replaced the handset. This was turning out to be an interesting day. The two cases were obviously connected, but why? These two people were rich, successful and they had very expensive tastes in cars, but you don't get your head blown apart for that.

Then there was Detective Lee Hunter. He didn't strike her as a contract killer nor a cold-blooded murderer. Yes, he was the main suspect, but he didn't seem to fit the classic profile. This was going to be a long and interesting case. She suspected that there would be many twists and turns before it was solved.

Outside My Place.
Monday Morning.

I opened the front door and was struck in the face by a howling gale and torrential rain - *'Another day in paradise then.'*

I managed to get a text off to the number left by the kidnappers, giving a grovelling apology, hoping beyond hope, that they would still give a toss and might want to talk to me. At least my phone was now showing 100%, so a dead battery would not be able to screw up my day, again!

I wanted to phone Ruth to try and make up for last night, but to be honest, I lacked the moral courage to face her. So, I did the next best thing, whimped out and sent a text. I really wouldn't blame her if she never spoke to me again. Not only did I let her down, but the police had been on the phone - not a good start to a relationship.

Anyway, off to the office. Try and engage the kidnappers and keep the police off my back. I needed to see what Adele was up to, call Kim and of course see if Ruth still wanted to see me. Should be a very good day all in all. For once, I was really looking forward to what lay ahead.

I jumped into the car. It was only parked a few yards from my door, but I was already half soaked, thanks to the wonderful spring weather. I pulled out of the carpark and set off to the office, but no more than half a mile into the journey, my phone buzzed. I stopped by the side of the road and pulled it out of my pocket and looked at the screen.

YOU HAVE THREE TEXT MESSAGES FROM – Unknown

TEXT MESSAGE @ 07:59 FROM - unknown.
MR HUNTER, APOLOGY ACCEPTED, BUT THIS WILL BE YOUR ONE AND ONLY CHANCE. NEXT SCREW UP AND THE DEAL IS OFF. I WOULD LIKE TO SEE WHAT YOU CAN OFFER FOR THE LIFE OF THE GIRL. IF YOU STILL WANT TO HELP, MEET ME IN THE SMALL CARPARK, FACING THE BEACH AND FOOTPATH, JUST BY THE SAND WORKS ON THE COAST ROAD. BE THERE IN 45 MINS.

My head whirled. I read the message three or four times. This was a lucky break indeed. I had to get to that meeting. I checked my watch - it was already 08:10. I knew where it was, but would I have enough time to get there?

I pushed the car into first gear and pulled away from the carpark as fast as I could. I managed to get to the first set of traffic lights just as an unmarked police car and a black transit van went screaming past - blues and twos on full blast - waking everybody in the whole neighbourhood. As I drove away, I checked in my rear-view mirror and it almost seemed that the unmarked car and van turned left into my flat's carpark? Must be the bend in the road that made it look like that. Why the hell would the local old bill, including an ARU in the black van want to go there?

By the time I reached the carpark, the rain had stopped and the sun had started to make an appearance. A black S-Class Mercedes was parked at the far end. There were only two other cars in the small carpark. All seemed quiet. A cyclist's rode by and I could see several walkers on the footpath making their way along the foreshore.

I pulled up opposite the Merc, cautiously stepped outside and made my way over. Before I got too close, the driver exited. He glared right at me. He must have been six feet ten - a huge man, not one to mess with.

"You, come over here."

Needless to say, I did exactly as he instructed.

"I will search you before you get any closer. Mr Brau doesn't like surprises and neither do I. Turn your mobile off and give it to me - and anything else you might have in your pockets."

Again, I did exactly as I was told. After going through my pockets and rubbing me down, he opened the rear offside door and ushered me inside. By now, I was feeling somewhat nervous, perhaps even frightened. If I screwed this up, Gwen would not be the only body floating in the local canal!

I slid inside. The car was dim with heavily tinted windows and the smell of leather was delicious. I cautiously turned to my left. There sat a man in his fifties, brushed back grey hair, Ray-Ban sunglasses, dressed in a very expensive dark blue suit and smelling of exclusive aftershave. He didn't turn to look at me. He just slowly inhaled and spoke in a low very well-educated and somewhat dry voice.

"My name is Mr Brau. Very glad you could make it this time and nice to meet with you, Mr Hunter. I gather you have a proposal for me. One that might be beneficial for all parties concerned?"

Yes, sir. I intend to find Mr Walker, deliver him to you in exchange for his daughter."

"Mmmmm, what makes you think you can deliver this man when my staff can't even find out where he is, Mr Hunter? I have expended considerable time and resources in pursuit of him, but to absolutely no avail. Consequently, I thought it prudent to take his daughter into my 'protection' until he came to his senses and handed himself into me, so to speak."

"I do have a few options, sir. Perhaps some avenues that you haven't explored. At least, it's worth giving me a chance - nothing ventured, nothing gained!"

"You have a point, Mr Hunter. It would seem such a shame to let the girl die. She seems such an innocent young thing. Right, this is what you will do. Today is Monday. I will ensure her safety until next Monday. You have until then to deliver this man into my custody by midnight on that day.

If you fail to do so, I will kill her myself, Mr Hunter. After strangling her, I will have her body dumped in the local canal. I will then take her mother and do the same.

Don't doubt me for one moment, Mr Hunter. I do enjoy killing people. That feeling as their life force leaves them. It's that look in their eyes, total fear and overwhelming panic as they know they are about to die, fascinating."

A shiver ran down my spine. I was used to people like this. I had dealt with them so many times before. But there was something about him. I felt fear in his presence, something that I have not experienced for many a long year. I was in no doubt at all that he meant what he said, especially about enjoying killing.

"That's clear enough, sir. I will have this man in your custody in plenty of time, don't worry. Whatever it is you need from him, you will have very soon, I am sure."

"I am sure you will, Mr Hunter. Now, if that's all?"

"If I may sir, I wonder if you could clear something up for me? One of my informants, we all called him Jenks, died. He was looking into this case for me. I don't suppose you might know anything about this?"

"Sorry, Mr Hunter. I certainly didn't authorise anything. I would undoubtedly know if anything had happened to your man. I wouldn't terminate anyone just for asking questions about me. A couple of threats or perhaps a beating would normally do the job. No, Mr Hunter. I think I can be sure that this was not down to myself or any of my staff or at least not under any instructions from me."

"Thank you, sir. That's very helpful. Now I must get on and find your man."

I left the back of the Merc, was handed my belongings and made my way to my car. I was sure that Jenks had been killed because of poking around this case. What did he say, "*that bit of info you asked for on that girl who's gone missing? You will never bloody believe what I have found out...man this is unbelievable!*"

Of course, the man in the back of the car might have been lying, but why would he? He had nothing to fear? He was used to dealing with this kind of thing. He certainly wasn't worried about me or anything I might want to say. I was not going to say anything and he knew it. Even if he had admitted to killing Jenks, I wouldn't dare report it. Not if I wanted to see tomorrow morning!

What the hell did Jenks find out though? What was so explosive that it had cost him his life? I had to try and find out. Whatever it was might lead to his killer. I owed Jenks that much at least.

The black S-Class Merc pulled silently away, carrying with it the man who controlled so much. Not only in his criminal dealings, but with the lives of a young girl and her mother. I had no doubt whatsoever that he meant to carry out the killings of Gwen and her Mum. I had to succeed and there would be no second chance.

The merc pulled out of the carpark and turned right towards the pier and off to wherever this Mr Brau had his office. I watched as it quickly accelerated away down the coast road. I wondered how much that car alone must be worth. Where did all that money come from? How many lives were ruined because of it? I pushed the 'Start' button on my Mondeo. It fired first time. As I put it into gear, I noticed another BMW X6. This one was following the Merc away down the coast road. These things are two a penny. There must be too much money around here. That's three I have seen in as many days.

As the two cars stormed off and out of sight, I turned my mind back to Jenks and his murder. Think Lee, there must be something else here. Whoever killed him and took his phone and laptop must have left a clue, a trace?

There was one thing about Jenks that stood out. Well, apart from his ability to find things out, that was his mouth. He just couldn't help himself. The old saying about him was, *'telephone, telegram or tell Jenks',* and the world would soon know. I wonder if he shot his mouth off to someone? A person he knew and possibly trusted? Perhaps someone in the underworld of drugs and minor criminals?

I looked down at my mobile - the screen was blank. I needed to turn it on, but I would only get distracted by all the stupid *'end of sales'* deals and *'please contact us, your email has been hacked'*. Strange how they always seemed to want money to unhack it!

I had to get to the office, think about Jenks, try and find Mr Walker and get in touch with Adele. That was a point. Why didn't she contact me last night? Not like her to leave things undone. A woman who openly wanted her husband dead would be way more insistent that that. Anyway, first things first, find the absent Mr Walker, Gwen's dad. Where the hell was he? Could he be dead already? That was a good point. If he was dead, perhaps all this was going to be for nothing. After all, I couldn't drag a cold, rotting body into Mr Brau's office.

I was halfway to the office when a thought suddenly occurred to me. Smelly Ken. Now there's someone who Jenks might have gobbed off to...I wonder. I often saw them together - usually exchanging the best prices for their drug deals or maybe the best person to go and buy stuff from.

Now Ken was one of those disgusting little weevils who inhabited the nether regions between life and death - not quite alive, but not quite dead. He spent most of his waking hours smacked out of his mind on some substance or another. Odd thing was though, despite his inhuman condition and disgusting personal hygiene, hence Smelly Ken, he was a kind of likeable guy, in an odd sort of way. Ken was not a bad person, just odd - under the radar, never really coming to anyone's attention. Just the way he liked it. He was just part of the scenery.

The thing was though, where the hell would I find Ken at this time in the morning? It took me a few minutes, but eventually I came up with the answer. The soup kitchen at the back of the old bus station. He was bound to be there, grabbing a cup of hot coffee, a piece of toast before he began his day of despicable activities. If I could speak to him before he disappeared into his psychotropic wonderland, I might get some useful information out of him – well, perhaps.

I pressed the loud peddle on the car and sped off towards the old bus station. It didn't take long. The morning traffic had now eased and a feeling of normality had resumed in Southport. I rounded the corner and drove into the carpark and to my delight, at the counter of the mobile soup kitchen, was the man himself - Smelly Ken. He was resplendent in his ripped trainers, dirty grey jogging pants and disgusting parker coat. As I exited my car, I wondered when he had last washed his hair. It might have been in this century, but it seemed very unlikely. He turned as I approached. A toothless grin spread across his face. Goodness knows how old he was, but to be honest it didn't matter - with his drugs and drink habits he wouldn't be around for much longer.

"Mr Hunter, come for a coffee? You'll have to pay you know. Nothing free for you posh folks here."

"I haven't come for a coffee, Ken. I need a word if I may."

He looked around suspiciously. It didn't look good talking to someone like me. The world in which Smelly Ken lived would never trust an outsider. It just wasn't worth the risk. He gestured with his eyes back towards my car. I obliged, turned and walked back.

"What's up guv'? Don't suppose you've got a couple of quid, do you?"

"I do Ken. I will sort you out, don't worry, but I need to ask you something. Have you heard about Jenks?"

"Yeah, some twat did him, guv'. Fuckin' shame. I liked him. Good guy was Jenks."

"He was, and I know you two were mates. Did he say anything to you, just before he was murdered? He was looking into something for me."

"Didn't say anything to me, guv'."

I pulled my wallet out and took a ten-pound note, waved it at Ken and asked the question again.

"Well guv', there was something. He said you had asked him to see what was about concerning some young girl. She had been taken from school. Some sick perverts, I guess, selling her into the sex trade...fucking twats."

"Yes, yes Ken. Stop making things up and answer my question. Did Jenks say anything to you?"

"Can't remember guv'."

I took another ten-pound note out and pushed it into his grubby hand.

"Now Ken, has your memory returned? Because if it hasn't, I am off. So, get thinking."

"It's like this guv' - Jenks came back to my place last week. He was fuckin' buzzing. He could hardly contain himself. I asked him what he had taken and he said nothing, it was something he had found out. Jenks had loads of contacts, knows everyone around these parts, know what I mean?

Anyway, he eventually calmed down and told me he had been poking about, asking questions for you like. You wanted to know about this kid who had been snatched, where she was, who had her and all that shit.

Jenks gets talking to one of his mates - I think his name is Dell - he buys stuff off Jenks - bouncing powder and Charlie - shit like that, sells it on to fund his own habit. Anyway, Dell had been asked to buddy up with some goon to snatch a girl for the big boss, whoever that is. They were shown some photos of the girl, you know, so they get the right one. Turns out that she is the best mate of this Dell's sister - goes to school with her. So, Dell says no fuckin' way! She will recognise him and that will be a bad thing, right! This guy agrees, slips Dell a few quid to keep his mouth shut and fucks off."

"Nice story, Ken, but how does that help me? Obviously, someone was asked to snatch the girl. After all, she has been taken."

"No boss, you don't know the full story. It was this guy who was trying to get Dell to join in. Dell knew him. He had done a few jobs in the past. Got well paid by this geezer, so Dell kept his mouth shut. But this was a bit too much for Dell...reminded him of his sister and all that, so he was more than happy to spill the beans to Jenks.

The man in question, the guy who had been trying to recruit Dell to do this job, was a cop. Yeah, boss a fuckin' fed. One of the local five O. Jenks couldn't believe it."

"Wait a minute, Ken. Are you trying to tell me that a local police officer is part of this?"

"Yeah boss, no doubt. Jenks was buzzing and it cost him his life. Man, you need to get this joker. Make sure he is locked up forever."

"Wait a minute, Ken. How sure are you that this Dell was telling the truth? Might just be a tale to get some money out of Jenks?"

"Listen boss, this is fuckin' guy...this guy is a cop, no doubt. No doubt at all. Jenks was buzzing, but he was also very frightened. For a very good reason as it turned out."

"I need to speak to this Dell. Ask him some more questions. Where does he hide out?"

"You'll be lucky boss. This news is all about town. Dell will be hiding. No one will find him. If I see him, I will tell him you are trying to find this cop. Do right by Jenks and that."

"Did Jenks say anything else about this cop?"

"Not much else. He was a cop... high up, not a plod on the street. Jenks thought he was working in Merseyside. A bit of a slimy twat, you know the kind. Dell did tell Jenks that the cop was up to his neck with the big crime boss - his right-hand man. He was one of the boss's enforcers. Didn't mind getting his hands dirty and knew how to use a gun if needed.

Dell was shit scared of him. Jenks did tell me that. I know Dell, he isn't scared of no one. He's a hard man, can take care of himself. Never been scared in his whole life, doesn't give a fuck about reputations. He was scared of this cop though. He wasn't playing any fuckin' games around him, no way."

"No names or descriptions?"

"No boss. Just what I told you. A cop, high up and bloody dangerous. This guy needs stopping. Can't be allowed to carry on. Get him boss. Do the fucker."

"I will do my best, Ken. Keep me posted mate. You have my number. I need to speak to Dell. If you find him, I promise it will be discreet - no names, nothing. Find him Ken. It's worth a few quid. Best day's business you will ever do. Find him and get in touch. Do I make myself clear?"

"Crystal, boss. I will find him, don't you worry. Let's do this for Jenks. Best mate I ever had."

I reluctantly shook hands and remembering to wash as soon as I could. I turned and got back into the car. He was right about Jenks. He wasn't a bad person and he certainly didn't deserve to die just for asking a few questions. As for the high-ranking cop, now that was a surprise and potentially a very difficult situation to resolve. I had to keep my wits about me. He had killed at least one person already. I didn't want to be the next one on the list!

Murder Squad Office. Southport Police Station.
Monday Late Afternoon.

"What do you mean DC Evans, you can't find him? You are a detective and very well paid. You have a high profile, one of the best this force has to offer. Well, that's the rumour. Please don't tell me he has gone missing. A two-bit private detective who spends most of his time grubbing about in other people's lives.

Get back out there and find him! I want him back here in one hour and if he isn't, Detective Constable Mike Evans, you will be back on community and school liaison by nightfall. Do I make myself clear?"

"Yes boss."

"Yes, Detective Inspector Smith. If you don't mind."

"Sorry, DI Smith. I will be back with our man shortly."

"Good answer. And take DS Shacklady with you. If you get lost or can't bloody remember what I have told you to do, I am sure she will point you in the right direction."

DC Mike Evans knew when to back off and get on with it. DI Smith was not a woman to be trifled with. He turned, grabbed his coat, and made for the stairwell. He would pick up DS Shacklady from the canteen on the way out.

The dark blue, unmarked Police Ford Mondeo pulled out of the carpark and set off along Lord Street. It was slightly grubby, perhaps one or two scratches down one side. To anyone who didn't know any better, it was just another car, taking a sales rep onto his next appointment.

"So, let me get this right, Mike - you have been looking for this Lee Hunter all day and have not been able to find him, anywhere?"

"Sharron, wherever he is, I haven't got a clue. If I didn't know any better, I would swear he knew I was coming. I have been to his flat three times, the Bold Arms - where he has lunch - his office, his next-door neighbours. I have all the patrols looking for his car and there has been nothing, not a thing."

"Not sure about that, Mike. He's ex-Met Police. He wouldn't do a runner, I am sure. He knows we would catch up to him in the end. You have been unlucky, that's all. Let's start again. Back to his place and see if anyone around there has seen him. Anyway, we need to get this murder sorted. It's a double homicide now, you know. The guy's wife was found in Derbyshire this morning with the same MO - three bullets in her head."

"Yeah, I heard. Who the hell would do that kind of thing and why? I know things get out of hand sometimes, but even the big gangs in these parts wouldn't normally go that far, and if they did, we would never find the bodies. We would have two missing persons, not two dead ones. The case would never be solved.

I have been trying to work it out all day. Is it a warning to someone? Are they trying to establish themselves or is one person trying to impress the boss? Why kill the wife? Surely, she's just a bit-part player. If anyone is involved in anything naughty, it's going to be her husband."

"We will get to the bottom of it eventually, Mike, and we better look good doing it. Eyes are upon us."

"Eyes? What do you mean?"

"Debs has had the gypsies from upon high. Some serious brass wanting this sorting out - no expense spared! Odd really, no clue as to why, but the pressure is on. There is no hiding what will happen to Deborah if she doesn't solve this case, and it won't be pleasant, I can tell you! To add to the confusion, the magnificent Detective Chief Inspector Mark Bruno, Operation Elm Tree, is joining us as joint chief, goodness knows why."

"What does that twat want, Sharron? He's next to useless. Never done a day's work in all his life. Just climbed the ladder on the backs of his staff. All he is going to do is screw this up. That's all he ever does. Then blames everybody else and walks away. How the hell has he managed to get details into the case? It's nothing to do with him?"

"I know, but what is Debs supposed to do? If she complains, you know full well what will happen. Bruno will complain to the highest level, Deborah will end up on gardening leave and Bruno will end up as the boss. If that happens, heaven help us all!"

"Why has he taken an interest in this case? What's he got to do with it?"

"Because it's high-profile, Mike. As I said, Debs has already had the *'get this done or else'* warning. Bruno must have picked that up and decided it will benefit him to be associated with it. He will ride this in all the way, take all the credit and criticise everyone else for being so slow, *'good job I was in charge'* kind of line! I can't think of any other reason why he would want to trouble himself. He's got nothing to gain from sorting this out."

"Just great! That's all we need. He was my first boss as a detective. He was head of the CID. What an idiot! And bent, I am sure. He used to try and get me to do lots of stuff and some of it wasn't completely kosher, but I was wet behind the ears and too fucking scared to say anything."

"Well, we don't know if he is bent, Mike. I wouldn't go around sharing that point of view. Mixing it with Bruno will get you sacked. No question about it!"

"We'd better keep our heads in gear then, Shaz. This is not going to be nice with that fool in charge."

The rest of the journey to Lee Hunter's flat was completed in silence. Neither detective was looking forward to their new joint boss taking over, but they had little choice in the matter and they knew it.

By the time they reached their destination, the rain had started again. The late afternoon had become dark grey and foreboding. The whole scene was slick and shining. The rain soaking everything not covered, including the dull grey concrete of the flats. It was a depressing and uninviting vista, forgotten by the progress of time and the degeneration of the area.

DC Mike Evans turned into the small carpark at the back of the flats. The windscreen wipers of the police pool car were by now on full speed. There were three other vehicles in the area - a rusty old transit van with no front wheels, a tired old Vauxhall Vectra with 'Taxi' and a telephone number emblazoned on the side. The third vehicle was a metallic black Mercedes S-Class, almost new. Its engine running, but no lights showing.

"Bloody hell! That's a flash motor for these parts, Sharron. Now that kind of car would do me fine, especially with a chauffeur."

"Yeah, it's nice. How much are they?"

"Got to be the best part of 85k Shaz, probably more. I have seen that car somewhere before though. I recognise those wheels. They are not original spec. They are 3k alone, plus the tyres."

"Come to think of it, so have I. Where the hell have I seen it? Maybe it belongs to one of the local drug dealers? Shall we knock on the window and introduce ourselves?"

"That would be fun, Sharron. Perhaps have a mooch about in the back? I bet we'd find plenty of stuff for a bonus nicking."

"Yeah, let's do it. Pull up behind him. He won't be expecting to see us here."

As DC Evans turned fully into the carpark and manoeuvred behind the Merc, it suddenly sprung into life. It's lights coming on. In a flash, it turned to the left and quickly moved off, through the gates and onto the main road.

"Oh yes, he's certainly up to no good. Shall we follow, Mike?"

"I want to Sharron, but I have Deborah's words ringing in my ears. We need to find our suspect. As much as a nicking of a local drug dealer would look good, finding the main suspect in a double murder would always look better. Leave them to it. Let's just concentrate on the job in hand, hey!"

"Yeah, you are right. We will come across that Merc again no doubt. Next time, he gets nicked."

"Right Sharron. You wait here. See if he pops out or tries to do a runner. I will knock on his door."

DC Mike Evans walked up to the concrete steps leading from the ground to the first floor and turning left walked to the last flat of four on that level. The door bore the repaired marks of the forced entry by the Armed Response Unit on his last visit. A cold shiver ran down his spine. He should have had an ARU here this time. This guy was probably still armed and dangerous, but there was no time to worry about that now. He knocked several times, but with no answer. He turned back to make his way to the steps when a woman popped her head out of the door next-door.

"Can I help?"

"Sorry, madam. I am looking for Lee Hunter. Have you seen him about?"

"Who are you?"

"Sorry, this is my badge. Detective Constable Mike Evans, Merseyside Police. It's very important that we speak to Lee. Have you seen him today?

"Nope, not seen him for a few days. Is he in trouble?"

"Trouble? No, we just want a chat that's all. You say you haven't seen him for a few days...when was the last time you spoke to him?"

"Well, it's Monday night...I would say, middle of last week? Last time I saw him was perhaps Thursday last? Something like that."

"OK. I wonder if I might take your name?"

"Yeah, it's Ruth Davenport. If I see him, I will tell him to get in touch. Have you got a card?"

"No problems, Mrs Davenport, here you go. It's got my office and work number. This one here ending in 1313 is the best to contact me on. It's really important that I speak to Lee. Please get him to call me."

"Thanks, I will. And it is Ms Davenport, not Mrs."

"Sorry, I stand corrected."

With that, DC Evans made his way back to the car, running the last few yards through the rain and slamming the driver's door behind him.

"No luck Mike?"

"No, nothing. The next-door neighbour popped her head out. Said she hasn't seen him since last week. Not sure that I believe her. For all we know, he could be in her kitchen right now or in any of the other properties around here. It wouldn't surprise me if he was back in London. We need to get back to the office and get the Met Police to start looking into his old haunts, and get a surveillance team in here just in case he turns up again."

It Has Been a Bloody Long Day.
Monday Late Afternoon.

What a day! Started off early, went to find Smelly Ken, lost my phone, well actually it had fallen under the driver's seat, then the car broke down. That's all I needed - plenty to do and no damn car - perfect! Fortunately, it was within a few minutes' walk from the Ford dealer, and since I had been talked into a comprehensive breakdown package by the spotty salesman, I managed to get a free hire car - bonus!

Well, if you could call it that. I lost my lovely Mondeo and gained a Fiesta, but at least I was moving again. Also, the lovely lady behind the reception desk helped me find my mobile. Good job she persuaded me that it must still be in the car, and her intuition was way better than mine.

"If you didn't turn it on, sir, and you haven't used it at all, it must still be in the car. Have you checked the glove compartment?"

"Of course, I have. Do I look stupid?"

The truth was, I didn't check the glove compartment nor anywhere else for that matter! There was just too much going on for my brain to work properly, especially when it came to errant mobile phones.

The problem was that things were beginning to overwhelm me. Find Gwen's dad by next Monday night, dissuade Adele from killing or getting me to kill her husband, find 30k for Fat Tony or I die, and try to make things up to Ruth. Not much, eh?

Where to start? Well, I decided to go for lunch, not in the Bold Arms, but over the road to the Hesketh. Maybe I might find Adele in there - no such luck. The white Fiesta wasn't such a bad little car though, so I went for a drive in the country to try and clear my head, and called in to my accountant. Necessary, but bloody boring. That's when I remembered that I hadn't switched my mobile on all day. Oops, it was now 7pm, better power it up and see who's been trying to call me.

There were eight missed calls from a mobile number I didn't recognise ending in 1313, and six voicemail messages from the same number. I deleted them without listening, they were probably some scams. Two calls from my bank - deleted them as well - a missed call from my sister - I will phone her back tonight, and a couple from Ruth. Now that's better.

I scrolled down to 'RETURN CALL' and pressed 'GO'.

"Hi, Lee. Where the hell have you been all day? The old bill has been here three or four times. What the hell have you been up to?"

"Sorry, what the heck are you talking about, Ruth?"

"The police! Just seen one off. Some detective constable wanted to chat to you."

"Sorry Ruth, but I haven't got a bloody clue what's going on there. They did pull me in last night about an incident, but my alibi checked out and that was the end of that, or so I thought. I guess they must have phoned you to confirm my whereabouts?"

"Yeah, they did. I wondered what that was about Lee, do you know?"

"Yeah, something about a Mr Francis Jackson Barnes. I wonder if they think I am involved somehow in whatever it is he has done. Goodness knows what. They wouldn't tell me. I guess they want to talk to me again. They have verified my whereabouts, so I don't know what else they think I know?"

"Well come home and I will make you a nice supper. I still have that wine in the fridge. Could be a nice evening."

I felt the hackles on the back of my neck starting to prick up. You develop senses like that after so many years in the police. Call it instinct, but you just feel when something isn't quite right. The one place the local police can find me will be at home. All they need to do is watch and wait.

"I can't afford to spend any time as a guest of the local police, Ruth. They can really mess you around if they feel so inclined. I haven't a clue what they want with me, but I have a very important job on, and I need to get it done by next Monday night. I can't afford to spend a couple of days being questioned about something I haven't done by some pissed off detective who can't find the real person they are looking for.

I need to stay out of the way. I know this sounds a bit Hollywood, but a life depends on me getting this job done and time is running out."

"Wow, sounds a bit James Bond! I like a bit of intrigue. It's like one of those novels I buy, or B movies on the movie channel."

"I can assure you, Ruth, that this is as real as it gets, and a young girls' life is on the line. I am bloody scared, I don't mind telling you, if I fail… I don't want to think about that."

"Lee, you sound really anxious. Sorry about those last remarks. I didn't mean to make fun."

"It's OK, Ruth. It's been a long day. I just want to lay back, relax and switch off for a few hours, and clear my head. Tomorrow I need to try and find someone who no one has seen for days. He may be on the run, hiding abroad, or even dead and I don't know where to start."

"Look, I am house sitting for my sister. She and her other half are away for a couple of weeks. I can meet you there. We can have a bite to eat, watch the TV and just relax. Worth a thought?"

"That's kind of you, Ruth. I certainly can't come home. The old bill will be watching my place for sure, but I can't involve you. That's not fair."

"You already have, Lee, and I am happy to help. Have you got a pen and paper? Here is the address..."

Of course, I didn't have anything to write on, so I tried to commit to memory the address she had given me. It was Haig Avenue, near to the football ground. I was hoping I would forget it by the time I got there as I really didn't want to involve her in this disaster of a job.

On the drive there, I couldn't stop thinking what all the fuss was about with the local police. Why were they so keen on talking to me? I couldn't give them any more information regarding Mr Francis Jackson Barnes. I didn't know the guy or anything about him. I tried to connect him with anything I was doing or anyone I knew, but there was nothing, nothing at all. The only thing I could think was he knew Jenks, but given the address DI Smith had given me, I doubted that very much.

There was also the problem with Ken Walker, Gwen's dad. Time was running out and I still had no clue at all on what I was going to do next. I decided to put that to the back of my mind and not to worry about that until the morning.

Tonight, I needed to contact Adele and see what she was up to. I sat outside the address Ruth had given me and waited for her to turn up. This was a good opportunity to make that call to Adele. I hadn't heard from her for a while and that was unusual for her. I picked up my mobile and thumbed through my contacts, found her name, and pressed 'CALL'.

The phone rang, but there was no answer. Goodness knows what she was up to at this time of night. I tried once more, hoping she would answer, but there was nothing. Again, the line just disconnected, leaving me listening to white noise. I was just about to stuff the mobile back into my pocket when it started to ring. I looked down at the screen and much to my surprise, Adele's name was flashing.

"Hi Adele. How's it going? We have not spoken for a while."

"Sorry, sir. To whom am I speaking to? This is Detective Constable Williamson, Derbyshire CID."

I sat there in the car for several moments. What had just happened? I looked down at the screen and sure enough it was Adele's phone, but who the hell was DC Williamson?

"Hello, sir. This is Detective Constable Williamson, Derbyshire CID. May I ask who's calling?"

"Erm, sorry DC Williamson. My name is Lee Hunter. I was hoping to speak to Adele?"

"Are you a family member or a friend of Mrs Jackson Barnes?"

Mrs Jackson Barnes? It took a second or two for the penny to drop. Mrs Jackson Barnes... Shit, that would make Adele the wife of Francis Jackson Barnes! This whole thing was becoming very strange indeed. Why the hell would Derbyshire CID have Adele's phone? Was she in their custody? Has she finally done the deed and killed her husband herself? I wondered if that's why Merseyside Police wanted to talk to me. Her husband was dead and she was blaming me for the murder?

"Sorry, DC Williamson. That's taken me by surprise somewhat. No, Mrs Barnes is a client of mine. Is she in trouble?"

"I am afraid, I can't be any more help with that, Mr Hunter. Not unless you are a close family member."

That last comment told a story. One that many a training course in the Met Police had taught me. This was a very serious issue indeed. I could easily deduce from it, that Adele was most likely in very serious trouble, or even dead! The question was, what was it? Was she a suspect in a crime or something way more serious?

"I see, DC Williamson. I need to find out what has happened to Adele. Who can I contact that might be able to help? I was involved in a long running case and it's important that I find out what has actually happened."

"I have your name and number, Mr Hunter. I will make sure someone contacts you shortly. Please keep your phone handy."

With that, the phone went dead. My head was whirling with the possibilities. Was the case involving Francis Jackson Barnes, which DI Deborah Smith had questioned me on, directly connected to the incident or even demise of Adele? After all, she was his wife. Has she killed him? Committed suicide? Or been killed in a car accident trying to escape the crime scene?

Of course, I could simply be jumping the gun. She could have been arrested for driving at 120 mph down the M6. I needed to wait, speak to someone from Derbyshire CID, stop making stories up. I decided to get out of the car and wait for Ruth. I had spent all day either sat in the car, in a pub or at the accountants. I needed to stretch my legs and my mind.

I had just closed the car door when the phone started to ring and without looking at the screen I pressed 'ANSWER'.

"Hello, Lee Hunter. I assume that's Derbyshire CID?"

"No, Mr Hunter. This is Detective Sergeant Sharron Shacklady, Merseyside Murder Squad. Listen, Mr Hunter. I need to speak to you face to face. Please can you come into the station at the end of Lord Street?"

"What the hell for? I have spoken to your boss about Francis Jackson Barnes. There is nothing else I can say."

"No, Mr Hunter. This is not directly related to that. Can you just pop over to the station now, please? I need to speak to you."

"And if I say no?"

"Well, I would hope you would try and help me out and pop in for a chat. Shouldn't take long."

"And if I say no?"

"I am sure it won't take long, Mr Hunter. No need to be like that."

"I will ask you for the last time - what will happen to me if I refuse?"

"Then I will need to take more formal actions, Mr Hunter, but I am sure it won't come to that."

"You mean you will issue a warrant for my arrest?"

"Mr Hunter can I... "

"Listen, DS Shacklady. I spent many a long year in the Met. I know how this dance goes, so let's get to the point, hey. Whatever you want to talk to me about doesn't relate to that parking ticket I got last week, does it? This is way more serious. Can I assume it's something to do with Adele and her current situation?"

"Can you just come into the station now and we can clear all this up, Mr Hunter?"

I pressed 'END CALL', got back into the car and drove back towards town. I could have evaded DS Shacklady and waited until morning, but to be honest, I couldn't be bothered. In any case, they would catch up with me sooner or later and then they would be really pissed off. So, discretion would be the better part of valour in this instance.

I felt really disappointed for Ruth though. I got a quick text off to her with a huge apology, and promised that our third date would certainly be better. I wasn't so sure, though."

Murder Squad Office. Southport Police Station.
Monday Night.

I found myself back in interview room four. It didn't smell any better than last time and the air conditioning still didn't work. They haven't told me anything about why I had to be here. One thing was for sure, I don't intend to stay for very long.

They were still using that old trick - *'make him wait, make him uncomfortable, make him panic'*. Of course, none of that was going to work. I did try to tell them about my past, but they weren't listening. So, nothing new there then!

Anyway, I sat back, sipped on my brown liquid and waited for the inevitable interview. After all, I had nothing to hide, did I? I kept checking the clock on the wall. A very generic white device with a second hand that seemed to take hours to rotate around. Eventually, more than an hour after I arrived, a woman in her late fifties entered the room with a case file under her arm. She was soon joined by a younger man, smartly dressed. It was DC Mike Evans, all full of his own importance. Odd thing though, those alarm bells started to ring again as soon as I saw him. I don't know why. Mistrust or suspicion? Not sure, but it wouldn't surprise me if he turned out to be a very bad apple!

"Right, Mr Hunter. This shouldn't take long. There are a couple of things we need to clear up."

"I am here to help DS Shacklady, but when you say, *'it shouldn't take long'*, that's police speak for, *'you are going to be here for ages'*, doesn't it?"

"Not necessarily, Mr Hunter, but there are a few points that we need to discuss. Firstly, there is some evidence that you might have been at a crime scene recently. Namely, 3 Claridge Road. What can you tell me about this?"

"Look, I have cleared this up once and for all. You have my movements for that night. They have been checked and all is fine."

"We just like to be certain about things, sir. Also, we have found an envelope with your fingerprints on it. It has some money inside. What can you tell me about this?"

"If you are talking about that cash Adele tried to pay me, it was about a thousand pounds, I would guess? It was for a job she wanted me to do. I refused, gave it her back and she drove off in her car. That's about it really."

DC Evans then decided to come to life. What the hell he thought he could bring to the party eluded me, but give the kid a chance, that's what I say.

"How do you explain that envelope being found at a murder scene, Mr Hunter?"

Now that did shock me - a murder scene. How did it get from Adele's car to a murder scene? Had she tried to use that money to pay someone else to do the job I refused to do?

"Not sure what you mean, DC Evans. I gave her the envelope back and she drove away. Not much more I can say about that. Check the CCTV camera around the back of the Bold Arms. You will see the meeting taking place, date and time, no problems."

"What was the money for, Mr Hunter?"

"That's client confidentiality, DC Evans, but sufficed to say I didn't want the job. That's why the money was handed back. Now, how it ended up at a murder scene, wherever that was, I have absolutely no idea. I suggest you ask Adele."

"We can't, Mr Hunter. She was the victim at the murder scene. That's where the envelope was found, with your fingerprints on it. To make things worse, her husband was found dead earlier on Sunday with one of your business cards by his side.

You see, Mr Hunter, there seems to be a pattern emerging here. Namely, evidence of your presence at two murder scenes. So, I ask you again. Why was an envelope with a considerable amount of money and your fingerprints found at a murder scene?"

This sent an almighty shock through my system. Adele, dead? Things had taken a dizzying turn. Her husband found murdered at home and Adele found dead later.

OK, he might have been murdered by Adele. She would be the main suspect for that. But then she was found murdered. That didn't make sense. How the hell had that all happened? Surely, they meant she had committed suicide, after killing him?

"You seemed shocked, Mr Hunter. Have you anything to say?"

"DS Shacklady, I have just put two and two together and I might have come up with five, but you are suggesting a double murder. One at home and another, well, somewhere else? Are you saying Francis Jackson Barnes was found murdered at home and his wife, Adele Jackson Barnes, was found murdered in her car?"

"We ask the questions, Mr Hunter. Now what can you tell us about this? You seem to be familiar with the scenario."

"I knew you were going to say that, DS Shacklady. It's just supposition on my part, being an ex-cop and that, you get a feeling for these kinds of things. To be honest, I haven't got a bloody clue what's happened here. Did she kill her husband and do a runner? Has a double hit been put out on both of them? Did her lover kill the husband, but then an argument broke out and so he killed her? You tell me. It's a bloody mystery.

I will tell you what the money was for, DC Evans. She wanted me to deal with her husband, perhaps even kill him, but I refused. That's why the money was handed back. I am not the squeaky-clean boy next door Detective Constable, but I am no hit man either, I can assure you of that.

I am more than happy to furnish you with all my movements for the last 48 hours. You already know about Sunday - the rest shouldn't be a problem."

The room went quiet. The two detectives looked at each other, then DS Shacklady turned back to me.

"Look, Mr Hunter, at this present moment, you are a suspect in a double murder. Letting you go isn't on the books at this present time. I am going to hold you for 24 hours and try to get to the bottom of this. Being an ex-cop, I guess you know the score."

I certainly did know the score and as the door to the cell slammed shut behind me, I contemplated the next 24 hours, damn it! That's going to knock another day off my deadline to find Gwen's father. The whole thing was going to hell in a hand cart. I couldn't imagine a worst-case scenario, and that's if they did let me out. They might just charge me and that would be the end for Gwen, her mother and for me.

Early Tuesday Morning.
Initial Case Meeting, Murder Squad.

Four people sat in the meeting room - DI Deborah Smith, DS Sharron Shacklady, DC Mike Evans and Senior Scenes of Crime Investigator, Kaye Marie. DS Smith sat at the head of the table and she drew the meeting to order.

"Right, what have we got? What do we know? What don't we know? Once we get these things straight, I will call a full department meeting and try to get this lot sorted out. I would also like to get the main work underway before that prat Detective Chief Inspector Mark Bruno slimes in to take charge. Right Kaye, what do we know?"

"Both Mr and Mrs Jackson Barnes were shot in the front of the head at close range. Both were shot three times with a 9mm automatic pistol. The lab tells me that all recovered bullets came from the same gun. Both were shot on or abouts last Sunday afternoon, or early evening. Both died immediately. There is no specific DNA evidence at this time."

"OK, Mike, evidence?"

"Not much on that front, boss. We found a business card in the house adjacent to the body of Mr Jackson Barnes that belonged to Lee Hunter. The other evidence is an envelope containing one thousand five hundred pounds with Hunter's prints on it. That was found in the glove compartment of Mrs Jackson Barnes' car. Someone took the CCTV videotape from the house and smashed the machine, so no chance of any recording. Mrs Jackson Barnes' car was found on a deserted road. No tyre marks, no bullet casings, sod all boss.

Whoever did this was good at their job and was very well prepared. They knew about the CCTV at the house, they knew exactly where to intercept or meet Mrs Jackson Barnes without being noticed. To date, there is no DNA, no prints, no CCTV and no witnesses. 'F' all boss."

"Right, Sharron. How's the interview going with our one and only suspect?"

"Yes, our darling Mr Lee Hunter, private detective and ex-Met Police. I checked with the Met and he was a detective chief inspector with 25 years in the job. He left of his own accord a couple of years ago, moved up here and started his detective agency. Apart from a couple of parking tickets, that's about it on his background. He seems to be a not particularly successful PI, who just gets on with his job.

He has plenty of corroborative evidence regarding his whereabouts on Sunday afternoon, and other times, including time dated CCTV from the Hesketh pub and the Bold Arms carpark. You can't get much better than that. As for the reason for one of his business cards being in the house next to the body, he has no explanation, other than Mrs Barnes was a client of his. As for his whereabouts on Sunday evening, that's very simple Debs, he was here with you! No way he could have got out to Derbyshire and then back here to be picked up by the uniforms at his flat. No way at all. There wasn't enough time!

He was seen in the Hesketh by the bar manager with the late Mrs Adele Jackson Barnes. That kind of backs up his story about her being a customer and perhaps the explanation regarding the money.

To be honest boss, I don't think he has anything to do with it. There is some circumstantial evidence, but nothing that can't be either ignored or explained away. In any case, why would an ex-Met police detective chief inspector go around blowing people's brains out? He can verify his movements for the whole day in question and there is no physical evidence connecting him. I think we are barking up the wrong tree boss."

Just as DI Smith was about to answer, the door burst open and to everybody's horror Detective Chief Inspector Mark Bruno walked into the room. He was wearing his normal dark suit and cream suede shoes. His hair was as greasy as ever and his pock marked face seemed to shine in the morning light.

"Morning tossers! Well, Mark Bruno is here now so you can all relax. Steady up, Deborah. I know I have that effect on women, but here is not the time or the place. Maybe later babes. Now what were you saying Shaz about pissing up trees? I like a bit of that you know, especially in the privacy of your own home, know what I mean?"

He made a clicking sound as he gave an over exaggerated wink at DS Sharron Shacklady.

"Well, if I live and die, it's DC Mike Evans. Does your mum know you are here? Shouldn't you be at school or something?"

DI Deborah Smith tapped the table as she tried to take control of the meeting.

"Right, sir. I think we have all had enough of silly banter. We have a double murder on and Detective Chief Superintendent Martin Kiff wants answers, and he wants them soonest. We were going through what we have, and to be honest, it's not much."

"Listen, Debbie baby. That fuckwit you have in the cells - what's his name? Lee Hunter - charge him and let the courts sort it out, done! Kiff has his answers, case solved, one big tick in the statistics for closed cases and we can all go the pub at lunch time. What's the problem with that?"

"The problem is, sir, we have no evidence to charge him with and the name is DI Deborah Smith, sir!"

"Sorry, DI Smith. Not getting enough at home? You should pop over to my place, I can sort that out for you. Who needs evidence anyway? His business card says he was there. His prints on the envelope tells me he was in the car with that bird Adele Jackson Barnes. That's it, case closed."

"The problem is, sir, he has alibis for the whole day in question including CCTV images."

"Fuck that! He could have tampered with the CCTV recordings. Charge him. Let's get him over to the magistrate's court and remand him in custody. Job done."

"It's not going to work, sir. They will throw it out."

"It will work DI Smith, because I say it will work. Now get the paperwork together and let's get this shamble on the road. What kind of department are you running? It's a fucking joke! How the hell you lot get anything done around here amazes me. Do you actually solve any cases?"

"We get things done, sir, by due diligence and meticulous attention to detail. Not to say absolute professionalism. What you are asking is wrong and it will fall apart. We are wasting our time even talking about it. He is not our man, so we need to find out who is."

"He is our man if I say so, DI Smith. You go on about professionalism, but seem to lack the basic grasp of rank structure. I am telling you to sort this out. Get him charged and get this case closed, and do it now. Do I make myself clear? If I need to tell you again, you are for the fucking high jump, DI Smith. A very fucking high jump."

Without uttering another word, he turned and walked calmly out of the room, leaving those present absolutely shell-shocked. The door closed gently behind him and the room fell into a deep and stunned silence.

DS Sharron Shacklady looked around the room before finally turning to DI Smith.

"Did that just happen or did I fall asleep and have a bloody nightmare? I know he can be a right knob, but that takes the biscuit. Surely, he doesn't expect to get away with that? There is no way the CPS or the local Magistrates are going to do anything other than throw the case straight out of the nearest window. You are going to see the superintendent about this, aren't you Debs?"

"Nope, I am going to let Hunter go. If I involve anyone else in this, goodness knows what will happen. I already have Chief Superintendent Kiff chewing my arse over this as well as that dick DCI Bruno. I am beginning to think there is conspiracy going on here. No one else is going to get the chance to screw this up any further than it already has been."

"I know I am a lowly detective constable boss, but isn't Bruno simply going to have Hunter re-arrested and then you thrown off the case? A man like Bruno is certainly not going to sit back and accept what you have done. Not in front of everyone?"

"You are right, Mike, but it's the right thing to do. It's the right thing for Lee Hunter, it's the right thing for me and the department. We are just going to look like fools if we do what he wants.

Get down to the cells Mike, and bail Hunter - normal conditions - give him the gypsies and throw him out of the front door. Best get a move on before Bruno decides to screw this up even further."

"Do you think that's a good idea boss? If he finds out what you have done, he will have all of us. I think we need to do what he says. Perhaps he is right about Hunter?"

"Get down to the cells now, DC Evans, and do as you are told!"

DC Mike Evans exited the room without any further comment. Again, the room fell into silence before Kaye Marie decided to break the hush.

"We all know about Bruno, but this is extreme, even by his standards. What the hell is he up to? Trying to stich someone up, in all probability, an innocent man? He was never going to get away with it, never in a million years. The courts would see to that. Is there something going on here? Has he got something on Hunter? I wonder if he knows something we don't?"

"I have to agree Kaye, but what the hell can Bruno know in connection to this half assed private detective? He is after making Hunter the scapegoat for these murders. I am not sure why though? It's never going to work. He is just going to make a fool out of the lot of us. That bastard is up to something and we need to find out what. This doesn't feel right. Even for Bruno this is extreme. We have to make sure it doesn't end up destroying us or Lee Hunter."

Outside Southport Police Station.
Tuesday Lunchtime.

I finally found myself standing on Lord Street, outside the police station. It was 12.30pm and I was starving. The car was exactly where I had left it, so I decided to grab some lunch and pay a visit back to see Smelly Ken. I was sure he knew where Dell would be hiding. I just have to bribe him enough to tell me. Dell was the one man who could connect things together in this case and maybe even give me a name or at least point me in the right direction to the bent cop.

I pulled my mobile out of the plastic 'property bag', along with my car keys. Well, actually the courtesy car keys, my wallet and some loose change. I stood next to the little white Fiesta, stared down at my phone and waited for it to come to life. As it did so, I glanced across to the police station. I could see through the heavy metallic gates into the car park with the myriad of yellow and blue marked patrol cars, two ambulances and several boring unmarked cars. They always seemed to be dark blue, slightly grubby and unloved. Perhaps that was deliberate. There were a couple of nice police motorcycles which I would love to have a go on, but I'd probably end up killing myself. There was a mixture of other vehicles, possibly belonging to members of staff, and another one of those bloody BMW X6's. Who the hell is earning enough money for one of them? They are paying cops way too much nowadays. I need to complain to my local Police Complaints Commission!

Anyway, my phone finally came to life. I knew when I turned it on, the list of missed call, texts and probably the odd threat from Fat Tony would bombard me. To be honest, I couldn't be bothered with all that crap. I needed to concentrate on getting Gwen back.

That's when thoughts of Adele rushed back into my mind. She has been murdered, and her husband. Who the hell did that? It made no sense at all? I had to decide if I involved myself in that nightmare. The police would be constantly on my back, I wouldn't get paid and who would benefit? No, let the local old bill sort that out. Leave it to them and walk away.

The trouble was I couldn't. Maybe it was the ex-police detective in me. Perhaps unresolved business, but it felt wrong just walking away. Another thing was the reaction of DI Smith and her team. It was obvious to all that I had nothing to do with the murders, but they couldn't leave me alone. Also, when that dumb DC Evans released me, he made it abundantly clear that they knew it was me and I would be back!

Why the hell did he say his boss, Detective Chief Inspector Mark Bruno would have me in the end? I thought his boss was Detective Inspector Deborah Smith? This smelled of something and I couldn't quite put my finger on it. I knew from experience that some pools of black mystery are not worth diving into. They are full of hidden rocks and undercurrents. This was one such pool, and not one that I should play with.

Damn it to hell. I couldn't leave it alone. Adele and her husband have been murdered and they were trying to finger me for it - why? What benefit would they get from sending me down for thirty years? Ok, they could claim a victory for their solved crimes statistics, but that's not how people like DI Smith worked! No, there was something else going on here and I was going to find out what!

Anyhow, I decided to turn the phone on with the rule, *'if it didn't begin with Ruth'*, I would delete it. Sufficed to say, I spent the next ten minutes pressing the delete key with three exceptions. Four texts from Ruth - she didn't sound too pleased, not that I blamed her! One voice mail from Kim Walker, saying that she has received another threatening message from her daughter's kidnappers. I must get back to her and soon.

The last was a text from Smelly Ken. Something about *"the sun is shining good man. It's Friday and what I got to say, what a fucker"*. I had no idea what that meant. I guessed he was off his head again, but it was probably a good idea to get back to him, maybe! He had taken the time to contact me. Probably he thought he was phoning someone else, but I couldn't ignore that text.

Right, prioritise - first phone Ruth. Take her to lunch, try and start again. Well, again, for the third time. Second, call Mrs Walker and try to convince her that everything was going well and not to worry. That was not going to be easy, but I would try, get my best lying head on and hoped it worked.

Lastly, call Smelly Ken and try and work out what the hell that text meant. It was probably not meant for me or for anyone else for that matter, but I would give it a go. It might prove amusing if nothing else.

With some considerable amount of apprehension, I pulled up Ruth's number and pressed 'CALL'. Chances are she would be at work. Even so, she was never going to speak to me ever again, was she?

"Well, if I live and breathe. It's Mr Mystery. The ever-vanishing Lee Hunter."

"Sorry Ruth. What can I say other than sorry. It wasn't my fault. Please let me explain, say over lunch?"

"Oh right! Like the last couple of times, you left me standing, followed by calls from the Merseyside Police Murder Squad. Just what a girl wants on a date - quizzing about a fella's whereabouts. What more could I have wished for? What an adventure!"

"Listen, I know I might be flogging a dead horse here, but I owe you a proper apology at least."

A long deadly silence followed. You know the one, just before the phone went dead, never to ring again. Of course, I wouldn't blame her, perhaps it was for the best.

"So, Lee Hunter, if I agree to meet you for lunch, are you actually going to turn up this time or am I going to be arrested for some terrible crime? I was going to dye my hair this afternoon, I can be at least certain that, that will happen. Or I can take a chance to wait the whole afternoon hanging around and not meeting you?"

"Please let me make it up to you, Ruth. I will pick you up. There is a great place in Birkdale we can chat, have a bite to eat, a glass of wine."

"I am nowhere near Birkdale, but I will meet you in the carpark of the Richmond on Scarisbrick New Road in twenty minutes. Surely nothing much can happen in that amount of time?"

"Deal."

I didn't get the chance to say anything else before the phone went dead. To be honest, I was happy with that. At least she was open to me grovelling and humiliating myself in a public place. That would be a good start, I guess.

I pulled up in the Richmond's capacious carpark. It was then I realised that I had no idea what her car looked like. I decided to get out and stand, very self-consciously and look around. She emerged from a silver Renault Clio, looked in my direction and smiled. Now that was a good start.

The lunch went very well, which made a change. A couple of beers, a half bottle of wine for Ruth and two hearty ale and steak pies. The conversation was a little ropey, but I wouldn't blame her if she slapped me across the face and walked out. Thankfully she didn't.

"So, what the hell is screwing with your life to such an extent that the Merseyside Police keep arresting you?"

"Well, they don't keep arresting me, but they do keep pulling me in for a chat. There has been a double murder and they think I have something to do with it, which I haven't by the way!"

"I didn't think for one moment that you did, and I certainly wouldn't be sat here if I thought you had. Why do they think you have something to do with it?"

"You tell me Ruth, because I haven't got a damn clue, other than one of the victims was a client of mine. But that doesn't turn me into a serial killer, does it? I just get the feeling they are trying to stich someone up for the murders. They are looking for a scapegoat, someone to pin this lot on, a quick fix to cover up the big picture."

"The big picture, which is what?"

"That's a great question. It's not the murder squad per say, there is something going on under the radar, someone or some people looking to cover something up. Look, it's probably just me being a suspicious old twat. I spent too much time running around after criminals and it's warped my mind. Take no notice."

"OK, let's talk about something else then. What else is happening in the private detective world?"

"Well, it's been interesting. I am on the trail of a young girl who has been kidnapped. I need to find her father though and that's proving very difficult. I need to get in contact with an informer of mine by the name of Smelly Ken. I will go and see him later. He might be able to help in another murder case. This time of a friend of mine by the name of Jenks. So, plenty to keep me busy and, of course, there is you and the blown dates. I would love the chance to make it up to you, please!"

She smiled the warmest and widest smile, took a sip of her red wine, and laughed.

"Lee Hunter, I have known a few men in my time, but I have to admit you are the most interesting. Even though the police keep ringing me at stupid o'clock in the morning asking questions about you. You can be very, very frustrating, but I must admit, it's not been boring.

I am a chiropodist. I travel about the town seeing to my clients' feet and I know that's not very glamorous, but it's a job. I see the same people and have the same conversations every day. Life owes me a bit of enjoyment.

I don't mind admitting that I need some excitement, something to look forward to, some fun, a pleasurable encounter. I am 52, I have been divorced for five years and have spent all that time building up my business. It's been hard work, but I have a long list of clients now, so I can't complain. In fact, I am about to put an offer in on a house, so all that hard work, the twelve-hour days and neglecting my kids is starting to pay off.

Things look rosy in the life of Ruth Davenport, or so you might think? For all the success and feelings of purpose and achievement, I still miss that companionship. Even if it's a serial killer like you. Don't get me wrong, I am not after Mr Right or a new wedding dress. Far from it, but it's nice to know there is someone special in my life. A person who you can have fun with, get drunk with, do stuff with, not a friend, I have plenty of them, but someone special."

"Odd you say that, Ruth. I was thinking the exact same thing. Since my divorce life has been busy in business and empty in life, if that makes sense? I wonder if you could see your way to giving me a second, sorry, third chance to be that special person?"

She laughed again. That smile was captivating. It was warm, inviting and full of happiness. I would never let her down again. She reached across with both hands and took firm hold of mine.

"I can see my way to giving you another chance, Lee Hunter. Even though I know I might well regret it. How about that bottle of red at my place and that meal I promised you, tomorrow night? The kids are at their dad's after school tomorrow. It's the rehearsal of the annual swimming gala. If you could possibly get to my place without being arrested again, say about 8pm?"

"That would be great. I will look forward to it. A nice evening and no bloody police."

As soon as I said that, I knew I might well come to regret it, but it was a date, and I was really looking forward to it. I paid the bill and we sauntered out into the carpark and over to her Renault.

"Well Lee, I have another three clients before I finish so I have to go, don't forget tomorrow and don't be late!"

I smiled, looked down at my feet like an awkward teenager and back into her eyes. She was smiling again and I so wanted to kiss her, but I had never been that confident around women.

Yes, I know I had been dishonourable in the past, but they were situations that just seemed to occur. Bumping into someone from work whilst out with friends, a drunken party or being thrown together on an operation.

There are millions of lonely people out there, people who just want some comfort, a warm and reassuring embrace. They need to hear that they are very special, even if they know it's not really meant. They ache to feel the excitement of seeing someone, receiving that late night text, waking to find that *"Hi, hope you have a great day"* on their WhatsApp. Life can become very dull or for some people - rejected by their partners, taken for granted - superseded by someone more exciting.

This was different though. This was turning into a relationship and I didn't have a bloody clue.

"Look Lee, are you going to kiss me or just keep standing there wondering what to do next?"

I laughed, stepped forward and kissed her. It felt so good, warm, passionate and genuine. I had forgotten how good it was to feel someone else so close to me, sharing one space, passion surging through us both. I could feel her back stiffen as the kiss became more fervent. I drew her ever closer as she ran her hands into my hair. I swear I could hear fireworks exploding overhead. It had taken me completely by surprise. I had not felt like this, maybe ever!

She pushed me back with a look of amazement written large in her eyes. Her mouth was open slightly and she held tightly onto my shoulders.

"Well, Lee Hunter. You certainly know how to make a girl feel hot inside. I almost forgot where we were. We will continue this tomorrow night. Now, I must go before I end up cancelling all my appointments this afternoon and take you home."

She turned, opened the car door and with a smiling backward glance, drove off out of the carpark.

I eventually managed to get Mrs Walker on the phone and reassured her that everything was fine, and to just ignore the threatening calls. I wasn't quite sure that she believed me, but there was nothing else I could do at his point in time.

"Just leave it to me, Mrs Walker. I will sort this out. I promise you. I am on the verge of finding your husband and Gwen will be released soon."

I felt terrible telling her lies, but she was so screwed up by all this that she would grab at anything I said just to make herself feel a little better.

It was almost 6pm before I managed get through to Smelly Ken. I wasn't quite sure which universe he was in, but it didn't sound like anywhere I had ever been. Still, at least he was awake, just about, and willing to see me. All I had to do was work out where the hell he was.

"Listen Ken, I need to talk to you right now. Can we meet for a drink or something?"

"Yeah man, sounds sweet. Got some dollar, cos' I is skint?"

"I have Ken, but where are you. Can I meet you somewhere?"

"That's cool, so long as I don't have to pay, cool man."

"Ken, you need to concentrate before I feel the need to beat you to death. Where are you?"

"I am here man. Where are you?"

"Right, I will ask you this for the last time, where are you right now?"

"You fuckin' stupid or something? I am at the bus station, right!"

"OK, stay right there. I will be over in twenty minutes."

"Yeah man, and bring some Vodka. I am thirsty."

"Will do, don't move! I am on my way."

It was never easy talking to a smack head, even when they were sober, but Ken was a special case, in fact a very special case! I couldn't help but liking him. He had a real shit start to his life.

His parents had left him to his own devices from the age of ten. They were never at home unless they were both pissed. There was never food in the house, clean clothes for him to wear, nothing at all. If he couldn't beg or steal it, he didn't have it and that included something to eat every day.

He was doomed from the start. He was dealt a real crap hand of cards in life. He just had to make the best of it. I often wondered if he had ever really known love and affection. Probably not. Just abandonment and emptiness.

Because of all that he was a lost soul, adrift in life's maelstrom, at the mercy of those that would take advantage, nothing to look forward to except an early death. He sank to the bottom of the pit, lost and with no hope of ever making it, and the worse thing of all, none of it was his fault!

I dropped in at the off-licence on the way to the meeting place. I bought a bottle of vodka, a dozen cans of strong larger and sixty fags. Seemed wrong somehow, I was just feeding his addictions, adding to the chaos in his young life, but this was the currency of his existence. It was as normal to him as fish and chips was to any regular person, but it didn't feel right. It never did!

I turned into the carpark at the back of the bus station. There were a couple of cars and a van, but otherwise it seemed quiet. The soup kitchen had gone, towed to another location in an endless attempt to bring a little sustenance to those not able to provide for themselves. Sitting on the little stub wall was Smelly Ken, looking exactly the same as he had done the last time I saw him. In fact, every time I saw him.

I pulled up next to him, got out and popped the hatchback on the white Fiesta. It didn't take him long to come and see what I had.

"Hey, sweet man. Love the lager and the fags. Let's open the vodka now. I feel like a touch."

"Just hang on Ken. We need to talk before you get blitzed out of your mind, again! You rang me earlier. What was it you wanted to tell me? Have you found this Dell guy? I really need to speak to him."

"Yeah boss, I have, but he's really scared. Jenks is dead and he thinks he will be next. So, no go. He's hiding and speaking to no one - not a chance."

"Listen Ken, I have to speak to him. He is the only person who may be able to save this young girl. I need to know what he does. I don't care what it costs or where or what I have to do, but I need to speak to him and speak to him now!"

"Look man, let me ring him and see what he says. Maybe he will speak to you over the phone?"

"Good idea Ken. Dial that number!"

I stepped back to give Ken some space. To be honest, I had to before I started to throw up. The bright afternoon sun and Ken are not a good combination. Eventually, and much to my relief, his call was answered. Ken wandered off with his mobile pinned to his ear. At least the lad was trying. I couldn't ask any more than that.

Eventually, the call ended. He turned and walked back towards me. He had the toothy grin on his face. Despite the appalling start this young man had to his life, he never lost that smile. Somewhere in there was a good human being. I promised myself that, someday soon, I would do my best to bring that person out into the sunshine and leave that desperate young man behind.

"Bit of a result here guv'. Dell will meet us. Says he trusts me and you, cos' you were a mate of Jenks. Says he has some news about that cop, but he is fuckin' scared guv'. We need to be careful."

"Don't worry, Ken. We will be. Now where do we meet him?"

"There is some wasteland, behind the old gas works, top of Russell Road. He said be there in twenty minutes. If we are one minute late, he fucks off. Understand guv'?"

"Right Ken, in the car. We are off."

We jumped into the car. Russell Road was at least twenty minutes away and we needed to get a move on or we would miss him! First thing I did was wind all the windows down. Don't you just love electrical systems?

We arrived at the appointed place with a few minutes to spare. A piece of overgrown waste land adjacent to the old gasworks. It was a typical scene - a broken chain-link fence, weeds a metre high, a couple of abandoned shopping trollies, but there was no sign of Dell.

I took the opportunity to have a look around, just in case we were being watched, but there was no one else about. I could hear the reversing horn of a lorry in the background, but other than that, it was a fairly peaceful scene.

"Right Ken, where the hell is Dell? It's past the appointed time. He should be here by now."

"Don't know boss. He said to be on time. I don't know. Let me ring him. He might be still at home, smoking some weed."

Ken pulled his rather dog-eared mobile from his coat pocket and made the call, but with no success. He tried several times without an answer. Finally, he stuffed it back into his pocket accompanied with a large sigh.

"Sorry boss, he isn't answering. Don't know what's happened?"

"Right, do you know where he lives Ken?"

"Yeah man."

"OK, we are going to his place. I am sick of this cloak and dagger crap. This is Southport, not the bloody Kremlin. James Bond isn't going to jump out at us any time soon and mow us down with some kind of super gun. Get in the car and we are off, now!"

"But boss, he doesn't want us to…"

"Ken, listen to me. Jenks is dead, murdered in his own home. I have the police chasing me over another two murders. A young girl has been kidnapped and I have been assured that she and her mum will be dead if I don't find her dad very soon! For goodness sakes, the body count could be five by next Monday - six if you include me! To add to all of this, there might be a rogue cop running around. That same cop might be trying to pin stuff on me or worse.

We are going to his place and he is going to tell me what he knows. Even if I must beat it out of him, do I make myself clear? It's like some kind of sick nightmare or a crazy Die-Hard film. It's bloody madness! This situation is way out of hand Ken. If Dell knows anything, he needs to tell me, no, he will tell me!"

Smelly Ken looked astonished at my outburst. He didn't know whether to run or just give in and do as he was told. It was several moments before he responded, eventually opening his mouth, spitting the words out one at a time.

"Right, boss. We best go."

Unsurprisingly, it didn't take long to find Dell's place - a broken-down old caravan, not far from the gas works. It had been somebody's pride and joy, a holiday home par excellence, but that was many years ago. The white exterior was now yellow with age, covered in part with streaks of dirt and green algae. One of the broken windows has been repaired with an old plastic sack and brown parcel tape.

"This is it, boss. Not much, but at least it's all his and no one bothers him here. Let me go and knock. You stay here, less chance of him doing a runner if he sees my face."

I had that same feeling looking at this rotten, broken-down caravan as I had earlier with Ken. Another life on the scrap heap with no chance of making it. I was prepared to bet the beginning of his life had been blighted in the same way as Ken's.

Ken knocked on the door, but there was no answer. So, I decided to join in. I had to admit to feeling angry by this stage. I was getting absolutely nowhere. People have died and the killing hasn't stopped yet.

I tried to peer into the windows that were still actually useable and not covered in black plastic sacks, old newspapers or filth. I couldn't see anything inside. The grime and crap made the whole interior grey and indistinct.

"Ken, stand back. I am going to kick the door in. If he is hiding in here, I need to find out."

"Yeah boss."

He stood back as I levelled a kick at the door to the caravan. It buckled and burst open without any real resistance. The smell from inside was overpowering - a mixture of unwashed clothes, dirty bodies, and rotten food. I took a deep breath before entering. I hoped it would be enough to sustain me as I looked for Dell.

It didn't take long to find him, laying prostrate on the floor of the caravan, in between the cooker and the bathroom was his body, surrounded by a pool of still wet blood. I was immediately frozen to the spot, unable to move either inside or out. The head had been blown apart - several shots had turned the cranium into an empty shell. Blood, brains, and gore sprayed upwards, covering most parts of the interior, including the roof.

It had that sickly smell of dried blood and body waste that often accompanies such an event. I felt the caravan move as Ken entered behind me and I wanted to shout out to him, but it was too late.

"Fuck man! What's happened? He's dead."

"Ken, carefully turn around and step out. Don't touch anything. Just go and get back in the car. We are leaving."

"But boss, he's my mate and someone shot him."

"Listen Ken, Jenks is dead, now Dell. Who do you think is next? You perhaps? Go and get back in the car. No one gets to know that you were here, or you will end up just like they did. I will drop you somewhere where you will be safe. Don't ask any questions. Just do as I tell you, understand?"

"Yeah boss, too fucking right."

There was no way Ken could go back to his place. My guess was whoever had murdered Jenks and Dell would be waiting for Ken to turn up. My head was beginning to spin with the body count. Adele, her husband, and now Jenks and Dell. They couldn't be connected, could they? No, no way. It was just a horrible coincidence.

The trouble was, every time someone died around here, the police put me in the frame. Eventually something was going to stick, and I wasn't going to wait around to find out what! I had to vanish for a while, talk to DI Smith at least, try to find out what was going on and more importantly, who was doing the killing. I wouldn't be able to do that from the inside of a police cell!

I did have somewhere in mind for Ken, but for me, now that might prove a little more problematic. We got back into the car and drove back to the main road. I would phone this one in, but not quite yet, we had to disappear first.

We drove out to Ormskirk. My little white Ford Fiesta might not be the most luxurious car I had ever driven, but the police hadn't cottoned onto the fact that I was driving it around. If they wanted to pull me in, they would be looking for my Mondeo, which was still in the Ford dealer in Southport. At least that had turned out to be a stroke of good fortune.

On the outskirts of Ormskirk was a new centre, a secure halfway house for recovering drug addicts. It was run by one of life's good guys, someone who would never judge or preach to you, a man who just wanted to help. We first met ten years ago in London. I was on a team looking for a missing girl. He came forward with some crucial information, it saved her life and solved the case. After a very messy divorce, he moved to start this job as the manager of the new centre in Ormskirk.

A few years later, we bumped into each other at a live music event in Southport. We stayed in touch, talked about our past lives, drank too much cider listening to live bands that no one had ever heard of, and congratulated each other in escaping the maelstrom of London. My hope was, he would take smelly Ken in and keep him safe.

"You're taking me where? I don't want no halfway house boss, no drugs there. I will be fucking done in."

"Ken, it's for the best. You will be safe. Better that than dead. Any case, it's time you started to think about life. The course you are on isn't a good one, and it won't last very long even if this murderer doesn't get to you first."

"Yeah, but boss, I'm not ready. It's going to be shit."

"Ken, you are going, and you will stay put, even if they have to lock you into one of their secure rooms. You are not going to leave there until I come and pick you up, so just deal with it!"

The rest of the journey was conducted in complete silence. Ken clearly didn't want to go, but he didn't want his head blown apart either. At least he had seen what was left of Dell, I was hoping that it was enough to scare him into doing what he was told.

Eventually we arrived at the centre. It was made up of four accommodation units and an admin block. I pulled into the carpark and drew up in an empty bay. The area surrounding the centre was well cared for with multiple flower beds and green bushes.

"You are going to like it here, Ken. You stay here and I will go and have a chat to Mike. He will take care of you."

Ken didn't reply. He just sat there like a petulant child, but this place was going to keep him safe and away from those murdering hands. There was also a certain amount of self-serving guilt relief in placing him here. It upheld that promise I had made to myself to help Ken, possibly the first person ever to have done so. Mike would surely work his magic on him. I was certain it would put him on the road to a better life, out of the gutter and away from drugs.

On My Way Back to Southport.
Tuesday Evening.

Mike Geil agreed to take in Ken. I handed him over like a lost pet I had found wandering the streets. I was certain he would never speak to me ever again, but this was the right thing for him. Mike laughed at the smelly bundle of rags I brought in. He promised to keep him safe, give him a bath and some new clothes. He also agreed to put Ken in one of the centre's secure rooms. At least this would prevent him from doing a runner and keep him away from those who would do him harm.

I phoned Ruth before leaving the carpark and told her to meet me at the Travel Lodge at the top end of Lord Street. It wasn't a particularly clever place to hide, but the rooms were cheap, and the fact that I had a discount card made it even better. I drove all the way back from Ormskirk, which took about 45 minutes. I had all the windows wound down in an attempt to clear the aroma of Smelly Ken. I was really hoping the 'parfum aux Ken' hadn't attached itself to me, especially as I didn't have a change of clothes.

Anyway, I booked myself into room 16, told the reception guy that my partner would be along shortly, went up to my room and jumped into the shower. The water was gloriously hot and with the gel I had bought from Tesco on the way here, I scrubbed myself clean.

I slipped on my new boxer shorts, also from Tesco, and lay down on the bed to reflect what had been a horrendous day. It was then that I realised that I had not yet phoned in the murder of Dell in his caravan. Shit, what was the best way to do this? I could ring 999 and report the murder. Trouble was, yours truly would be, yet again, the number one suspect. No, that was not the way. I could just leave it. The smell would alert some dog walker and they would phone it in. Again, I would end up getting the blame. No, there was only one way to tackle this - phone Detective Inspector Deborah Smith!

I nervously reached for my phone, searched for her number and after withholding my own, pressed 'CALL'.

"DI Smith. Can I help?"

"Hi Deborah. This is Lee Hunter. The man who seems to be taking the blame for every murder in the borough. I have something to tell you."

"Ah, Mr Hunter. How are you?"

"To be honest, I am knackered and sorting this case out is more than I can cope with. However, there is something I need to tell you and I need to explain why."

"OK, well, if you call into the office in the morning, I will book us a room and we can have a chat."

"Not so fast Inspector. What I am about to tell you is extremely serious. If I show my face anywhere near the station, I will be clapped in irons and thrown into a very deep dungeon.

Today I found another dead person. It was clear to me that he had been murdered. Now before I give you the full details, I need to explain a few things, and some information and thoughts of my own. Are you willing to listen?"

"Go on."

"Firstly, can I ask you a simple question? I understand about the need for discretion, but a simple answer would be most useful to me and to you."

"Listen Mr Hunter, I have no need to explain to you..."

"Di Smith, let me stop you there! I know what you are about to say and the need for me to come into the station, but that's not going to happen. I am in the middle of a nightmare. People and friends are dying left right and bloody centre. I am terrified that either myself or another friend will be next, so please listen to what I have to say. After that, I will do exactly what you want me to do, and I bet it's to come into your police station!"

"Ok Mr Hunter, you have my attention. Please go on."

"First question - was my friend Jenks shot three times in the head?"

"He was."

"Right, well another acquaintance of mine has been murdered in the same way. His name is Dell, a drug addict and minor pain in the arse. He lives in a caravan on some waste ground, up past the old gas works. I found his body earlier today. You need to get some SOCO'S up there ASAP.

These two murders are connected to the disappearance of a young girl by the name of Gwen Walker. I have been employed by her mother to find her and bring her safely back home.

I asked my informant, Jenks, to dig about and try and find out whatever he could. He did find something and whatever that was, cost him his life. I thought that the info died with him, but it turns out that another informant - the aforementioned Dell - was also aware of that same information.

Dell had been employed to kidnap Gwen Walker, but refused, and was paid off to keep his mouth shut. It was only when Jenks and Dell got talking, I guess over a bottle of scotch stolen from the local off-licence, that the truth began to come to light."

"And that truth was?"

"The man who had tried to engage Dell to kidnap the girl, was in fact a cop. A local and senior police officer, probably a detective. It is my opinion that this detective is working for a local gang and is probably responsible for the murders of both Jenks and Dell. This opinion has been confirmed by another associate of mine who is now in safe custody, as both he and I fear for his life.

This story may sound a little too far-fetched for your taste, DI Smith, but putting all the details together and talking to those involved and the fear that all this has generated, I am certain that I am correct.

I believe that Dell and Jenks got together, got off their faces on goodness knows what and talked a bit too much about the kidnapping and this bent cop. Perhaps Dell asked for some more money from him to keep his mouth shut, perhaps even Jenks got involved in that blackmail - he was certainly dumb enough - and of course the inevitable happened. They were both silenced, permanently, I believe by this cop.

DI Smith, you have a problem, a huge one. Please believe what I have said. I am on the way to solving the kidnapping. The cop most certainly works for the gang who have Gwen. They won't let her go until they have her father. I know not why, but I guess he owes them something or has something they want back?

Now if I come in to see you, I will most likely be the next one with three bullet holes in my head, of that I have no doubt. If I stay out here, I can carry on trying to find and get Gwen back to her family. I might even be able to put a name to the bent cop. I won't be able to do that from a cooler in the morgue!"

The was a long silence before DI Smith finally replied.

"Mr Hunter, I have no doubt of your innocence in the murder of Jenks, or the cases of Adele Barnes and her husband. I am even willing to accept your innocence in the apparent murder of, what was his name, Dell? I do have to admit that murder seems to follow you around though and in truth, I do need to meet and formally interview you here at the station.

However, in the light of your allegations relating to a corrupt police officer and the kidnapping of Gwen, it might be more beneficial to wait for a while yet. Added to this, your apparent fear for your life and the help you might be able to provide in these cases, perhaps having you at large may be more helpful, at least in the short term.

You see, Mr Hunter, the information you have provided might well be relevant in other cases. None of which I am at liberty to discuss. This information is all part of a larger picture, a jigsaw. You have some of the pieces and I have a lot more!

Perhaps we can work together, on this one occasion, and complete the whole scene, before more lives are needlessly lost. But first, Mr Hunter, I need to know who the alleged corrupt officer is, and I need to know very quickly. Do I make myself clear?"

"Perfectly, DI Smith, but first I need to do some more investigations to finally identify who it is. It will do no good simply accusing someone without the proof. They will be alerted to what we know and will therefore take steps to keep themselves in the clear."

"That's for sure, Mr Hunter, but if there is a corrupt officer in my department, then I need to know who it is."

"Understood. But please bear one thing in mind, no one ever said that this officer was in your department!"

There was a long silence before she replied to my last comment. I wondered what else she knew that she wasn't telling me? If she had suspicions about a bent cop or their involvement in crime, then I should know. I put that to the back of my mind. No matter how many times I asked her, she would never disclose anything more than she absolutely had to.

"Right Mr Hunter, this is the deal. One, you phone me at least three times a day and keep me updated. Two, you don't get involved. When you know who this person is, you phone me, and we will make the arrest. Three, I need to know everything you know, so no holding back. It's important that I have all the details. Four, when you find Gwen, tell me. We will get her out, not you! Finally, you don't, under any circumstances, go steaming in, no matter what the situation. The last thing I want is another dead body, namely yours. And no more answers than I have now. Do I make myself abundantly clear, Mr Hunter? There is no latitude or discretion in any of these conditions, understood?"

"Completely, DI Smith. I will phone you in the morning and set out my plan for the day."

"I will look forward to hearing from you, Mr Hunter."

The phone went dead. I must admit my last statement about setting out my plan for the day sounded very impressive. The fact that I did not have a bloody clue what tomorrow's plan was, made me both smile and shiver at the same time. This was becoming very real indeed. People have already died. I had no clue of how to find Gwen's dad and now Detective Inspector Smith wanted me to phone her three times a day.

Do you ever get that feeling that you have jumped into a pit that you can't get out of or run up a blind alley and now find yourself trapped? That's how I felt right now, boxed in and totally screwed. I've made promises to Fat Tony about the money I owed him, the mysterious gangster in the back of the S-Class Merc, Mrs Walker and now DI Smith. I needed to come up with some answers, and tomorrow would be a damn find time to start!

The stress of the last few days, the comfortable bed and the cleansing feeling of the hot shower had begun to take effect. My eyes felt heavy and my mind slowly drifted away, into dreams of murder, Jenks and Dell, bent cops, corruption and fear. That poor girl Gwen, and what that man would do to her and her mother if I didn't find the father. Dreams, more like nightmares to be honest, dark places, terror and dread, pools of rancid blood, more killings to come, that was for certain.

My black dreams were interrupted by a distant knocking. I opened my eyes with a start and gazed about. Where the hell was I? The room was in complete darkness and I was totally disorientated. My mind and my senses scrambled about trying to fix on anything familiar. That knocking came again and I sat up. The bed felt soft and comfortable beneath me and I put my hands down in an attempt to steady myself.

"Lee, are you going to let me in or is this another blown date? I must admit that I should be getting used to it by now, but it is bloody annoying."

That was Ruth. What was she doing here? Come to that, where was here?

"Right, I am going to knock once more then I am off."

It was then my mind started to reboot itself - Travel Lodge, room 16. Ruth was here, just like I asked her. I reached over and fumbled for the bedside light and switched it on, I had no idea what time it was. My guess was after seven. That must have been the first deep sleep I had in over a week.

"Hang on, I am on my way."

I got up and went to the door, giving a passing glance at the Fire Evacuation Orders on the back of the door. I pulled the handle down and opened it. The bright lights of the corridor beyond made me squint.

"Well, Lee Hunter, at least this time you are partially clothed. Are you going to let me in?"

I blinked several times and stood back as Ruth walked past me into the room. She hit the main light switched and the blast of light stung my eyes.

"Well shut the bloody door and no need to thank me for the chips! I thought you might be hungry. Now put some clothes on and sit down. I will get this kettle going and we can eat. I am starving."

I stood there, still half blinded by the light and partially disorientated, but I did as I was told. Slipped on a clean T-shirt, courtesy of Tesco again, and sat at the end of the bed. The smell of the chips was heavenly and the boiling water liberated the aromas of coffee. That made me feel relaxed and happy once more. Ruth dropped a towel in my lap, closely followed by some chips in grease-proof paper. They smelled of vinegar and salt and I breathed it in deeply.

"Right, well eat up whilst they are hot! Budge over, I will sit next to you here. It feels like ages since the last time we met that night. We had a little too much to drink that time. I don't want you thinking I drink like that all the time."

I laughed. Her female voice played gently on my senses. She had no reason to apologise for that night.

"Another thing Lee, do you know anyone with a swanky BMW? I think it had an X6 badge on the back. It's been outside our flats on and off for the past couple of days. I can only assume they were looking for you?"

I stopped eating and turned to face her, "Did you recognise anyone inside?"

"I couldn't see who was inside, the windows were blacked out."

"Any chance of the reg number?"

"I knew you were going to ask me that. Sorry I didn't take a note, but I will next time. I will text it over."

"OK, anything else of note?"

"Nope. I have been really busy the past couple of days. Customers coming out of the woodwork. Shouldn't complain I guess."

I smiled. Listening to someone else's day was wonderful. So far away from what I had been through.

"Tell me every little detail. I need to escape from this case."

She smiled, took a deep breath and began. I sat there captivated. I had forgotten what a normal existence was and it made me very envious indeed.

Liverpool Marina.
Tuesday.

The boat swayed gently at its moorings. It had been a glorious day. The first of the summer insects had been playing on the surface of the water and the odd fish jumped to take first helpings of the feast to come.

He sat on the flybridge of the Fairline Corniche 31. The evening chill had begun to set in. Thoughts of tonight's evening meal and the remainder of the red wine began to consume his thoughts. He gazed out from 'Pier A' at the many beautiful boats. He wondered if anyone here had the same story as he did, but he doubted it very much.

He noticed a couple tidying the deck of their pride and joy. Another guy reversing his boat off the pontoon, ready for an evening cruise. A large cruiser had just entered the marina, brought a couple of sexy young things draped over the bow of the million-pound gin palace.

He was safe here. Only one person knew where he was and they would never give that information to anyone. A slight shiver ran down his body, but he refused to move. The chill was increasing as long shadows had started to stretch out across the water. He was just about to give into the cold when the phone in his pocket began to ring. He thrust his hand into his shorts and pulled out his iPhone 12.

"Hi, how's it going? It's beautiful here. You need to come down and join me. What a glorious day."

"Listen Simon, I wish I could, but you never know who's watching. Anyhow, I need to be here just in case there are any developments."

"I know, but an overnighter would be ok, surely? We could get drunk, have some fun, know what I mean?"

"I would love nothing better than that, but I can't. It's too risky. We will get the chance again be assured of that. Then we can have all the fun you want."

"Listen Kim, just pack a bag with a couple of things and get down here. It will be lovely."

"Darling, I can't. What if they find Gwen? I need to be here."

"Don't worry! I know that lot and they won't do her any harm. They will get bored and dump her on the outskirts of town somewhere."

"I hope you are right, Simon. This plan of yours could go terribly wrong. We could lose Gwen and I don't know how I would cope with that."

"Gwen will be fine! Don't worry! Get yourself down here and I will make you feel all relaxed, I promise."

"OK, darling. Let me plan a few things first. I will ring back tomorrow."

"Don't forget, Kim, I will be waiting with bated breath. Can't wait to hold you again."

"Same here Simon. Give me a couple of days."

"I will look forward to it my darling, and don't forget your basque and stockings. You look so sexy in them."

"I won't Simon. They will be the first things I pack!"

He pushed the phone back into his pocket. Aroused by the thought of his wife in her sexy lingerie, he pushed back into his seat, oblivious to the advancing chill. He gazed dolefully into the distance, musing over the disappearance of Gwen. She wasn't his daughter. She was baggage from a previous relationship of Kim's. He had resented Gwen for that. He couldn't quite figure out why. Perhaps she has been an encumbrance, an inconvenient third person in his relationship with Kim?

In any case, he couldn't quite convince himself that he gave a damn what happened to her. He made all the right noises, but he knew the men who took her are far from getting bored and releasing her. They would certainly kill her if they didn't get what they wanted.

The problem was, he was most certainly not going to give himself up nor give back what he had taken. The inevitable conclusion, therefore, was that Gwen was going to die, and probably very soon. It sometimes troubled him as to why he didn't feel any level of guilt or responsibility for this.

He has been a lifelong career criminal, not petty, small-time stuff, but major crime. Big drug importation, laundering millions in cash and best of all, corrupting senior police officers. It has been continuous, non-stop and the stress of living like that has eventually overwhelmed him. He had to get out before he was shot by a rival gang or locked up for the rest of his life.

The trouble was, the money and privilege that this life had given him was not easy to leave behind. Hence his decision to move a lot of the gang's money to an offshore account which only he knew about. Of course, he had not figured on them taking Gwen. He had just presumed they would come after him.

The plan was for him and his family to hide away. Things would be fine and they would never find them. The plan went terribly wrong when one of the gang's accountants almost immediately spotted the missing cash. This left him with no time to enact the escape plan and before he knew it, Gwen was taken. So, he hid away on his boat, left his wife to pretend to be none the wiser and hoped everyone fell for the *'my husband has disappeared'* story!

This brought him back to his original thought - did he really give a damn about them? He had the money, he was hidden away safely, he could just disappear and live a life of luxury on some far-flung island. Sure, they would certainly kill Gwen and most probably Kim too, but did he really care? Was he truly concerned about that?

He looked out across the marina again. The evening closed in, the light dimmed and the chill increased to such a level that he decided to go inside and prepare his evening meal. He descended to the rear cockpit, making sure that he didn't miss any of the steps and kept a firm grip on the stainless-steel handrails.

"Do I really give a shit about them? My first priority is me. I will end up dead for certain if I screw this up and they will never let Gwen go unless they have me? No, fuck it, I am off. Leave them to their fate. Why should I care?"

Travel Lodge Southport, Room 16.
Wednesday Morning.

By the time I managed to shake myself awake, it was past 10am and Ruth had disappeared off to her first client of the day. The chips we had the night before developed into a trip down the pub, a walk to the off-licence on the way back, and to be honest, I can't remember much beyond that.

Anyway, it must have been a good night as I had that lovely warm feeling all about myself. Mind you that could have been caused by the excess booze from last night. In any case, I had a smile on my face and that was a good start to the day. I had a quick wash and shave (yes, razors and shaving foam thanks to Tesco yesterday) and got dressed.

First job of the day was to call on Kim Walker down Stretton Drive. Well, it should have been a call to DI Smith, but she would have to wait. I needed to ask Kim Walker a few questions about her husband. The gangland boss, Mr Brau, had Gwen and I needed to know why. I had asked her that question before, but I refuse to believe that she had no idea whatsoever as to why. That simply didn't make any sense. She must have at the very least an idea of why and possibly the actual answer.

I resolved to call without telling her. Perhaps my surprise appearance at her front door might take her slightly off guard, perhaps! I jumped into my Ford Fiesta and set off. It wasn't far - turn right off Roe Lane, down Wennington Road, second right into Stretton Drive. Kim's house was about halfway down on the left-hand side. I guess it was built in the 1930's. A very pleasant house in a classic middle-class neighbourhood. I assumed that none of the neighbours knew what her husband really did for a living as they made their way to the office in the morning.

I stopped, quickly jumped out of the car and ran up to the front door. The less time she had to prepare for me the better. I knocked and waited. It wasn't long before the door opened and there stood Kim Walker in her white bath robe, wet hair and no makeup. She was a very attractive woman even just out of the shower. Mr Walker was a lucky man indeed.

"Oh, Mr Hunter. I wasn't expecting you. Erm, I have just got out of the shower. Can I help you?"

"Yes, can I come in? I need to ask a couple of questions?"

"Not really, Mr Hunter. I have an appointment. Can you phone me later?"

"This won't take a minute, Kim."

I didn't give her the chance to reply. Using an old police trick of mine, I gently manoeuvred my way passed her and into the hall. They used to call it the *'Ali shuffle'*, after the great boxer. As I turned, the look on her face was priceless - utter astonishment and bemusement - exactly what I wanted.

"Can we go into the living room, Kim? As I said, this won't take long?"

"Erm, well, this is very inconvenient."

"That's ok. Let's go and sit down."

I didn't give her a chance to reply. I set off for the front room, opened the door and went inside. The room was immaculate - leather furniture, expensive crystal ornaments and the biggest TV I had ever seen. The only thing out of place was a Samsonite suitcase on the settee. It was bright red leather with shiny locks. Whilst the top was closed, it wasn't fastened - curious! She followed me in, her face red with a flustered look. She didn't want me there, which was exactly the reaction I needed.

"Mr Hunter, I have to get ready. Are you sure this can't wait?"

"No, it can't. Shouldn't take a minute though."

She looked down at her white bath robe, naked ankles and feet and quickly looked back at me.

"I need to get dressed, Mr Hunter. Sit down, I will be back when I am properly attired."

"Be my guest Kim. I am not going anywhere."

She turned and marched out of the room, leaving me looking at the bright red suitcase. So, she was going somewhere then? Curiosity got the better of me. I had to see what was in that case. An overnight stay or something longer? Why was she going anywhere? For goodness sakes, her daughter had been taken, and if it were me, I wouldn't be going anywhere.

What the hell was she up to? Last time I had spoken to her, she was beside herself with fear. Now she was going on a jolly? Didn't make sense. Right, let's have a look in that case. There might even be a booking form in there. I quickly moved over and flipped the top back. What I saw shook me to the core. On the top of a small stack of clothes was a very sexy black basque, two packs of black stockings and a pair of handcuffs.

What the hell was going on here? One minute she couldn't think straight because her daughter had been kidnapped, the next thing she was off for a fun weekend with her boyfriend. I bet her husband didn't know about this, not that it was going to make a difference to his prospects. Mr Brau was going to see to that.

My mind wandered for a few seconds. Typical of me really. In the middle of a life and death situation, and all I could think about was Mrs Walker in her basque and stockings. Still, it didn't make sense. She didn't seem the sort to have a boyfriend. Not that you can really tell. It was often the most inconspicuous folks that had the most fun!

I carefully dropped the lid back into place, sat on the chair furthest away from the case and waited for Mrs Walker to reappear. It was some considerable time before she returned, flouncing back into the room in tight jeans, a partly see-through top, heels and all her hair and makeup done to perfection. She looked at the case, studied it for a second or two before turning to face me.

"Now, Mr Hunter, how can I help? I have an appointment, so please can you make this quick."

"I can see that you are impatient to be off Kim, so perhaps I will phone you later and discuss your daughter's situation in more detail. In the meantime, I do need an answer to a couple of questions."

"Mr Hunter, as you can see, I have an appointment that I am already late for. Please can this wait until another day?"

It was then that the truth hit me, like a proverbial ton of bricks. That epiphany was truly wonderous. It was pleasing to think my old and alcohol ravaged brain still worked from time to time. This beautiful creature stood in front of me, hair and makeup perfectly done, sexy lingerie in her case, wasn't going to meet her boyfriend. No, she was going to meet her husband!

I had to think quickly. This was my one opportunity to find him - the man at the centre of all this trouble. All I needed to do was follow Mrs Walker and she would lead me directly to him. I had to play it cool and give no indications of my thoughts. I was excited, but I mustn't let her know.

"Look Kim, I am really sorry. I will phone you later. I can see you are busy. It was very inconsiderate of me to call on you without ringing first. There was nothing really urgent. I was just passing. I will leave you to it. Have a nice day."

Did I really say, 'have a nice day'? Anyway, without any further delay, she showed me the door. We said our goodbyes and I drove away from the house. I had to take a chance in which way she would go, but I figured back onto Roe Lane and from there, who the hell knows?

It wasn't that long before she emerged, looking furtively left and right before she threw her case into the boot of her green MX5. At least the car would be relatively easy to follow. Trouble was, would my little Fiesta keep up?

We headed north, towards Ormskirk. It reminded me of smelly Ken. I wondered if Mike had managed to weave his magic on the little oik, or had he done a runner in the middle of the night? I would call in on the way back. At least he was safe there. I was certain that Mike would phone me if anything untoward had happened.

We crawled through the town, off toward the M57 and routes leading to Liverpool. Surely, he wouldn't be hiding so close to home? That would be ridiculous. Maybe he was banking on Mr Brau and his men thinking the very same? I suppose when you think about it, even if you hide 100 yards from home, providing you kept a low profile, no one will ever find you. So long as he wasn't somewhere he was known to frequent, a second home, caravan, girlfriend's house, then he should be fine. That's where they would be looking.

Anyway, on we pushed into Liverpool itself. Magnificent city with a long history, fantastic buildings, music and of course the River Mersey. Without any prompting, I began to sing 'Hey Jude' - love that song, love the Beatles. Eventually we ended up in the docks area. Thankfully, my little fiesta had managed to keep up, although it did smell of burnt oil and the fuel light had come on.

We eventually came to the entrance to Liverpool Marina. I let her pull into the carpark, get out of her car, grab the suitcase from the boot and make her way to 'Pier A'. Once she had gone through the gate, I parked in the carpark and got out. I watched her walk to a large cruiser berthed on the end of the pier.

This was it. I have either found her husband or her boyfriend. I was desperately hoping that it was the former. If this was him, I could contact Mr Brau and Gwen would be released by tonight - job done! But it wasn't going to be that simple, was it?

Mrs Walker was in there. If Mr Brau's goons turned up for her husband, the chances are, they would take her at the same time. After all, she was playing the ditched housewife, with no clue about her husband or where he was. If Brau suspected that she was in on whatever her husband had done, he would kill her as well, and Gwen would certainly end up at the bottom of the local canal.

No, I had to be patient. I had promised Brau that I would deliver him by Monday, so there was no immediate rush. Take your time Lee - don't screw this up. I had that small photo Mrs Walker had given me of her husband. So, first things first. I had to make sure it was him. The one ace I had was that Mr Simon Walker didn't know what I looked like. If I waited until his wife left, I could simply knock on the boat's door - if boats have a door - and make some excuse as to my presence. If I was able to identify him, I would make the call to Brau and Mrs Walker would be nowhere near when they turned up to grab him - great plan.

There were two problems though, I never could wait, and the second was the boat itself. What would happen if they simply sailed away? I couldn't follow them in my little Ford Fiesta, no matter how good it was, and they could literally go anywhere. With a rising sense of panic, I decided to risk going down to the boat itself and trying to peek inside - what could possibly go wrong?

My chance wasn't long in coming. I spotted a man leaving his boat and walking up the pier towards the locked electric gate. I would meet him there. With a courteous smile and a well-aimed question about sea conditions, he didn't even notice that I didn't have a pass. As he opened the gate from his side, I slipped through, wishing him a safe journey home as I did so.

The pontoon seems oddly unstable. I was never a water baby, much preferring dry land. I always felt much safer there. Another thought then struck me - What happens if they decide to go for a walk? There certainly wasn't anywhere to hide out here, and jumping in the marina was definitely not an option. No, it was too late. I was on the pontoon. I needed to find out who she was meeting and I had to do it now.

Eventually I arrived. The Fairline Corniche was moored against the end of the pontoon. I gently swayed as a breeze wafted across the water. The curtains had been drawn, so I was not hopeful of seeing inside, but I had to persist. Gwen's life depended on what I was able to accomplish. I quietly got closer to the vessel. If I couldn't see inside, perhaps I might hear something. Any clue would be very welcomed.

It quickly became obvious that there was no chance of seeing inside. All the curtains were tightly drawn, but I could hear voices. I needed to concentrate - try to pick out a name in the muffled conversation. I heard the popping of a Champagne cork. That was good news. People do get very loud when they have plenty to drink. As the boat swayed, the voices became more audible as the conversation and laughing increased.

"Wow! You look good, Kim. I have forgotten how damn sexy you are in that outfit and those stockings - I could eat you alive."

"Well, that's a promise I aim to make you keep. I haven't come all this way just so you could look at me. No, sir. You are going to make it up to me, and you need to take your time - lots and lots of time."

"Oh Kim, I am ready to explode. Come and sit on my knee."

"No, I won't. You need to get on your knees and beg me. After all, you don't want me to go back home, do you?"

After that, the conversation became too muffled to understand and shortly afterwards, there wasn't any conversation at all! So, it was back to plan A - wait until she leaves, and go and knock on the door, and see who answers. One thing was sure, they wouldn't be sailing away any time soon. Not if he was on his knees and begging her!

The Office of Detective Inspector Deborah Smith.
Southport Police Station.
Wednesday Evening.

There was a knock on the door and DI Smith looked up from her computer. She could see DS Shacklady through the Georgian wired glass panel in the door. She was pleased to see Sharron. Deborah had been sat behind this damn computer for way too long. A friendly face and human voice were more than welcome.

"Come in, Sharron! No, on second thoughts, we are off to the canteen. I am bloody starving."

DS Shacklady stood in the open door, "before we go boss, I need to tell you something in private."

"Come on in, Sharron. Let me guess, it's something to do with that prat, Detective Chief Inspector Mark Bruno?"

DS Shacklady laughed as she closed the door behind her.

"How did you guess boss? He has been creating trouble behind closed doors. It's about letting that private detective go - what was his name, Hunter?

Bruno has been into Superintendent Watkins office gobbing off, saying that you let a known murderer go. Says he should be put in charge of the whole team, not just this case.

Good job Superintendent Watkins thinks he's a complete dickhead as well as us. So, he called me in and warned me about Bruno. The problem he sees though is, Bruno won't just stop with him. If he doesn't act, he will go up the chain until someone does listen to him. He promised DCI Bruno that he would investigate it and launch an internal enquiry, which of course the Super won't! This won't last long though. As soon as Bruno realises that he has been lied to by Superintendent Watkins, he will go higher up, so we need to sort this murder case out ASAP."

"You are right, Sharron, and thanks for the warning. With a bit of luck, Bruno will be the next name on the murderer's list. In the meantime, we need to get cracking.

Because of the identical MO's, there are now four victims in this case - Mr Francis Jackson Barnes, his wife Mrs Adele Barnes, and two local druggies - a guy called Jenks and his mate Dell. Difficulty is, that detective you spoke of, Lee Hunter, knows them all and makes him an ideal prime suspect. Two problems with that - firstly I am certain he had nothing to do with it, and secondly, he is an easy target for that dick Bruno."

"And if he has his way, our detective, Lee Hunter, will be going down for the rest of his life for the four murders."

"Yes Sharron, and the real killer gets away scot free. What we need to do is work out what the hell is going on."

"Listen boss, why is Bruno so interested in the case anyway? He's got nothing to gain from any of it. In fact, he's only going to lose when the truth comes out. It's not like him to put his career on the line over something that won't gain him any extra kudos. Even if his name is on the *'solved case'* paperwork. Now he's being obstructive, trying to divert the direction of the case. Truth is, he could lose his job for that."

"I have already thought of that, Sharron. That's not like Bruno. Something is going on - something so important that he is willing to risk everything for it."

"Well, the only thing 'going on', as you put it, are these four murders. Are you suggesting boss that Bruno is doing the killings?"

"No, I don't think so, Sharron. He is a complete tosser, but he is no serial killer. Perhaps he is covering for the real murderer though. The question is, why are the Barnes' murders and the two druggies' murders connected? Or aren't they? A married couple -in the millionaire bracket, successful businesses, fabulous lifestyle - and then Dell and Jenks - two down and out smackheads who got nothing, amount to zilch, forgotten by society?"

"Well, they are connected boss. The three shots to the centre of the head and forensics have confirmed the same gun in each murder. All four people were killed by at least the same gun and, in all probability, the same person."

"OK. So why is Bruno trying so hard to screw up the investigation? Trying to nail it on Lee Hunter? What's he trying to cover up? That's what we need to find out Sharron, and do it fast before he has us thrown off the case and goes and stiches someone right up for this!"

"OK, so how do we do that? Bruno will find out if we try to investigate him, even informally? He has too many contacts around this place. He knows everyone. One false step and he will be all over us."

"I have been thinking about that and there is one possibility, Shaz. I am going to use young DC Mike Evans. I am going to ask him to get closer to Bruno, be his friend. Bruno will lap it up - plenty of sexists talk and fantasising about shagging the admin girls, build his ego up - he'll be Bruno's best mate in fifteen minutes.

He might be able to get a feeling of what is going on, especially if Bruno thinks he is on his side. DC Evans needs to position himself to appear to be his agent, in our department. We can feed Bruno information through Evans and see what comes back."

"Are you sure Bruno is going to fall for it, boss? I know he is a complete knob, but he isn't stupid?"

"He's stupid, Sharron, believe me. He just needs the right circumstances and any intelligence he might have will simply disappear. Even if he doesn't fall for it, and wises up to what we are doing, can't be any worse than the situation we are already in."

As the two women left the office on route to the canteen, Deborah picked up her mobile and sent a text to DC Mike Evans:

BE IN MY OFFICE IN ONE HOUR. IMPORTANT JOB FOR YOU. YOU ARE GOING TO ENJOY THIS ONE.
DI SMITH.

By the time DC Mike Evans knocked on DI Deborah Smith's door, the evening was beginning to close in. It had started to rain outside and Evans felt sticky from the short walk from his car to the station main door.

He drew a deep breath before entering. DI Smith was an excellent detective and his boss, but she had a reputation of suffering fools very badly. Since joining her team, just a few months ago, he has felt her wrath on more than one occasion. To be honest, it was normally his fault.

"What the bloody hell have I done this time? I am sure I got everything right in the Barnes' murder?"

He pushed the door open, somewhat nervously, and went inside.

"Mike, glad you could make it. I have a little job for you, just down your street. Take a seat and let me explain."

He listened to his boss with some trepidation as she explained what she wanted him to do. There wasn't any pressure on him to comply, but refusing wasn't really going to be an option either.

"So let me get this right, boss. You want me to cosey up to DCI Bruno, be his best mate, even offer to be his eyes and ears in this department. I am not sure what this is going to achieve? Why would he even contemplate such a thing and what are you getting out of it?"

"Trust me, Mike. Bruno is an egotistical, narcissistic, self-important knob. I bet he licks himself clean every night, just like my cat, and anything or anyone who plays up to his tendencies will quickly become his friend.

I need to know why he wants to sabotage the case and what is his motivation for taking control of my department. He is risking his job, and even his liberty by stitching up Lee Hunter. Whatever he is up to, is very important to him. More important than anything else in this world. I have known Bruno for many years, and the very last thing he would do is risk is his plumb job and fancy title.

You need to find out what he is up to before he dicks Lee Hunter, and probably me as well, and we'd both end up in Strangeways Prison. This is serious Mike. I need you to get this done. Buddy up to him, play to his weaknesses. Offer to be his eyes and ears in this department. Say you hate me - female boss, cramping your style - use anything you need to. Just don't make it too obvious, and our future conversations are face to face, not on email or text. I wouldn't trust that twat not to be monitoring that either.

Start right away. Go storming into his office. Tell him how I am ruining your career. Say I am a man-hater, a sexist bitch - he will love that. Tell him you want to be on his side, help bring me down, do everything you can for him in this case."

"And if he throws me out and tells me to get on with my job?"

"Then do exactly that, but I bet he won't. He won't be able to pass up an opportunity like that, guaranteed!"

Liverpool Marina.
Still Singing 'Hey Jude'!
Wednesday Night.

By the time it was dark, the rain had started in earnest. Not only that, but it was cold, very cold indeed. I was wishing I was back in the Travel Lodge with Ruth. The deluge hammered on the roof of my car, bounced off the tarmac of the carpark and ran in little rivulets towards the marina.

I was now convinced that Mrs Kim Walker would be staying for the night. There was no way she was going to leave that boat and risk the slippery pontoon. I was resigned to the fact that I would have to return in the morning and continue my vigil. It wouldn't matter if Mrs Walker had left by then. I could simply go and knock on the boat's door and ascertain who the man was. The problem was, what would happen if her husband left with her and disappeared to pastures new? They could sail away, move to a new hide out and they both could simply disappear into the sunset.

No, I couldn't pass up this opportunity. I had him cornered. I dared not let him slip away. So that was it. I was in for the night - come storm or calm, and it looked like storm. I pulled my mobile out. This would be another excuse for Ruth. Any time soon she would probably give me the big 'heave-ho', and to be honest, I absolutely deserved it. So, I dialled her number and hoped for the best!

"Lee, I was expecting your call earlier. Where the hell are you? Don't tell me, in the local police station?"

"Actually Ruth, I am parked in a marina in Liverpool. It's pissing down and I am freezing cold. I have a suspect under surveillance and I dare not let him slip away. So, tonight is off I am afraid."

"I have to say, Lee, that I have heard some crap in my life from men, all kinds of excuses, but yours are by far and away the best. So good in fact that they must be the truth. You simply couldn't make them up. Look, tell me where you are and I will bring something to eat. We can keep watch together. I have always wanted to be an undercover agent."

I broke into a wide smile. Despite all the excuses and messing about, she still wanted to see me.

"Ruth, you are one in a million. I will send the address. Put it into your sat nav."

"I know I am, and you don't deserve me, but I am a sucker for dumb excuses. See you soon."

As Ruth pulled out of the carpark at the rear of the flats, a shadowy BMW X6 followed silently in behind her. It followed her out of Southport and towards Ormskirk. she didn't notice it, until it was too late!

I woke just before midnight. It wasn't as cold as I thought it would be and thankfully the rain had stopped. I wiped away the condensation from the inside of the windscreen, just in time to see two people advancing up the pier in front of me. They were gently lit by the lights either side of the wooden pier. It looked oddly romantic to see them hand in hand in the dim yellow light. Their walking made the wooden pontoons bob up and down and the boats swing gently at their moorings.

It was then I remembered about Ruth. I guess she decided not to come over. I didn't blame her to be honest. Once these two had moved on, I would give her a call. Just in case she had got lost or something.

The couple eventually arrived at the security gate, stopping for a moment before pressing the exit button. The galvanised meshed gate swung gently open with a muffled buzz from the electric motor. They advanced out onto the carpark, turning to face each other under one of the security lights. Kissing passionately, running their hands up and down each other's backs - so close they almost melted into one.

It was then that I realised who I was looking at. It was Kim Walker. A shock ran through me. This was it. My chance to finally work out who she had come to see. I took a deep breath, calmed myself to concentrate. I looked at the couple. The security light was a lot brighter than those on the pontoon. If only they would let each other go, I could catch a look at his face. It wouldn't take more than a split second for me to positively identify him. Just be patient - take your time!

Eventually they came up for air, holding each other but then standing back, looking longingly into each other's eyes. It was then that I finally recognised him. It was the man himself, Simon Walker. I felt my mouth drop and I took in a large breath. This was it. I had him, and soon Mr Brau would also.

I decided to go back to the Travel Lodge. Simon Walker wouldn't move now, not with Kim leaving. He was going to stay here for a while yet. He would wait until things settled down - safer that way - then grab his wife and daughter and make a run for the hills, as fast as his legs could carry him!

Detective Inspector Deborah Smith's House.
Southbank Road, Southport.
Thursday Morning, 5am.

The phone on the bedside table began to buzz and it danced across the surface, finally dropping onto the floor. It was still pitch black in the bedroom and the heating hadn't come on yet - the damp hung about in the cold air.

She awoke with a start, blinking her eyes, trying to work out what was happening. Was this a dream or was it reality? The carpet muffled the buzzing of her phone, but there was no mistake in its electronic hum. It might have been on silent, but it shook her out of her slumber with a ruthless irrevocability.

Still shocked at the sudden change in her circumstance, Deborah tried to understand what was going on. Her private phone played some stupid ringtone from the installed options, but her work phone was on silent with vibration. She screwed her eyes closed one more time, hoping to go back to sleep. After all, who the hell would phone at this time in the morning? It must have been a dream.

She had just drifted away as the noise started again - a muffled buzzing, somewhere under the bed. Sitting up she cursed and fumbled for the bedside light. The sudden shock as it illuminated caused her to close her eyes and curse once again.

"Where is that bloody piece of junk? How come it's on the floor? This better be good."

Leaning out over the side of the bed, she grabbed at the errant phone and pushed herself upright, pulling the duvet closely around herself.

"Whoever this is, it had better be very important indeed, if you want to keep your job and pension. Now what do you want?"

"Erm, sorry boss, but there has been another incident."

"DC Evans, what the fuck is going on? Tell me this is a joke, right. Do you have any idea of the time?"

"Sorry boss, but the night staff phoned."

"Oh well, there's a thing. They clearly don't have anything better to do. Now, you are a big boy DC Evans. Deal with it and you had better hope I get back to sleep, otherwise, you will be facing the worst day of your life when I get into work."

"Boss, no, you don't understand."

"No, DC Evans, you don't understand. My mouth feels like I swallowed the bottom of a budgie cage, my back is aching and I should be fast asleep dreaming of Marcus. Now I suggest you stop talking, and go and sort this 'incident' out before I get up, come into work and beat you unconscious."

"Boss, there has been another murder, and it's the same as before - three shots to the head. He has struck again."

The conversation stopped with and abrupt jolt. Suddenly Deborah was wide awake. She sat bolt upright in bed and drew in a deep breath.

"OK Mike, where?"

"Ormskirk, boss. On the road towards the M57. A woman in her late forties by the name of Ruth Davenport. She was found by a patrol just after midnight. She has been shot in the head, three times. The doctor in attendance puts time of death between 10 and 11pm or thereabouts.

She was a chiropodist - no record, not connected to any crime scenes, drugs or illegal activities - nothing boss. Just a woman doing her best in life! One thing though, she was the next-door neighbour to that detective, Lee Hunter."

"What? This man is starting to annoy me. Surely he can't be connected to all five murders?"

"Boss, I am beginning to think that tosser DCI Bruno has a point. This is gone past a coincidence. You might be associated with the murdered man and wife, but have nothing to do with it, or the two druggies, but not the whole damn lot. What has this Ruth Davenport got to do with anything? She isn't a millionaire or a druggie? No, boss. DCI Bruno is right. This all points to Lee Hunter. He's your murderer!"

"No, Mike, he's not. It doesn't feel right. In any case, he has a cast iron alibi for the first two murders, including being in the cells at the time! I know what this looks like and I know why Bruno is barking up that particular tree, but it's not Hunter."

"Well, as soon as Bruno finds out about this latest murder, he going to have Hunter brought in and charged. Of that I have no doubt. If he has his way, and he normally does, Hunter will be in front of the Magistrates by lunchtime and in Strangeways by the weekend!

We have a genuine serial killer on the loose and the top brass will be watching everything we do. They will want a resolution to this as soon as possible boss. They won't want this splashed all over the press any more than it needs be, making them look like a load of idiots.

They will certainly put DCI Bruno in charge now and he will have all the authority he needs to get it done. There will be serious crime people from all over the region knocking on our door. The shit has just hit the fan boss, and we are in the way."

Deborah put the phone down on the quilt, she had to think, clear her mind, the decisions she was about to take would be the most important of her life.

"OK, Mike. Get the team up and into the office. We will have the first meeting at 7am in the main briefing room. Contact DCI Bruno and tell him what's happened. Tell him about the meeting. Leave it to him who else he calls, but make sure Sharron and Kaye Marie get the invite."

"Will do boss. See you at 7am."

Travel Lodge Southport, Room 16.
Thursday Morning.

My phone rang somewhere off in the darkness. I had downloaded *'Hey Jude'* and set it as my ringtone. It was this tune that snapped me awake. I reached out and fumbled for the phone, forcing my eyes open to see who had disturbed me and the screen showed a very familiar name.

"DI Deborah Smith. No, I am sorry about not phoning you, but...."

"Hunter, just shut up and listen to me very carefully. There has been another murder - exactly the same as the previous four and it's got your name all over it. I have just got out of a meeting with my team explaining what has happened and to whom.

I have been told that Detective Chief Superintendent Martin Kiff will now be having oversight of the case, along with a certain DCI Mark Bruno. Both of these men are complete idiots, and probably as bent as they come, but they do know how to stich someone up just to get the case solved, and that man is probably going to be you.

I don't know what they intend to gain from dicking you for this lot. After all, if we do have a serial killer on our hands, he's not going to stop just because you have been banged up in prison until hell freezes over, is he? No Hunter, these two have always been as thick as thieves. They are up to something and you are going to pay for it. Trust me."

"DI Smith, thanks for the heads up, but I must ask, who is the latest victim?"

"There is no easy way of saying this Hunter, but it's someone you probably know - Ruth Davenport."

I suddenly felt sick to the core. I couldn't believe what DI Smith had just told me. Ruth murdered, why? I had a rush of guilt surge through me like a flash forest fire consuming everything in its path. Names and faces thundered through my mind, people who I knew - Ruth, Jenks, Dell, even Adele Barnes - all dead. They all knew me, most were friends. Were they dead because of that? Was this all my fault?

A voice was trying to call out to me, somewhere off in the distance, beyond this roaring sound in my ears.

"Lee, are you alright? Did you know this woman well? Can you shed any light on why she was killed?"

My whole world seemed to fall into a black hole. All I could think about was Ruth, and by the simple fact of her association with me, she was dead. How many people have died because they knew me? How many have paid with their lives because of my actions?

Jenks was dead because I wanted some information. Dell was dead because Jenks had spoken to him. What about Adele and her husband? They have been killed in the same way. Was it because Adele had been seen talking to me? Now, there was Ruth, my next-door neighbour, murdered. Her life ended for nothing other than an innocent relationship.

I wanted to throw up, run out into the street and beg someone to kill me. What the hell was I doing messing about in people's lives? Who the hell was I to think I could solve cases and bring the guilty to account? For fucks sake, an innocent girl was languishing somewhere, the prisoner of a gang, and I had promised to find her father and if I didn't, she would be the next one to die. What was I doing? I wanted to run, find a dark hole to hide in and pretend none of this was happening. The trouble is, it was happening, and I was in the middle of it all!

That same voice was still trying to forge a way through from somewhere beyond the black whirling cyclone where I now found myself. It was the same persistent and urgent voice, pleading for my attention.

"Lee, are you still there? What about Ruth? Did you know her? It's important that I know."

I tried to pull my mind into some kind of shape, organise my thoughts and concentrate on what I need to say and do.

"Yes, Deborah, I did know her. We were seeing each other. I was on a stake out last night and she was supposed to be meeting me there. I fell asleep, and by the time I woke up things started to happen. I was going to call her later this morning and I just assumed she had decided not to come over to the marina, stay at home and get an early night."

"Lee, we need to talk. I have to try and put this case together. Things don't add up, something is going on that I don't understand. I don't want to talk on the phone, especially mobiles, so can we meet somewhere?"

"Deborah, I am not that stupid. I can imagine the scene as the thirty armed cops come running towards me as I get out of my car. No, I need to find out what's going on and I need to stop these murders!"

"Lee, there are five dead people. All of whom were killed in the same way with the same gun. One thing connects them all together and that's you. What makes you think you will live long enough to sort anything out?

If I wanted to find you, all I need to do is wait until some patrol finds your dead body somewhere. Let me guess, with three bullet holes in your head, all shot from close range with a 9mm pistol.

No, Lee Hunter. I need to talk to you and preferably very soon before someone blows your brains out, because that is what's going to happen to you and that's an absolute guarantee!"

I had to think for a while. Was she just setting me up or was there some truth in what she said? *'Things don't add up, something is going on'* - why would she say that? What did she mean? I was lost. Dead bodies all around me. Perhaps it was time to reach out before the next innocent person got their life ripped away from them?

"So, why won't you just arrest me and throw me in the cells? What is it that's stopping you from doing that?"

"I don't want to talk on the phone, Lee. Surely you can appreciate that. Let's meet in a public place, somewhere you feel safe. I can explain, please just give me a chance."

"There is a mobile soup kitchen cum coffee place behind the old bus station at the end of Lord Street. Meet me there in twenty minutes. If I even suspect anything, you will never see or hear from me again, do I make myself clear?"

"I am on my way, Lee. No ambushes or arrests, I promise."

I left the car in the street in front of the Travel Lodge and made my way to the appointed place. I had been there often enough to know where the local druggies hid in order to take their stuff. There were some dark places, hidden passageways, recessed corners from where I could easily see what was going on without being detected. The local addicts had chosen this place well. They couldn't be seen by the local drugs squad.

I found such a recessed place, chased off the couple of smack heads loitering and waited to see what was happening. Shortly after, she arrived in an unmarked, dark blue Ford Focus. She got out and looked around. She couldn't see me, but I could see her, and more importantly what was going on around the area. I left it a few minutes before venturing out. To be honest, I didn't really care if it was a stich up, the thought of all those dead bodies had drained my strength, and all I wanted to do was cry out and die.

"Ah, Lee. I was beginning to wonder if you had second thoughts. I am glad to see you didn't."

"Let's cut out the crap, Deborah. Time is running short and I need to know what's troubling you."

"Well, we could grab a coffee here or somewhere less germ ridden. I don't fancy my chances after drinking something made in that place, do you?"

"Let's just sit in your car. I need to listen to what you have to say. If I feel there is some mileage in our relationship, then we can go somewhere more convivial."

"That's a deal. Follow me."

The car door slammed shut. I must admit to feeling somewhat claustrophobic sat in the old Ford Focus. Not for the first time I felt uneasy and trapped. If this was a set-up, there was no way I was getting out of it.

"OK, Lee. Thanks for agreeing to meet me. There is no point in hiding anything. There is no time for that crap and too many people are already dead. To show good intent on my part, I will begin.

I am sat here because something is not right in this investigation. Games are being played and lies are being told. I must admit to not having the faintest clue as to why this is happening, but it is.

My team has been taken from me by two very senior officers and they seem intent on blaming other people, including yourself for these murders. We had a meeting this morning and a pair of corrupt, self-serving fools are now running this investigation. A certain Chief Superintendent Kiff and his slimy side kick, Chief Inspector Bruno, have full control of what's going on. They seem to be set on a completely unconnected rambling investigation, with no relationship to reality and no real purpose, other than to cover something up. I don't know what or for what reason, but they have all the levers of power, and there is nothing I can do about it, or so they think!

The strangest thing is, we obviously have a serial killer on the loose - five murders and counting. They are after you, Lee, and I know not why. But if they do manage to lock you up for that lot, it's going to mean the rest of your life in jail. Also, the killer will still be out there and free to kill again and again! So, what do they expect to gain from blaming you? Within a week of you taking up residence in Strangeways Jail and there will be another killing. I don't understand."

There was a long silence. Both parties looked out of the window. Grey clouds scudded across the sky, occasional bright shafts of sunlight stabbed earthwards, bringing a pleasing glow to the town below. This was a point in time when decisions had to be made, alliances needed to be forged before someone else paid the ultimate price.

"Listen Deborah, this is not my case. But they are my friends, or at least three of them were. I need the murderer brought to justice, for the sake of Ruth, Jenks and Dell. They didn't deserve to die just because they knew me.

There is one possible answer to your quandary - maybe those police who are trying to stitch me up for this are the murderers, or at least one of them is. That would answer your question about a serial killer getting away with it. If I were banged up in Strangeways, then the murders would stop. The bent cops would throw their guns into the River Mersey as everyone involved in this case would be either dead, or in jail - case solved. They would seem to have been right all along. It was me after all. But the real question is, why the hell are they doing this in the first place? Why are they killing so many people?"

"That's what I have been trying to answer, Lee. If it were about drug deals gone wrong, then I would say OK, Dell and Jenks fit the bill for the killings. If it were about money laundering, perhaps Adele and her husband, but what the hell has Ruth Davenport got to do with it? None of this makes sense, Lee. And why have they picked you as their scapegoat? I just don't understand it."

There was another long silence. I knew that this was the time to put all my cards on the table. If this case was going anywhere, I need to start talking about what I knew and I had to start now. There was always the chance that this was a set up, but I had to take that gamble.

"Right, Deborah. I have more information about this case than I have disclosed so far. Here it is, everything I know. Perhaps it will make sense to you or maybe it will add to something you already know.

I was contacted by Kim Walker about her missing daughter. The local old bill was getting absolutely nowhere with the case, and things were getting very techy. I was expecting the girl to be found dead in the local canal at any moment.

I asked an associate of mine, Jenks, to see what he could find out about the case. Just to give me a head start in the investigation. He tried to tell me what he had found, but was murdered before he got the chance to tell me the whole story. He did manage to say that a senior police officer had been involved. That same senior officer that had tried to recruit Dell to kidnap the girl in question. Both Jenks and Dell are now dead. Coincidence? No, I don't think so.

I am certain that these two men, lowlifes some might call them, not missed by anyone, below the radar of society are dead because they knew something. They knew the identity of that senior police officer, that dirty cop. A man or woman who was working for the local crime syndicate, organising murders, kidnappings and goodness knows what else. It was information that could not be allowed out. The identity of a senior police officer involved with the local syndicate? That would have been dynamite. They had to be silenced, kept from telling what they knew, the bad cop and the syndicate had to be protected, no matter the cost.

They died and someone presumed that they wouldn't be missed, but they were missed because they were my friends. They might not have been doctors or architects, but they were human beings. Just like you and I, Deborah. They've had a shit life, maybe a choice on their part, but they didn't deserve to die. Never, never! So, I will find out who killed them and I will avenge their deaths, because if I don't, no one else will. No one else cares and that's what this bent cop is hoping for.

Anyway, I managed to make contact with the gang who had the young girl, Gwen Walker. The boss is a Mr Brau - probably known to you? Anyway, he promised to release the girl if I found her father who has supposedly taken something belonging to Mr Brau. I assume a bag full of cash!

My aim was to gain the release of Gwen. To be honest, I don't give a shit about her father. Why would you put the life of your daughter at risk and refuse to give yourself up when she has been taken? At the same time, I hoped to get closer to the gang. Maybe, just maybe, I could find out who this bent cop was, turn him in to you lot and ruin his life for ever. Well, that plan was working just fine. In fact, I have found the father and I was just about to turn him over when you phoned me. I guess he would be dead body number six by now!

At least the young girl, Gwen, would have been released and safely to returned to her mother. Maybe they could have forged a new life together.

As for Adele and her husband being part of this story, sorry, can't help you there. Perhaps they were part of the original swindle perpetrated by Simon Walker. The father of the kidnapped girl. Perhaps Mr Brau ordered their killings because of that. The fact that I was working for Adele was merely a coincidence, but I became a very convenient scapegoat. But their murders are certainly connected, same MO, same weapon, in my opinion, same bent cop!

Ruth was killed because she knew me. Perhaps they were worried that I had told her everything I knew. Maybe it was a warning to me, to keep my mouth shut. In truth, I think I was next. The only reason I am talking to you now is that they haven't found me yet."

Another silence descended on the car. This time a deep stillness. Both people knew that their next moves would certainly mean the difference between life and death, perhaps even theirs.

"Thanks for being so honest, Lee. I agree with your last statement. I would offer you protective custody, but I think that would be a fatal mistake, given what we both believe. So far, as the murders of Francis Jackson Barnes and his wife Adele Barnes are concerned, there seems to have been several inconsistent or suspicious financial activities on their accounts. Including two hundred and fifty thousand pounds going into their account, and then straight out again. This was followed by half a million, and then five million, in and out. It went into a totally untraceable offshore account!

Maybe it's just putting one and one together and coming up with five, but I wonder if this is why they were killed? Gwen's father was the accountant, and Mr and Mrs Barnes were just part of the plan, facilitators. Perhaps they were members of the crime syndicate. I suspect they were there to launder money through their businesses. It's maybe something they had been doing for a long time, until the big one came along - a chance to be free of the syndicate for ever?"

"That would explain a lot, Deborah. It would also tie the five murders together. Nice job, but the main problem still exists. Who the hell is the murderer? Who is the bad cop? We need to find out before he kills again, and in particular, me! The problem is, we have no evidence at all. I don't suppose this cop is walking around with the very same 9mm pistol in his glove box. I am certain he won't turn himself in and tell us all he is sorry, so how the hell do we catch him?"

"Bait, we are going to use you as bait in order to lure this bent police officer out into the open! The problem with this plan is, it's very probable that it will go horribly wrong, and you will end up in the morgue with the other five dead bodies. I can't think of any other way though, Lee. I can't trust any of the senior officers in this case. Damn it, I am not sure who I can trust."

"So, what am I supposed to do with the father? I know where he is. One phone call and he will be picked up by the mob. With a bit of luck, Gwen will be released soon afterwards."

"When does this Mr Brau want an answer?"

"He said by this Monday. Believe me, Deborah, I am certain that she will die. As will her mother if he doesn't get his hands on the father. Mr Brau is a man of his word. He wouldn't hesitate for one moment to kill both of them, just for the pleasure of seeing them die. He is a psychopath. We don't have much time."

"Right, I need to know where the father is. I can have him picked up and detained on some trumped-up charge. At least that way, we will know where he is. He can't do a runner and we can use him as a bargaining chip if necessary.

We have got to get this thing moving, Lee. Three days and we run out of time. We end up with five dead in the morgue, and Gwen and her mother in the canal. This shit storm is about to get worse if we don't get a grip on it. And to be honest, I don't know who's going to help us. We need to do this by ourselves.

I know that you and I can be trusted, my Sergeant Sharron and my SOCO Kaye, but who the fuck else, who knows? One thing I do know, one false move, one minor mistake and we end up dead. Don't doubt that at all."

The Syndicate.
Mr. Brau's Office.
Thursday Night.

The office was large and opulent, reflecting Mr Brau's taste for Oriental art. In particular, jade statues along with embroidered silks. The dark oak furniture and panelling enhance a feeling of richness, but also a dark menace. Mr Brau sat in his large leather chair smoking a sizable cigar, watching the smoke gently rise and dissipate as it reached the panelled ceiling.

The three men stood in front of their boss, wondering what his mood really was. Things had generally gone to plan. The problem was, the accountant Simon Walker and the missing millions were nowhere to be found. Mr Brau had already expressed his displeasure at the situation, and has made many threats as to what would happen if both the accountant and the money didn't arrive, and very soon!

He dubbed out his cigar with a deliberate action before sitting back in his chair in order to address the three men standing in front of him. He looked each one of them straight in the eye. One glance from this man struck a deep and irrevocable fear. He was not to be crossed or argued with. His vengeance would be swift and without mercy.

Speaking in a low and slow manner, he began to address the three men. Not looking at anyone, he simply gazed about his office, occasionally alighting on one of his favourite objects. This made him smile. He engendered a faraway look, as if he recalled the thrill of acquiring something of such value and beauty.

"Gentlemen, I need not remind you of the unfortunate situation we now find ourselves in. A substantial amount of cash seems to have disappeared from the company's accounts, something that is particularly vexatious to me. As you can imagine, I would really appreciate this missing money to be returned, as soon as possible.

Now, I do pay you three gentlemen a substantial retainer to help get such unfortunate incidents corrected, along with the punishment of those responsible. After all, what is life without the rule of the law? Or at least my law. If people think that they can do as they please then where the hell would we be?

Now, from reports I see that the couple helping us to legitimise our income, Mr and Mrs Barnes have paid a heavy price for their misdemeanours - namely helping to steal our hard-earned money. You inform me that two local scumbags are also no more as it seems that they knew too much, along with the girlfriend of one Lee Hunter. This Lee Hunter has promised to deliver the main criminal in this episode. He has until Monday to fulfil his part of the bargain.

It would appear that you three, very well-paid individuals, are delivering nothing more than dead bodies. I have several employees that could do this for me at a fraction of the cost. So, I have to ask myself - what the hell are you really doing for me, except draining my bank account of money?

Gentlemen, I need results and I need then now. I will give you until midnight on Saturday to find Simon Walker and present him in this office, in the exact same spot where you are standing right now. If this doesn't happen, I will personally come and find you, tie you to the back of my car and drag you all about this town until the flesh is ripped from your bodies. Just before you die, I will rape each one of your wives in front of you, before pouring petrol on them and setting them on fire. As they burn, I will slit the throats of your children, their blood gushing onto the floor, and the screaming of your burning wives will be the last things you experience before you die.

Don't doubt me gentlemen, I will do this. And I will enjoy every second of the process. Go and find this bastard, Simon Walker, and bring him to me before I send my men out to find your families. You are all intelligent and inventive men, well trained, resourceful with access to a great deal of intelligence and information. It shouldn't be beyond you to find him. Now go back to your offices, turn on your computers, talk to your associates and bring Simon Walker to me. Are there any questions gentlemen?

Without so much of a word, the three men glanced at each other, turned and walked out of the office. They were escorted out of the building by two large and very intimidating thugs. The front door was opened for them, and they left, turning down the main street and towards the BMW X6. As they reached the vehicle the security systems disengaged and the doors unlocked.

"Well, gentlemen. Shall we go for dinner before we go back to the office? We need to talk, try and formulate a plan. We can't get this wrong. Brau will do exactly as he says. We know that from experience. The three of us should be more than enough to finish it off. That prat, DI Deborah Smith, will take the blame for a botched investigation and Lee bloody Hunter will rot in jail for the rest of eternity."

"Listen, what about the forensics? Kaye Marie is damn good. She will have that side of things done to perfection. That could discredit what we are trying to do and point the finger at one of us perhaps?"

"No problems there. I can pay a visit to forensics, check things out, make sure that we are not implicated. I will go through what she has done, ensure that Lee Hunter is firmly in the hot seat for the whole lot."

"Good, well use my authority to get what you need and don't rush. Make sure all the T's are crossed and I's dotted. We can't afford any kind of fuck up, not now! Right, that's that settled. Now let's get down the pub and have something to eat. I am starving."

The BMW X6 sped off down the main street, narrowly missing a mother pushing a buggy, much to the amusement of the three occupants. They were indeed untouchable, brimming with confidence and self-assurance. This job would be wrapped up very soon, they would be considerably richer, and Mr Brau would be happy and reunited with his money. Lee Hunter would be doing life x5 and DI Deborah Smith would be working security at the local clap clinic.

Nothing and no one could stop them now. It was inevitable. They will win and the status quo would be re-established. The bodies in the morgue would be turned to dust at the local crematorium and no one would care.

The Home of DI Deborah Smith.
Southbank Road, Southport.
Thursday Night.

They sat in Deborah's lounge. Three on the leather settee and two in the very comfortable armchairs, with the coffee table in the middle. They were the only people she really trusted. Perhaps the key to resolving the situation. It had been difficult asking them to join her, not because she didn't trust them, she did, but this inclusion could cost them their careers and, in all probability, their lives.

Deborah was in no doubt as to the potential consequence of this plan, but there didn't seem another way. She has resolved to fight fire with fire, confront this evil head on before it destroyed her and her friends. It was not just her, but the service itself. It had to be cleaned, scorched and sterilised of this evil - this corrupt cancer that was eating it alive.

She took a deep breath before addressing the little gathering. As she looked around, she could see and sense feelings of unease. One thing was for certain, they would not let her down. They would fight to the last.

"Right guys, for the benefit of our guest, let's introduce ourselves. Lee, you go first."

"OK, thanks Deborah. Lee Hunter, Private Detective. I guess it's my fault that you are here tonight. I spent twenty plus years in the Met Police before leaving a couple of years ago."

"Kaye Marie, Chief Forensic Specialist. I am here because Debs promised me lots of free wine. Not sure if I have been had though, let's see!"

"Sharron Shacklady, Detective Sergeant. Strange that, Debs promised me a cuddle with her new puppy. I don't see a puppy, do you Debs?"

"Marcus Cooke, Inspector, Thames Valley Police C.I.D. Debs said there was a half marathon on tomorrow, along the sea front. Strange I haven't seen the posters though."

There was a ripple of laughter as the five people looked around the lounge.

"OK, sorry about that folks, and Kaye. There isn't as much wine as you can drink, there is no puppy Sharron, and Marcus, there was a reason for the invitation, but it has nothing to do with running a half marathon.

No, the real reason is trust and you three are it. The only people I can trust right now. The reputation of Merseyside Police and my department are at risk, as is the liberty of Lee Hunter. There is a serial killer on the loose and we believe this person to be a senior police officer. I can have a guess as to the identity of this person, but we are here to ascertain the exact identity with evidence and proof beyond any doubt whatsoever.

I am not in the game of stitching people up with guesswork and questionable methods. Just good solid police work. It might be that there are two bent cops - we will find that out - but for now, we are working on the idea that there is just one.

He has certainly killed or been involved in the deaths of five people. I have their particulars here. These murdered people have jeopardised the security of one of the country's biggest crime syndicates, and some have been responsible for the disappearance of over five million pounds.

A young girl, by the name of Gwen Walker, has been kidnapped by this gang to make her father give himself up, and in all probability, with the money he has stolen as well. Lee has found the whereabouts of this man. One Simon Walker. Marcus has had him picked up on the pretence of a protective custody enquiry. He is being held at a station in Bicester for his own protection, or at least that's what Marcus has told him. This is both highly irregular and against all the protocols known to man. We know that we can't just walk into another force's patch and pick someone up without prior consent, but it was the only way we could think of to ensure the safety of Simon Walker, and keep him where we can get our hands on him if necessary.

As you all know, we can only hold him for maybe 24 or 48 hours before we need to formalise the protective custody paperwork. And since we have absolutely no evidence of anything, we will have to let him go by tomorrow evening or the Saturday morning at the latest. That means, we must sort this mess out by that time because once released, he will do a runner and will never be seen again. Any questions thus far?"

Sharron Shacklady was the first to speak, rubbing her chin in astonishment at the revelations.

"If we knew where he was, why didn't we just leave him there and keep him under surveillance?"

"Good question Sharron. Given the current situation with the murders and the potential bent cop, submitting such a request for surveillance officers would certainly have drawn attention to him. I have no doubt that the order would have gone out to pick him up and deliver him to the syndicate. We would have lost him and his daughter forever, along with any information he might have. I had to use Marcus and Thames Valley Police. Hopefully there will be no connection and he might just make it through the night."

"So, what are we doing to try and find this bent cop, Deborah?"

"Well Kaye, I have DC Mike Evans sucking up to one of the main suspects. Namely Detective Chief Inspector Mark Bruno. Hopefully he can get close enough to open this case up, perhaps even get the evidence, so we can close this traitor down once and for all."

"Who's this girl who has been kidnapped?"

"I will let Lee fill you in on that, Marcus."

"OK Marcus, and thanks to everyone in particular to Deborah. This case is huge. Let's hope we can solve it before more people lose their lives. The girl is Gwen Walker. The daughter of the man in question and the guy you have in custody at Bicester.

I struck a deal with the head of the crime syndicate, Mr Brau. He agreed to let her go if I delivered Simon Walker to him. I spent quite some time finding him and I was just about to give him up when Deborah called. It is my opinion that Simon Walker has something of great importance to the syndicate - probably the five million Deborah spoke of.

There have also been the five murders, which include three very dear friends of mine. I am certain that they are also connected to this case. I am in no doubt that a senior cop is involved, and the name of that person was found by one of the murdered friends of mine. That cost him his life, along with another friend. This case must be cracked before more people end up dead.

By a sheer twist of fate, I ended up involved in this maelstrom, by trying to find a missing girl and working for a woman who is also now dead. It was just a boring afternoon and I had no idea of the shit storm heading my way. Talk about hindsight, but if I knew what was about to happen to me, I would have run as far away as possible.

That said, three of my friends are dead. This I will not run from. I will find their killer and bring him to justice, and if I can't do that, I will kill him myself."

The room went silent. The thought went through everyone's mind - if this person was a high-ranking cop, would they ever be able to nail him? If he has remained undetected this long, who's to say he would ever be brought to justice? Who's to say that they would be able to do it? Deborah circulated the documents - information on the case - what evidence they had and material on the murdered people. It contained everything they knew. It wasn't much, but it was all there was. It had to be enough!

"So, Debs, I have come to have a cuddle with your new puppy that doesn't actually exist. That has traumatised me beyond belief, and now to add to my ordeal, I am being drawn into a scheme that will either end up in me being shot or thrown out of the police forever.

We are chasing a bent cop. We have no idea who this might be. Oh yes, he might have murdered five people thus far. A young girl has been taken and she will be murdered also, if we don't let the boss have her father, who will certainly be murdered once we hand him over. Marcus has transgressed numerous rules and regulations regarding arresting people in other force's territories, and now we are holding said person on some trumped-up protection blag.

Well, call me an old fuddy duddy, but this looks like a whole world of pain just about to drop on my newly dressed hair and fuck it up for all time, or am I getting the wrong end of the stick here?"

"Sharron, you are correct, and I had no right to ask you here. But you guys are the only people I can trust. If we don't do this, he will get away with it and that's not going to happen. There comes a time in everyone's life and careers when you must stand up and be counted, even if the heavens are just about to fall on you.

This is one of those times, and if anyone wants to leave now, I will think no less of you, but it won't stop me from getting this done."

Kaye Marie stood up, cleared her throat and she addressed the group with all the authority and strength she had.

"I think Debs is right. I am the only non-cop here, but this has to be done. Five innocent people are laying on those stainless-steel racks in the morgue. I have examined each one of them, each with their heads blown apart, just enough of the brains left to fill an egg cup. I wonder who the last person was that they looked at as the flash of the gun ended their lives. I am willing to bet it was the same face, the face of this bent cop.

We cannot let this person get away with it. They should be above such things, instead they are wallowing around in murder and treachery. They are laughing at us, the forces of good, and all those men and women who put on a uniform and risk their lives every day to keep us all safe. If we walk away now, we are spitting in the faces of those photos on the wall of our fallen heroes who have died in the line of duty.

I know the risks we are now looking at, and the possibilities that might befall us, but I for one need to do this. If I end up dead with my brains splattered all over the place, at least I know that I tried my best."

An energy grew in the room. Kaye had said what most of the group had been thinking. This was the time. They had to put a stop to the criminals who called themselves police and upholders of the law. It wasn't going to be easy, but no one said it would be. It was simply the time to act, because no one else would.

Travel Lodge, Room 16.
Friday Morning.

I woke up early, perhaps before 6am. To be honest, I hadn't slept well all night. I just couldn't stop thinking about Ruth. In all this nightmare, she had been an absolute rock and completely innocent. She had nothing to do with any of this corrupt filth nor these men who perverted the badge and the name of the police. To add to that, she has been murdered for no reason other than she had known me. What the hell did someone think that would gain them? What advantage would they benefit from by killing an innocent woman?

I had determined one thing though, if they didn't get this man, if he ended up at large, I would track him down and kill him. I wouldn't do it quickly either - real slow and painfully. He was going to pay for what he had done and pay very deliberately indeed.

Oh Ruth, shit. She was a mother. Who was going to tell the kids? Who was going to look after them? Of course, it would be the family liaison officer, but that wasn't going to help them much. No mother, no future. Just like Smelly Ken, Jenks and Dell. I had a burning hatred inside, a fire that was only going to be quenched in one way and it wasn't going to be vaguely legal!

I wish I could just walk away and pretend this wasn't happening. Just leave it to others, and to be honest, if it hadn't been for Ruth, I probably would. Anyway, that was all too late now. The plan had been agreed on and we all have our part to play. The one lingering thought though was the old saying, *"if it can go wrong, it probably will."*

It would start with Kaye Marie. She would be the first into the office, find Detective Chief Inspector Mark Bruno and tell him that Sharron would be late as she has a lead on the kidnapped girl's father. Tell him some hazy story about a boat in the marina in Liverpool - just try and get his juices flowing. Of course, he may not be the bent cop they were looking for, but if he wasn't interested in this story then at least they knew to look elsewhere.

Marcus would take up station at the marina. See who turned up once the 'secret' had been let out by Kaye. Sharron would find and keep an eye on Detective Chief Superintendent Martin Kiff, the other protagonist in this pool of bile and sewerage. The consensus of opinion was that he wasn't their main man. Bent yes, but not a murderer. Perhaps a man for a future investigation, but not for the murder of five people.

Deborah would contact her man on the inside, DC Mike Evans, and see what he has been able to dig up on his new best mate, Detective Chief Inspector Mark Bruno. She would ask for a quick out of office meeting this morning. Somewhere they could talk in private and away from prying eyes.

I was the 'back stop'. Be there for when I was needed. In other words, stay out of the way and we will contact you! I was happy enough with that. I was confident that Deborah and her team had all the bases covered. They have the advantage of surprise. No one would suspect the trap awaiting them. All they needed to do was fall into it.

With a bit of luck, by the close of play today, the murderer would be in the bag. Mr Brau would have the hairy finger of Merseyside Police's finest pushed up his nose, and Gwen would be released.

So, all in all, a very profitable day. So, why couldn't I shake this feeling that we had overlooked something? You know that sensation when you leave the house and you know you have forgotten something, but you don't know what it is, and it's only when you get into town you remember. I just couldn't put my finger on it. The trap has been laid. The bent cop wouldn't be able to resist getting his hands on Simon Walker and drag him off to chat to Mr Brau. Surely that bent cop would either be Detective Chief Inspector Mark Bruno or possibly Detective Chief Superintendent Martin Kiff. There was no one else even close to being in the frame and even if it was someone else, he would turn up at the marina and they would nab him, simple!

So why didn't I feel comfortable about all of this? Why did I have that, *'no, no it's not right'* feeling? I put it to one side. It was because of losing Ruth and it had me completely on edge - knocked me off – yes, that what it was, right? Just get on with it, Hunter. Let's get to my holding place and wait to be called. It's just the stress and the regrets about Ruth.

So off I went, winding my way through the early morning traffic - commuters off to work - not one of them cognisant of the events unfolding in their town. By the time they returned this evening, it would be over. Bent cops in the cells, Gwen back with her mum, and goodness knows what would happen to her dad.

I guess I must have lost concentration a little - my mind mulling over the grand plan and still with those nagging doubts in the back of my mind. I was shaken back into the real world by the blaring horn of a car on the roundabout at the end of Lord Street. I immediately stamped on the brake pedal and open my eyes wide. It was suddenly obvious what I had done - drifted out onto the roundabout without looking to my right.

There sat in a white Mercedes was a young man looking very angrily at me. He had a red face and even though I couldn't hear him, it was obvious what he was shouting in my direction. I held my hands up and apologised as he gave me a two fingered salute and drove past, and away at the next exit.

Feeling rather silly, I continued on my journey and off to the Bold Arms carpark, where I had been told to wait. I hadn't got one hundred yards down the road when it suddenly hit me. It came like a bolt from the blue - the reason I had been feeling uneasy all morning. It had been triggered by the young man in the white Mercedes, who I had pulled out in front of on the roundabout.

It's that bloody expensive BMW - the one I had seen several times, the BMW X6. I had seen it when I met Mr Brau, when Mrs Walker had been walking down Lord Street, and in the carpark of the police station. And Ruth said she had seen it in the carpark behind our flats.

Did that BMW X6 belong to a cop? And more importantly, the bent cop? No one gets into the station carpark unless they are on official business - absolutely no one.

So, the car might well lead to the perpetrator, whoever owns that car is more than likely our man, or at least someone who knows what's going on! I had to find out who the owner was but how? No point in ringing the station and asking. They would never tell me.

OK, think Lee. Who's going to know who that car belongs to? Who can I call? DI Smith. She will know or at least she can ring the station and find out. OK, give her a call. I punched her name into my phone and pressed 'CALL'. The number connected and rang but with no answer. Right, she is busy with that guy she was meeting. What was his name, DC Evans? OK, ring her number two - Sharron Shacklady. She might know. I pulled up her number and pressed 'CALL' once again.

"DS Shacklady."

"Hi Sharron, it's Lee Hunter. I wonder if you could answer a question for me?"

"Yeah Lee, no probs. How can I help?"

"I noticed a fancy BMW X6 in the police carpark, and to be honest, I think I have seen the same car following the missing daughter's mum. Also, Ruth said she noticed it in our flat's carpark, and I also noticed it following a meeting I had with Mr Brau. It's probably nothing Sharron, but I can't shake this odd feeling I have about it. Do you happen to know who it belongs to? These cars are rare Sharron, very rare. It might be a clue to the identity of our man."

"BMW X6, yeah, it belongs to Mike Evans. How the hell he can afford such a motor I don't know. He just tells everyone he inherited some money from his nan and decided to treat himself. Bloody liberty if you ask me. I can't afford any decent car, just an old rust trap which just about gets me to work in the morning. That jumped up prick won't even give me a lift, even though he drives past my house most mornings."

"Are you sure about that, Sharron? It belongs to DC Mike Evans?"

"Absolutely certain, Lee. There aren't any other sixty-thousand-pound cars in the station carpark I promise you. That car belongs to DC Mike Evans, no question about it."

"And to be clear Sharron, Deborah is meeting Evans this morning? Somewhere away from the office, no cover and no help?"

"What are you saying, Lee?"

"I think this Mike Evans has got something to do with all of this, and to be honest, it wouldn't surprise me if he was our man. We need to get to Deborah sooner than later. Stop this meeting from happening. I have tried to ring her - no answer. If Evans is the murderer, I wouldn't put anything past him, especially if he thinks, even mistakenly that Deborah suspects him of anything!"

"Surely not, Lee. He's just a young DC - nothing special. He hasn't got enough sense about him to do anything like this. He's not that intelligent."

"Trust me Sharron, most of the criminals I've met didn't have a bunch of university degrees. One thing many of them do share though is an ability to get things done, even if it means killing people who stand in their way. Don't underestimate this young man. He may be more than capable of being that dangerous. It doesn't take any amount of intelligence to pull a trigger!"

There was a long silence. I could sense Sharron's mind whirling with the possibility of DC Evans being the bent cop. Also, he was meeting Deborah this morning. They had to get to her, warn her of their fears, get her away from him and to a safe place.

An Industrial Estate in Southport.
09.40am

The darkness was overwhelming. There was a dull throbbing pain in her back and a woozy, drunken feeling. She felt both sick and claustrophobic. The heavy hood that covered her head restricted her breathing. It felt clammy and hot. Panic was not more than a moment away.

She tried to think - what's happened? Where was she now? Why couldn't she move? She tried to stand, but the burning sensation around her wrists pulled her back. Her feet refused to move - they seemed fixed and out of her control.

She could hear talking somewhere behind her. It was muffled, almost unintelligible, but there was the odd word she recognised. Something about the police, and then there was an angry exchange. Why was she here? What was the purpose? None of this made any sense and that light-headed feeling washed over her again and the darkness returned.

She wasn't aware of the passage of time. All she knew was her consciousness slowly returning. Gradually, at first, but then more rapidly, like exiting a tunnel, the light returned. She took several deep breaths. She had a need to blow away the blurred edges of her mind, open her awareness and push back the darkness.

Her senses opened up, gathering what information it could - sounds, tastes, even smells. At first there was just darkness and silence. There was nothing to hold on to, no anchor to fix in her mind. As she settled and her perceptions grew sharper, she became aware of something out there, beyond her blindfold.

At first it was just a noise - an indistinguishable sound, something different. There was a flutter of pigeon's wings on the external structure of the building. That wasn't it. A sound of rain on the roof, pattering gently and unceasingly, but that wasn't it either. No, this sound was rhythmical and continuous. Eventually she identified it – crying. Someone close to her was crying. It sounded like a woman's cry - higher in pitch than a man. Maybe a younger woman or even a girl?

She tried to spit the gag out from her mouth. No luck at first, but eventually she managed to dislodge it, working her chin above its clawing grip. She drew in another deep breath. There was crying, but what else was out there? She was utterly lost. There could have been ten people stood right in front of her, ready to strike at the first word she uttered. She drew her fears in close and decided to act. Gently, she spoke, reaching out into the abyss.

"My name is Detective Inspector Deborah Smith. I don't know why I am here, but I am sure help will arrive soon. Can I ask what your name is? Why are you here?"

At first there was no reply, but the crying did stop. At least whoever it was had reacted to her questions.

"I don't suppose you are Gwen? We have been looking for you for a while now. Is your name Gwen?"

"My name is Gwen, but we can't speak. They will come and hurt us and we have to be   quiet."

"I understand that Gwen, but if we are to get away, I need to understand where I am. That way we can plan an escape. Are you tied up like I am?"

"No, I am free. I was tied up at first, but they let me go. I am locked in now. I have tried to get away, but the doors won't open and the windows are right up near the roof."

"OK, Gwen. Can you come and remove my blindfold? I need to see where I am. Don't worry. If anyone asks, I will say I managed to shake it off."

"They will hurt me again. They hit me sometimes. I don't want them to hit me again."

"Don't worry, Gwen. I am a police officer. They won't hurt you anymore, but I have to see where I am. You need to pull my blindfold down."

There was a shuffling sound from somewhere nearby. Deborah couldn't see if anyone was close, but her senses suggested a person standing right in front of her. She desperately reached out. Was that someone breathing? Was she just imagining it?

"Are you there, Gwen? Why don't you just reach out and pull this bag off my head? You can then go back. They won't know you did anything to help me. I don't even think they will care."

With a sudden start, the light returned. Deborah closed her eyes as the brightness caused a stabbing pain in her brain. She tried to blink it away, setting off tears, blurring what vision she had. She blinked again and again, and slowly everything started to return to normal - the light, colours and vision opened before her.

She was sat in the middle of an empty industrial unit, on a grey concrete floor, corrugated steel roof and lines of narrow windows just below the roof line. The whole building was around one and a half stories high, with heavy sliding blue doors at one end. Perhaps wide enough for a van to enter when open. Facing her on the gable end was a single blue door. It looked substantial and backed in steel plates. This was a secure place. No one was supposed to enter or leave it without the keys.

In the corner was a dirty young girl - hair tangled, clothes grimy and covered in dust. She had a white trainer on her right foot and just a sock on her left. There was a blood stain to the right of her mouth and her eyes were open and full of fear.

"Hi Gwen. My name is Deborah. We are going to get out of here, don't worry about that. My colleagues will be looking for me and they will find me. I promise you. All we have to do is get ready. Let's start to plan for that, hey. In the meantime, tell me about yourself. What have they done to you? Have you any idea of where we are?"

"They tied me up, just like they have to you. A man came in and hit me. He tried to get me to ring my dad, but he wouldn't answer his phone. What's happened to my dad? Why do they want to speak to him?"

"I am not sure, Gwen. Perhaps they just want to ask him a few questions. I am sure everything will be fine. Did they say who they were? Did you see the same man every time?"

"Yes, he was a horrible man. He kept hitting me. He said they would kill me if I didn't get my dad on the phone. Sometimes they bring me some food and a drink, but they don't want me to call anymore."

"That's better then. I am sure they don't intend you any harm, Gwen. When they say they will kill you, it's just a threat. Don't worry. Do you hear any noises outside? You know, lorries, trains anything like that?"

"It's quiet in here. Sometimes there are perhaps train noises, but they are far away. Otherwise, nothing at all."

"Right, well, we need to get on, Gwen. I need you to untie me. We are not going to get away from here with me fastened to this chair, are we?"

Gwen didn't get the chance to respond. The sound of a key entering the lock in the small blue door brought proceedings to an end. The door opened with a squeal and in entered a man. He stood about six feet tall, perhaps a little more, dark brown hair, strong muscular build, dressed in a white T-shirt, jeans and trainers. He locked the door behind him, pushed the key into his jeans pocket and without taking his eyes off Deborah, walked slowly towards her.

He stopped right in front of the her and glared right down at her. He didn't display any emotion at all. Eventually he took a breath and spoke.

"Well, DI Deborah Smith, what brings you here? Oh yes, I remember. You were drugged. Yes, that's it. You were in the middle of an investigation and you are trying to find a man of interest to my boss. You see, Deborah - you don't mind me calling you Deborah, do you? My boss is very keen indeed to talk to this man. In fact, he will do everything and anything to find him.

To that end, he has asked me to come in here and have a chat to you. See what you know about his whereabouts. Thing is, my boss said I could use any means necessary to get you to talk, and he means anything! To be honest Deborah, I don't usually beat women. It's not part of my nature, but you know what it's like. Your boss wants something, so you have to do as you are told.

Anyway, enough of this chat, hey. I need to get on. Now as I said, I am not in the habit of beating on women, so I am going to leave, go and get something to eat, buy a birthday present for my niece. I will be back in a couple of hours, around 11.00am and we can have a chat then. Gives you time to think about it!"

Without another word, he turned and left the industrial unit, locking the door behind him. The silence in the unit was deafening. Deborah knew when threats and intimidation were real, and this man was one hundred percent genuine. There was no doubt what would happen in an hour or so when he returned. They have that time to escape and they have to make it.

The Bold Arms Carpark.
10.00am

They all crammed into my white Ford Fiesta. First DS Sharron Shacklady, closely followed by the Senior SOCO Kaye Marie. There was an air of fear and I could almost taste it. It was 10.00am and the whole plan had already gone to hell. No one could reach DI Smith, and DC Mike Evans has also disappeared.

Sharron drew in a deep breath and tried to calm the situation.

"Right, first things first - what have we done and what do we know? Kaye, did you manage to find Detective Chief Inspector Mark Bruno? Did you inform him about the possible location of Simon Walker?"

"I did. I found him in his office just after seven. I brought him a coffee, we had a chat - well, he tried to chat me up - slimy bastard. Anyway, I spilled the beans about the possible location for Simon Walker in the marina. I reminded him that he was the father of the missing girl and maybe there was a link? I also slipped in the meeting Debs was having with DC Evans. He didn't seem that bothered to be honest. Said I should go and tell the missing persons team about Gwen's father.

He then asked me out on a date. Said I would really enjoy it. I told him to go and play with himself and left the office. I watched him for a while, and he just scoffed his croissant, drank his coffee and stared out of his office window. He didn't do anything after that. Just gazed into the distance. Next thing you called me and I made my way here. What's going on, Shaz?"

"Right Kaye, I was tasked to find and keep an eye on Detective Chief Superintendent Martin Kiff. Turns out he is in hospital today, on a last-minute knee operation. His secretary said he was called in this morning and should be out later today and back at work next week. It was at that point that Lee phoned me. Seems we have overlooked something and that might be very significant indeed.

Do you remember that flash car in the staff carpark, BMW X6? Well, that belongs to DC Mike Evans, and Lee thinks it has been seen at several of the crime scenes. Just a coincidence? Possibly, except those motors are 60k minimum. If you see one in your area, you have probably seen the lot!

Now, what has this got to do with anything? Well, Evans has got that private meeting this morning with Debs, and guess what? We can't get in contact with her! Could be her phone has gone flat or might be she has left it in her car. Could be that Evans is our killer!"

"Oh, come on Shaz. Evans is a bit of a dip stick, but he's not a homicidal killer. No way. Debs has lost her phone or something. She is probably on her way back to the office. Anyway, DC Evans is not one of our suspects. He is Deb's man on the inside, trying to find out if Bruno or Kiff are the bent cops. What possible motive would he have? Why would he turn into some deranged killer? He is a DC in the murder squad, nothing more."

The conversation was going nowhere and time was running out. Perhaps Kaye was right. Maybe we were jumping to conclusions, adding one and one and coming up with six. However, I have spent many a long year in the Met and my hackles were up. This didn't feel good. Kiff was in hospital and Bruno was wishing his life away staring out of his office window. Absolutely nothing suspicious there!

Now Evans might be a knob, but I just couldn't shake off the feeling that he was more than just a detective constable. It was easy to assume the quiet guy in the corner was exactly that. I have been proved wrong on that score on more than one occasion. It's called hiding in plain sight - keeping a low profile and not drawing attention to yourself. That's how serial killers get away with their crimes for so long. Nobody ever suspected them in the first place!

This wasn't the crime spree of a serial killer. This had gangland written all over it. Five dead, all killed in the same way. This was the work of a hit man and someone who enjoyed his work. If it was Evans, he was no deranged killer, he was an ice-cold executioner. And the last person to meet him was DI Deborah Smith. I took the opportunity to jump in and try to get this nightmare sorted out.

"Look Sharron, our first priority is to find out what the hell has happened to your boss. My guess is she met Evans and he has taken her. Maybe in panic, because she was too close to him. Perhaps he is getting to like his work too much, but we need to find her and fast."

"OK, so where do we start? We don't even know where she was meeting him and we don't even know if anything has happened to her. She might be back in the office pigging out on a chocolate doughnut for all we know."

"Right, well, best make a start. Kaye, phone Marcus. See if he knows where the meeting was. Don't panic him. Just say you need to see her. Sharron, get to the office. See if she is pigging out on that doughnut. We can take things from there."

It wasn't long before Kaye and Sharron came back to the car with their answers. It was much as I expected. Deborah has not returned to the office and they confirmed that her phone was not on the network. They haven't seen her all day and were not expecting her to return anytime soon.

Kaye had some better news. Marcus said that the meeting between Deborah and Evans was supposed to take place in Walker's café on Wesley Street, at about eight this morning. At least this was a start, it wasn't much but it was all we had.

"Right, Sharron, get on to the station. We need everyone looking for Evans BMW X6. Wherever he is, Deborah won't be far behind. Get them to put a trace on his phone and anything else they can. We don't have much time. We must find him and fast.

Kaye, get onto Marcus. Tell him it's probably Evans and in all likelihood, he is on the way to the marina. If he thinks Simon Walker is on the boat, then Evans will have to go and check it out. He has no choice. Marcus is going to need backup. Evans is more than just a serial killer. He will certainly be armed and he won't hesitate in using whatever force he sees fit. Is there any possibility that we can get some armed officers out there, Sharron?"

"Yeah, leave it to me. I will call my ex-boss. He owes me one. In fact, he owes me lots. Especially after the flower show debacle. Oh, and those interesting photos of him and the journalist's wife. I think it's time he paid me back and I am certain he will do so. It won't be the whole Armed Response Unit, but it will have to do."

"Why don't we just call this issue in and get the senior managers to sanction everything we need?"

"Because Kaye, the senior managers are Detective Chief Inspector Bruno and Chief Superintendent Kiff. If they are part of all this, can you imagine the chaos it would set off? Can you envisage what would happen to Marcus sat alone at Liverpool Marina?"

"Good point, Lee. I guess we are all alone. So, where do we start?"

"Firstly, Sharron is going to make those calls. Can we find Evans? Get some protection for Marcus and does anyone know where Deborah is? Next, Kaye you are going to that café. Ask the staff what they have seen. Have a look at the CCTV. Do whatever you need until we have the answers.

In the meantime, I am going to see Mr Brau. Not sure if he is going to help. He might even feed me to the fish in the Liverpool canal just for asking, but I have to try. I know where Simon Walker is. Mr Brau needs Walker. He might be willing to help us out and he might even be able to find out where Evans is."

We broke up, off to our appointed tasks. To be honest, I didn't have any great expectations about our success. My guess was Deborah was already dead. Evans has not hesitated thus far in killing anyone who seemed to be a threat, even if it was a down and out drug addict that posed no risk at all. We had to try though. Perhaps Mr Brau would be able to come up with some information that would lead to Evans. My fear was, he would simply put a bullet in my head for asking. That was, after torturing me to find out the location of Simon Walker!

I pulled up the last conversation I had with Brau on my phone and typed in my question.

MR BRAU.
WITH REFERENCE TO THE TASK OF FINDING THE PERSON OF INTEREST.
I AM PLEASED TO INFORM YOU THAT I NOW HAVE HIS LOCATION.
IF WE COULD SET UP A MEETING, I WILL BRING YOU FULL DETAILS.
THIS WILL ENABLE THE RELEASE OF GWEN.
I WOULD, WITH DUE RESPECT, ASK FOR SOME HELP FROM YOURSELF. WE HAVE A MISSING POLICE OFFICER. I WONDER IF YOU MIGHT BE ABLE TO ENQUIRE AS TO HER WHEREABOUTS?

I pressed send. I wasn't particularly confident of a reply, but as my dad used to say, *'if you don't buy a ticket, you won't win a prize'*. Thing was though, the prize here was the life of a police officer. But in gaining that prize, it would cost the life of the father of Gwen Walker. I pushed the phone back into my pocket and hoped for the best, but expected the worse.

It wasn't long before Sharron got back to me. She had arranged for three armed officers to meet up with Marcus. This was a huge lift and a relief. At least he would be safe now. We didn't want to lose two of police's finest in one day!

Eventually Kaye called in. There was no CCTV footage of the meeting between Deborah and Evans. But the staff in the café said that they thought that a meeting did take place between two people matching their general descriptions early this morning. It was a very busy period. People on their way to work, some night staff from the hospital getting some breakfast, a couple of mums on the school run. All seemed well, plenty of smiles, a couple of coffees, nothing untoward. They said that two people had left together. Nothing more to report as everything seemed fine.

I pressed end on my mobile. It wasn't long after that I received another call which turned out to be an absolute bombshell. It was one of those earthquake moments. Once in a lifetime event that just took your breath away.

When I first heard it, I couldn't believe what Sharron was telling me. It simply didn't make sense. It threw everything we knew into absolute chaos. It felt like we were beginning to see a light at the end of the tunnel, but it turned out to be a train coming in the opposite direction.

When I received the phone call, I simply couldn't begin to digest what she was telling me. If this was right, and I had no reason to believe it wasn't, we were in even greater trouble than I first thought - if that was indeed possible!

"Sharron, say that again. I am not sure I got that?"

"I know. I couldn't believe it myself, but I have confirmed it with the desk Sergeant. At 07:00 this morning, Detective Constable Mike Evans rolled up with an arrest. Some smack head that had been dealing contaminated Gamma Hydroxybutyrate. Some kids had got really sick and a possible manslaughter charge was pending. Because Evans was on an early shift, they had roped him in on a drug bust. He brought one of the dealers in, booked him at the desk and had gone upstairs for some breakfast.

I asked the girls in the canteen - he was there for about an hour, made a couple of calls and then went back to the cells. Lee, he wasn't at the café with Deborah. It wasn't him!"

I wanted to open my mouth and say something, but nothing seemed to come out. If it wasn't Evans, then who the fuck was it? We were thrashing about in the dark, no credible information, no leads and not a bloody clue.

"Hang on Sharron. So, it wasn't Evans, so what? That still doesn't change anything. Deborah is missing, probably taken by whomever she met. She would only have met a credible contact. Someone she knew from Southport Police. We just need to work out who. Evans was in the station, Bruno was staring out of his office window and Kiff is in hospital. It's not me, you or Kaye, who the hell does that leave?"

"The only person who knows what we are doing is Marcus. But I am certain it wasn't him. He would never harm Deborah."

"Sorry to tell you Sharron, but no one is above suspicion here. Thirty seconds ago, it was DC Mike Evans. Now you tell me? No one else knows what we are doing. Deborah kept it that way. We are the only people who knew the plan."

"In that case, Simon Walker is already dead as is Deborah, and probably Gwen Walker. If it is Marcus, then we are finished. He met Deborah this morning, he killed her, went back to Bicester, grabbed Simon Walker and the rest is history."

"You might be right Sharron, but there is one more possibility. I need you to ring the station again and ask them a question."

An Industrial Estate in Southport.
10.30am

"Gwen, listen. We have maybe thirty minutes before that guy comes back. We need to get out of here. There must be something you can think of - anything that might prove useful to me, anything that will help us get out of here. What's that over there? The small room with a red door?"

"That's the toilet, Deborah. They unlocked it so I can use it when I need to. There is no window. Just the toilet and a sink. There is no way out of there."

Deborah looked at the cubicle. One obvious fact was that it didn't reach all the way to the ceiling. In fact, it was only five or six feet short of the glass windows at the top of the prefabricated walls. She looked about the unit, taking it all in and anything that could assist in their escape - two chairs, some rope, a brush in one corner - this might just be enough she thought, but will we have enough time?

"Right, Gwen. You are going to help me. We are getting out of here, but we need to be fast. He will be back very soon, we need to act quickly, and we need to start now. You go and grab that brush, collect up all the bits of rope and take them over to the toilet."

"What are we going to do, Deborah? There is no way out of that toilet, believe me, I have looked."

"We are not going out of the toilet, Gwen. We are going out over it. We can get this chair on top of that cubicle, reach up with the brush. Perhaps we could break the glass and get out. We can make an escape with that rope, and those rags they used to blindfold and gag us. It won't reach to the ground, but it might be enough to stop us hurting ourselves. We need to get out quickly and I can't think of any other way."

They both looked up at the narrow glass windows high up near the roof. It would be almost impossible to get through them, but it was all they had. It would have to work - come what may.

They threw the brush, rope and rags on top of the cubicle. Deborah pushed Gwen up on top and passed her the chair. Using the other chair Deborah scrambled up. They were both in position - this was it, their only chance.

"Right Gwen, cover your eyes. I am going to reach up with the brush and break that glass. We can then use this chair to boost ourselves up higher and get out of that window. Tie together the ropes and rags. We need it to be as long as possible, Gwen, so take your time."

Balancing very precariously on the chair, Deborah reached up with the brush. Its long handle reached only just high enough to touch the glass. Swinging it as hard as she could, Deborah hit the glass, but there was no effect. She swung again and again, hitting the glass with every bit of force she could muster. Eventually, cracks started to appear, and for one last time, with every bit energy she could summon, she swung the brush and hit the glass.

There was a shattering explosion and pieces of glass showered down on them. A few seconds later, they could be heard hitting the concrete area outside of the unit.

Clouds of dust and cobwebs followed as the two women curled up as tight as they could.

"Yes, Gwen. We have done it. Now, we have to get outside and down on the other side. Trouble is, only one of us is going to be able to do it. I am going to boost you up to that window. Just squeeze through it. Tie your rope onto the frame and climb down outside. Then make a run for it. Head for anything that looks inhabited - another unit, a house, caravan - just get out there and call for help. Do you understand?"

"No, Deborah. You have to come with me. I can't do this by myself."

"You have to, Gwen. The only way out of that window is if I stand on this chair and you use me as a ladder. Once you are out, there will be no one left to help me. You need to summon help, Gwen. I can't help you with that."

"Then I will stay here. Use me as a ladder. I can't leave you behind."

"Gwen, listen. They will be back soon, then we are both in trouble. I can't leave you here. You have to go and get some help, so let's get busy."

With tears in her eyes, Gwen gathered up her makeshift rope and climbed up onto the chair with Deborah. Following her instructions and using the Deborah as a makeshift ladder, she scrambled up. She was just able to get her hands onto the window frame and with Deborah's assistance, scrambled though the opening. It was a tight fit, but after tying the rope onto the broken frame, she pushed herself though.

She was gone in a second. Deborah could hear her scrambling as Gwen descended the outside of the building. It would be very dangerous. The building wasn't very high, but the rope was much shorter than was needed. Eventually the noises stopped. Deborah waited to hear from Gwen, but there was nothing.

"Gwen, are you alright? Did you get down safely?"

There was nothing but silence. Has she sent this young girl to her death? Why didn't she go in her place? In Deborah's job, there were always decisions to be made. Sometimes life and death decisions, but has she made the right call this time? Was this young girl laying injured or worse outside the unit?

"Gwen, are you OK?"

Again, nothing but silence. A sinking panic enveloped her. She has made the wrong decision. She has failed in her duty to protect Gwen.

"Deborah, I am OK. I've hurt my ankle, but I think I will be fine."

A hot wave of relief flowed through Deborah. The sound of that girl's voice came as a huge relief.

"Thank goodness you are OK, Gwen. What can you see?"

There are more industrial units, but they seemed to be abandoned. There are no cars or vans, no people anywhere."

"Right, well, you need to get away, try and find a road. See if there are any signs of life anywhere. Go now Gwen! He will be back any minute now!"

The Bold Arms Carpark.
11.00am

"Sharron, I want you to ring the station to see if anyone knows Chief Superintendent Martin Kiff's private number. Let's see exactly what he is doing today. You need to speak to someone who you can really trust. I mean really trust Sharron!"

"What? You think it might have been him Debs met this morning?"

"It's worth a try."

"Sorry you guys, but aren't we missing the point here?"

"What's that, Kaye?"

"Debs set up the meeting with Evans, not with Chief Super' Kiff. How the hell would he know to meet Debs in the café?"

"Because Evans and Kiff are working together. Evans was on a dawn raid this morning, so he couldn't go. He phoned Kiff, tipped him off and he met Deborah early at the café. Perhaps Deborah knew nothing about the substitution until it was too late. She was either taken by Kiff before the meeting or immediately afterwards.

If I am right, we need to know if Kiff is at home after his hospital appointment or if the whole thing was just a cover for the last-minute meeting with Deborah."

The two women stared at me. If I was right, then we had proof that this thing went to the very top. If that was the case, it might be almost impossible to put this particular fire out. As they discussed the possibilities of who might know Kiff's number and who they might trust to hand it over, my phone went off.

With a start, I looked at the screen. It was a withheld number. I wouldn't normally answer, but given the circumstances, I thought I should. I slipped out of the car and pressed 'ANSWER'.

"Hello, Lee Hunter."

"Mr Hunter, so nice to speak to you once again. It's Mr Brau here. I wonder if this is a good time to have a chat?"

"Certainly, Mr Brau. Now is a good time."

"Right, Mr Hunter. Well, in that case, I will come straight to the point. It would seem that a friend of yours might know the whereabouts of a certain person of interest - namely Simon Walker. It has come to my attention, that this friend is presently a guest of my organisation. I am sure she will be more than happy to disclose the whereabouts of Simon Walker, once my men have spoken to her, if you get my meaning, Mr Hunter!

However, never let it be said that I am a cruel or an unfair man. I am, therefore, more than happy to give you the opportunity to hand over the location of Simon Walker before your friend is interviewed by my staff. It goes without saying that should you give me this information yourself, your friend will be released with immediate effect. Oh yes, I will throw in Gwen Walker as a measure of my good will and generosity. Now, there's an offer you can't refuse, Mr Hunter."

I shuddered as my brain tried to comprehend what Brau had just said. So far, as I understood him, he had Deborah and Gwen, and he was just about to beat the information from Deborah as to the whereabouts of Simon Walker. I on the other hand could simply hand over the location and they would be released. It seemed very simple, but I knew from experience, that this type of situation never was. Of course, Brau wouldn't release anyone until he had Walker in his evil grip. I had to think quickly. I could give him the location, buy some time. Obviously, Walker wasn't there, but it would slow things down, give me some more time to think. It would buy a few precious hours to unravel the mystery, put pressure on the likes of Evans or Kiff.

"Mr Brau, I do apologise for not getting back to you sooner, but you are right. I do have the location of Simon Walker. What with everything, I didn't have time to contact you. Anyway, I am more than happy to disclose that to you now.

Just to be clear Mr Brau - Gwen Walker and Detective Inspector Deborah Smith, currently guests of your organisation, will be released once you have Simon Walker?"

"They will be released as soon as I have Walker. I give you my word, Mr Hunter. I also promise that they will not be harmed in the meantime. So, you can rest assured that no 'interviews' will take place.

However, I also guarantee you that they will both die should anyone else become involved or should someone try to rescue them. Additionally, if I receive a visit from the boys in blue, they will die, without mercy and in horrendous circumstances. I hope you also understand what will happen to them if you send my men on a wild goose chase, Mr Hunter. I don't like to waste my time, so any information you give me needs to be correct. Do you understand me, Mr Hunter?"

"Perfectly, Mr Brau."

I walked back to the car. The two women stared at me. It was obvious on my face what I've just done. I had no choice though. I had to buy some time, otherwise Deborah would have the information beaten out of her. That I could never allow to happen. Kaye was the first to ask the obvious question.

"So, what happens when his men turn up at the marina and he isn't there?"

"Let's hope they hang about for a while, buy us enough time to try and figure out where Deborah and Gwen are. It's all we have Kaye. There is no other way of sorting this out."

"Why can't we just phone the station and mobilise the whole Merseyside Police Force?"

"Because we don't know who we can trust. Evans and Kiff are right at the centre of all this. If they suspect what has happened, they will call Brau and that will be the end of Deborah and Gwen. No, we can't trust anyone. We have to play this close to our chests. We dare not involve anyone else."

"I will phone Marcus. Get him away from that marina. We don't want him getting involved."

"Good point, Sharron. Tell him to hightail it back to Bicester. He needs to be close to Simon Walker, just in case we need to move him. Tell him we have this thing in hand. We will sort Deborah and he needs to be away. Being close to this isn't going to help him, Deborah, or us!

Did we have any luck with Kiff's telephone number?"

For the first time, I glimpsed a smile on Sharron's face.

"I did and you will never guess. I phoned and his wife answered, said he wasn't home. He was on a course in Coventry. Oh, Chief Superintendent Kiff, what a complex web you weave. In hospital, at home or on a course? Do make your mind up!"

A silence fell over our little group. For the first time we had an opening. Kiff was now right at the top of our list, but this time we had proof that he wasn't doing what he claimed to be. Now don't get me wrong, he could be on an undercover job somewhere or he could simply be off with his girlfriend having some fun, but it was a break and one we had to investigate.

Also, it was the first time the hackles on the back of my neck were quiet. When we first discussed Evans, it didn't feel right. He didn't quite fit the bill. Evans was a follower, not a leader. He certainly did play a part in all of this, but he wasn't the main man. He wasn't intelligent enough for that. He also didn't strike me as a cold-blooded killer. Don't ask me to explain, but you get to know people like that. They have a certain air about them, like an unsettling lack of emotion.

As for Chief Inspector Bruno, he never struck me as a mass murderer either. More like an arse licking ladder climber. He was that slimy office jerk who would try to chat up your wife or run to the boss when you had done something wrong. Yes, he would assassinate your character, talk behind your back if it meant climbing the ladder of success, but a cold-blooded assassin, no not at all.

On the other hand, Chief Superintendent Kiff was one of those men who would never push his head above the parapet. A quiet operator, a guy no one suspects of anything, a blameless life, easy going, never part of any kind of controversy. I knew men like him - faceless ghosts in the system. It all started to make sense now.

He has probably been part of the underworld for many years. Perhaps right from the first day he put his uniform on. Quietly working behind the scenes, feeding the gangland bosses with intelligence, occasionally benefitting from leads they provided, enabling him to 'solve' crimes and propelling him up the career ladder at an extraordinary rate.

The trouble was, he has gotten used to the benefits. The boss's yacht in the Bahamas, cash pay outs, protection from the mob, young hostesses at secret parties. This was all fine whilst he was working, but he was now on the brink of retirement and the big bosses wouldn't want to know him anymore - a retired cop was no use to them! So, he had to make that one last payday, that grand finale, and getting the reward from Mr Brau for retrieving the money stolen by Simon Walker would do him nicely.

The trouble was, things had got out of hand. Obtaining a million pounds for getting Mr Brau's money back seemed easy. All he had to do was snatch Gwen and Simon Walker, job done! That's where things had started to go pear shaped. Firstly, Dell and Jenks found out about him. What choice did Kiff have then? They had to die! Then Mr Brau found out that Francis Jackson Barnes and his wife Adele were assisting Simon Walker with the swindle. The order went out to kill them both and Kiff had to obey.

I am sure he never intended things to get so far out of control, but once the ball started rolling, he simply couldn't stop it. He was now in deep. Brau would have him and his family shot if he didn't comply. Additionally, there was so much evidence available about his involvement that there was no escape, even if he turned himself in.

When Deborah contacted DC Evans to arrange the meeting at the café, he had to turn her down because of being called in to assist on a dawn drug bust. Maybe DC Evans suggested a meeting with Chief Superintendent Kiff. Of course, Deborah would not have assumed too much. After all, Chief Superintendent Kiff was not suspected of any wrongdoing.

The focus of their attention was on Chief Inspector Bruno. He was the man in the firing line - the one they all suspected as the bent cop! DC Evans was her man on the inside, or so she thought, so perhaps he had contacted Kiff. He was a senior officer - very well liked and trusted. Perhaps DC Evans had passed on any information he had on Chief Inspector Bruno?

Anyway, it seemed likely that Deborah met Kiff at the café. She was taken from there or shortly afterwards. She is now in the claws of Mr Brau who was using her as a bargaining chip. I have no doubt about what he would do to her and Gwen once he found out that Simon Walker was not at the marina in Liverpool.

We have no idea where the two women were, so any attempt at a rescue would prove impossible. I had to come up with a plan - one that would lead to their rescue. The trouble was, I didn't think that plan existed!

An Industrial Estate in Southport.
11.30am

A vehicle pulled up outside the main doors of the industrial unit. Deborah could hear its tyres crunching on the grit and rubbish that lay all about the place. She had a feeling of impending doom. Clearly Gwen has been unable to find anyone who might have assisted, and now Brau's henchman have returned.

She spun around, for one last time, trying to find some way of escape, something that might assist her, but there was nothing. Instinctively she ran over to the toilet cubicle and grabbed the broom. She knew this wouldn't hold the thug off for long, but it was all she had.

She could hear her heart pounding in her chest. If it pumped any harder, it would surely burst. The adrenaline coursed through her veins and arteries. She might not win this fight, but she would not die for a lack of trying. There was the slamming of a door, perhaps two. They had come in force, '*some kind of hard men, hey.*'

Just before the storm, a silence descended over the whole scene. Tiny particles of dust spun aimlessly, tumbling over and over in the beams of sunlight pouring in through the windows. It all seemed somewhat surreal. It was not supposed to end this way. She had dreamed of retiring with Marcus. Maybe moving abroad somewhere - Italy was a favourite. Now there would be only suffering and certain death. There was no way she was escaping this. A tear rolled down her face as pictures of her family and friends flashed through her mind. She would miss them all.

She could hear voices coming from outside - talking amongst themselves, growing louder and quieter as they moved around. Why haven't they entered? What were they waiting for? She was an unarmed woman. They were several men. Next there was banging on the door. She could see it moving slightly. This was it. They were coming in. Then their voices became louder, distinctive and not what she expected.

It wasn't the local northern accent of the man who had spoken to her earlier. This was a different accent altogether. It was distinctive, it was not northern English, it was strong Irish. It didn't seem to make sense. Why would the local gang employ Irish to do their dirty work? That's not what normally happened around here. In any case, where was the thug who had threatened her? Why wasn't he coming through that door?

"Listen, sweetheart. We can't open the fuckin' door, so we are going to ram it open with the van. So, stand back!"

She shook her head in disbelief. Had she just heard that right? Ram the door open?

"Oi! Did ye hear me? Get away from the fuckin' door! It's comin' in!"

There was no more warning, and with an almighty explosion followed by the screaming of twisted metal, the large blue doors flew open. The dust and noise combined into a cacophony of chaos and anarchy. She threw herself to the floor, more in fear rather than self-preservation.

The noise rolled on as the huge doors crashed to the floor. The screeching of tyres and a revving engine just added to the whole scene. She dared to glance upward.

Through the dust she could make out the fuzzy image of a white transit van, no more than ten feet away. The doors flew open and two men jumped out.

"Well, darlin', are yer' comin'? Or just waiting till that fucker kills yer'? Dis friend of yours said he was comin' back, so we thought we would get 'ere first."

Deborah scrambled to her feet, still shocked at the recent events. In between coughing the dust from her throat and clearing her eyes, she caught sight of a familiar figure standing outside the unit. It was Gwen. She had the biggest smile on her face. She has done well and she was very proud.

"Come on, Deborah! We need to go before that man gets back. Jump in the back of the van. These guys have been really helpful."

Deborah jumped into the back of the white transit van. The back was dirty and full of old plastic sacks, builders rubbish and a couple of broken window frames.

"Sorry, darlin'. We were on our way to recycle this on the other side of the industrial estate, if you know what I mean. Your kid waved us down, told us what had been going on. So, we decided that today was a day of good will toward men - oh and women of course. Any case, never slap a woman! Fuckin' right! We had to come n' rescue yer' - not let that idiot fuck yer' up!"

Deborah turned around to face the man. An Irish traveller for certain, and she had never been so happy to see one.

"I have to thank you guys. You have certainly saved our lives. We need to get away from here quick. Can you get me back to the police station on Lord Street?"

"No problem luv'. Jump in! Get us there in no time."

The back doors of the van slammed shut. The engine roared into life and with a crunch of the gearbox, the van pulled away.

"Well done, Gwen! I didn't think you would make it so quickly."

"I was running as far and as fast as I could, but there was no one else on the estate. It seemed abandoned. It was then that this white van came roaring towards me. I think they were on the way to tip all this rubbish somewhere on the estate. Anyway, I held my arms out and they stopped. They didn't believe me at first, but once they realised that I was alone and just how far out of town this place really is, they said they would help."

"Good job they came your way, otherwise we would have been lost for sure. I have never been so happy to see a couple of gypsies on their way to tip a load of rubbish."

They were home free, they have done it, but without warning the whole environment seemed to turn sideways. The rubbish in the back of the van flew in all directions, as did Deborah and Gwen. There was a terrible screeching and banging as the dust from the rubbish flew into the air and chocked their lungs. Up and down they bounced, then onto one side and then the other. The noises were almost painful - a mixture of bending metal and breaking class filled their senses.

Gwen banged her head and a spray of blood shot across the chaotic space. Deborah fell backwards onto something sharp. The pain shooting up her neck and then down into her hips. She pushed out with her arms, trying to brace herself, stop the tumbling, and the feelings of intense nausea. It had little effect. She fell again, this time against her shoulder and a piece of broken glass jabbed itself into her arm. She felt warm blood trickling down.

Eventually, the confusion and chaos stopped in an instant of deafening silence. As quickly as it began, the whole world came to rest. The rubbish in the back of the van settled all around them. The dust whirled in disarray and a smell of diesel and burning oil filled her nostrils. She wasn't sure if she had lapsed into unconsciousness or just emerged from the stunned shock of what had just happened.

She looked about her. Gwen was half buried to her left, blood coursing from a head wound. She was clearly unconscious. Deborah tried to push herself up right, but at first the pain in her back and arm were too much to bear.

"Come on, get a grip Deborah! I know this hurts, but you need to get out of here, so get up now!"

The pain in her left shoulder ripped into her consciousness. She turned to see a shard of glass, about six inches long, sticking out of her upper arm. The urge to pull it out was almost overwhelming, but she knew better. The throbbing pain in her back was almost as bad, but more manageable. She could ignore it, at least for the short term.

She ripped the sleeve of her blouse off her left arm with her teeth and the still functioning right hand. Wrapping it around the top of her left arm, she tied it as tightly as she could. This increased the feeling of intense pain, but the blood flow slowed. At least she would stay alive for a little longer.

There seemed little she could do for Gwen. She was half buried buy the rubbish in the van, but she was breathing. Her pulse was strong and regular. Deborah's first priority was to find out what the hell had happened. The van was on its side - that was clear, but what was the reason?

She kicked at the back doors with both legs. It wasn't long before they sprung open, allowing light and a gust of lifesaving fresh air into the rear of the vehicle. Blinking the dust from her eyes, she cautiously peered outside - first to her left and then to her right, but there was nothing to be seen. Then a familiar voice came from behind her.

"Well, Detective Inspector Smith. Now, what the hell are you doing in the back of a pikey van? Trying to escape perhaps?"

The feeling of absolute terror and dread washed over her. The voice was that of the man who had gone for lunch. He has now returned, and he would not be as polite and courteous this time.

Deborah slowly turned to look at her tormentor. He was standing behind her with a sickly grin on his face.

"So, DI Smith. Where were you off to? A bite to eat? A trip to the supermarket perhaps? Good job I saw your van leaving the front of the unit, but these Irish aren't the best drivers you know. Drive straight at them and they panic. The van swerved to one side and turned over - fun to watch. Anyhow, the guy in the front seems very dead to me, so we can have our chat now with no threat of being disturbed. Once I have finished with you, I think a little fun with young Gwen is on the cards. I am looking forward to that.

Look at your arm, DI Smith. Come let me pull that glass out. No, on second thoughts, I will use it during my interview. I think twisting it and pushing it in and out might well help with your answers. What do you think detective?"

"Listen here, whatever your fucking name is, I will find you and I will throw you in prison for the rest of your life. If you kill me, my colleagues won't stop until they catch you and make sure you spend the rest of your miserable existence in the deepest black hole they can find."

"Not sure about that, detective. We have friends in high places, including your police force. Strings will be pulled and favours called in. I am sure I won't be spending anytime at all in one of your '*deepest black holes'*. You see, things are never quite what they seem. The truth is, we run this manor, not you boys and girls in blue. You have never really been in charge. We have just allowed you to think that way.

The public like to see you lot parading up and down in your flashy police cars, directing traffic, jumping out on drug busts and all that stuff. It's good publicity. Keeps the funding coming from government, but that's all show. It distracts everyone from the truth, and that is, we are in charge not you! Still, it allows us to get on with the real business of making money, DI Smith. That's what counts - making money.

The trouble is, people like you get too close and that screws everything up. You try and stop us doing what we do best. I am never quite sure why you insist on doing it. It never actually works. We still go on, making money, paying senior cops, politicians and the like. Why do you bother?"

"We bother because we want to serve and protect those people out there who trust us to do the right thing. Keep people like you from doing them any harm, keep them safe at night. I know there will always be bent cops, MP's, local councillors - money talks after all. But most people want to do the right thing and we will succeed. One day you will all be behind bars."

The man started to laugh. Slowly at first, but then almost uncontrollably.

"Detective, I do so love your view of the world, but from the beginning of time, our side has always had the upper hand. We have all the money, all the influence and everything that people want. You will never succeed because human beings don't like being controlled. They don't want someone watching their every move, demanding taxes and telling them '*no'*. You see, your side has nothing people really want. We on the other hand do, and the most potent weapon of all is freedom, and we have unlimited supplies of it!"

She was just about to reply when an image appeared from behind the man. In a flash, moving within feet of him, an Irish voice rang out as he swung something, bringing it down on the man's head.

"I might not have fuckin' freedom you twat, but I do have a piece of scaffolding tube."

The metal pipe hit him so hard that a gush of bright red blood shot out in all directions, splattering on Deborah's face and blouse. He immediately collapsed to the ground, without a noise or reaction. The Irish traveller hit him again and again until the man on the ground did not react.

"That'll teach yer', yer' fuckin' twat! It's my best van and you fuckin' wrecked it. And you've done me in, mate, I'll give yer' freedom - freedom from livin'."

Outside Southport Police Station.

The three of us sat in my car. The rain hammered on the roof, making a dull drumming sound. The sky had that dark grey, foreboding feeling. It seemed to suffocate any thoughts of happiness or joy. The windscreen had by now steamed up. At least people couldn't see in. I wasn't sure why that was important, but it made me feel a little more comfortable. We had to finalise our plan - this was a one-shot pony. If we didn't get this right, the whole thing would turn to crap and very quickly.

"Right, Sharron and Kaye, our first priority is finding out where Deborah is. If we don't do that soon, Mr Brau will have her throat cut once he finds out his men are on a wild goose chase. Make no mistake about that. We also need to know where Chief Superintendent Kiff is. The last thing we want to do is go rushing in like a herd of zebras only for Kiff to get spooked and do a runner.

So, three priorities: One - locate Kiff. Two - locate Gwen. And three - find out where DI Smith is being held. Now Sharron, is there a couple of people in that station right now that will help us, no questions asked, and no doubt about their honesty?"

"I can do better than that, Lee. One of Deborah's mentors is Chief Superintendent Watkins. He's one of the bosses here at Southport. They have always worked well together. He was her manager in the CID when she first became a detective. I could give him a call. I am sure he will help. He's a good guy. Debs has already spoken to him about that idiot Bruno and his involvement in this case. He is no lover of idiots and he is as honest as the day is long. So, he will be more than happy to help us, I am sure!"

"Right Sharron, then give him a buzz. Let's get this thing going before we run out of time. Kaye, have a saunter up to the Murder Squad Office and find DC Evans. Attach yourself to him. Don't let him out of your sight. He must not get away. Do I make myself clear? Wait until reinforcements arrive and do whatever is necessary, but keep him here and away from the phones. And in particular, his mobile."

I turned around to speak to DS Sharron Shacklady, but she had exited the car and was already on her phone talking to someone. Her facial expression alluded to the urgency of her task and the importance of getting it done. Her friend and colleague was missing and time was running out. It wasn't long before she gave me a big thumbs up and a radiant smile. I assumed that Chief Superintendent Watkins had come to the party.

Kaye Marie also left the vehicle, moving purposefully towards the main entrance of the station. She knew her task and she would not let Evans off the hook. I felt hugely proud of them, and I was sure this was the beginning of the end. It wouldn't be long now before Deborah and Gwen Walker were safe and sound.

"Right, Lee. Chief Superintendent Watkins is sending a couple of officers to grab DC Evans. They will throw him in the cells and charge him with corruption or something. It probably won't stick unless we can dig up a load of evidence, but at least he will be isolated for the time being. Watkins will get the Anti-Corruption Unit over from Liverpool. They need to take charge of this. It's their baby now.

As for Kiff, Watkins will try and find him and come up with some reason he needs to attend the station. He is sure that he will come in. Once he has them both, the Anti-Corruption Unit can get a grip of them, and they can try and pry some info out. Perhaps Evans will crack. Maybe he will give up Deborah's location?"

"Great work Sharron, but I am not sure we have that kind of time. Anti-Corruption Unit's likes to do their job *'by the book'*. We simply don't have the time to wait for that method to deliver up results. We need to find them now!"

"What do you have in mind?"

"Find Chief Superintendent Kiff. He is the key to all of this. He needs to know that we know everything, but we will help him and his family stays alive."

"I agree, but how the hell are we going to do that? He's supposed to be in hospital or in Coventry on a course, or goodness knows where."

"Get to Chief Superintendent Watkins. He will be able to contact him for sure, Sharron. We have to know where he is!"

I didn't have to repeat myself. Sharron sprinted off towards the main doors of the station. I was alone now. Both Sharron and Kaye were inside the building on their respective tasks. For the first time that day, I felt isolated. My thoughts began to turn to self-doubt. After all, it had been a couple of years since I left the Met and I was no longer a serving police officer. I had no right to endanger the life of others. To be honest, I was surprised they even wanted to talk to me, let alone carry out my instructions. I just hoped and prayed that I was right. If I wasn't, goodness knows what would happen.

I took a deep breath and consoled myself that we were doing the right thing. DC Evans was the owner of the BMW X6 - that was now confirmed. The vehicle had been seen in suspicious circumstances by me and others. Kaye had spoken to DCI Bruno this morning, so he couldn't have been the person Deborah met. Also, he had shown no reaction to the tip off Kaye had given him for the meeting, so he was now in the clear.

The only person now in the frame was Chief Superintendent Kiff. It had to be him - the man with a million excuses. All we had to do was find him. I was sure he would cough the first time we put the question to him about Deborah and Gwen. We could promise him a degree of immunity, assure him of the protection that would be afforded to his family. I had been involved in cases like this before. By and large, they followed a similar path of panic, regret, tears and capitulation. I was in no doubt that Kiff would go the same way.

It had to be at least thirty minutes before Sharron came out of the building. She had that smile on her face again, that sight made me feel a great deal better.

"Well Sharron, how's it been going in there?"

"Great news! Chief Superintendent Watkins has taken charge. He has called in the Anti-Corruption Unit and they are on the way. DC Evans is in the cells, protesting his innocence. Chief Superintendent Watkins is questioning him as we speak. Hopefully we will get an answer about Debs and the girl very soon.

As for DCI Bruno, no idea where he's gone. He is still signed in, but he could be anywhere. I guess Kaye will find him shortly. He's probably in the basement somewhere molesting some young PC, promising her a rapid promotion if only she would shag him.

Chief Superintendent Watkins has left an innocuous voice mail for our man Kiff. Something about a golf competition this weekend. He is sure he will reply to that. Once he does, the tech guys can trace the call and bingo, we have him!

He has the undercover team looking through their files. Perhaps they might have identified where Mr Brau might keep some of his victims. They are not too optimistic, but it's worth a try. You never know. All we can do now is sit tight and wait!"

"That's great work Sharron but I don't like sitting about and waiting. I am going to phone Mr Brau, make up some cockamamie story about Simon Walker telling me where he has hidden the money. Try and convince him that Walker doesn't want anything to do with it anymore. Maybe he will bite. I can swap myself for the women, then I can sit it out and wait for the cavalry."

I wouldn't recommend that, Lee. This Brau guy is a vicious killer. He won't hesitate in slitting your throat. In any case, he will only give up the girls until he knows where the money is. In all probability, Debs, Gwen and you will all end up dead!"

"Can you think of a better idea, Sharron? If you can I am more than happy to listen."

I opened my mouth to speak again, but to be honest Sharron was absolutely right. My plan was not really a plan at all. It was a suicide mission. There was no way Brau was going to let anyone go before that money was back in his account. To be honest, he wasn't going to let anyone go even after the money was returned and I knew it!

The silence was overwhelming. We had reached the end of the line. There was nothing else to do now but wait. The rain started again and myself and we retreated to the relative safety of my little Ford Fiesta. I closed the door and turned to Sharron, but as I did so, her phone began to ring.

"DS Shacklady."

There was a silence before a shriek followed.

"Debs, where the hell have you been? Are you safe? How the heck did you get away? What about Gwen? Is she with you? Lee Hunter is here. I am putting you on speaker phone."

"Hi Lee. I am ok, thanks Shaz. No thanks to some fucking lunatic heavy sent by Brau. It's a long story, but he was going to beat information out of me, and probably Gwen, but we managed to escape. Some Irish travellers came to my rescue. They busted me out of an industrial unit other side of Marshside. Anyhow, we are OK. Kind of. We are on our way back to the station. Should be there in about forty minutes."

"That's great news, Debs. I have got Chief Superintendent Watkins on the job. He has taken charge, called in the ACU. We have banged up DC Evans in the cells. Let's see if he talks. We are looking for CS Kiff. Once we have him, we can really get to work on this case. Oh yes, Marcus is on his way back to Bicester, so he is safe. He's going to look after Simon Walker. Things are looking up."

"That's great, Shaz. Glad Marcus is out of the way. Things were looking very dangerous indeed for everyone. One question though: why are you after Kiff? What's he got to do with this?"

"He's the man you met this morning. Surely you remember that?"

"It wasn't Kiff who met me this morning. I have no idea what that old fart has got to do with the case?"

"Hi Deborah. It's Lee Hunter here. What do you mean, it wasn't Kiff? He's the main man, he is Brau's puppet. It's clear to us now, he is also the killer!"

"Sorry to piss on your chips, Lee, but it wasn't Kiff who I met this morning. I am at a loss to understand what you mean. Do you think Kiff is that hit man you are looking for? Hang on, what bloody conclusions have you come up with? Are you trying to tell me that Chief Superintendent Kiff is our man? Sorry to spoil the party guys, but you are way off the mark with that one!"

A cold and intense silence permeated the vehicle. The fact that the rain was hammering on the roof once more had gone completely unnoticed. If I was hearing this right, we weren't even close, and to be honest I feared the answer to the next and most obvious question. The only person who could accurately answer was DI Deborah Smith, and if she was about to give the answer I thought she was, then we were really in trouble.

Sharron and I looked at each other. Had she also guessed what Deborah's answer might be? Was she feeling the same level of dread I was?

"Deborah, Sharron again. So, if it wasn't Kiff you met this morning, who the hell was it?"

"Are you two completely stupid or what? It was that slimy screw ball, Detective Chief Inspector Mark Bruno. Who the hell did you think it was going to be? Prince bloody Charming?"

Again, the silence invaded the space. I looked at DS Sharron Shacklady. Her mouth was just as wide open as mine. There was no doubt that she was just as shocked. This news was an absolute disaster. Not just because we have Chief Superintendent Watkins and his team looking for the wrong man, but Senior Scenes of Crimes Investigator Kaye Marie had gone looking for Bruno, who had turned out to be the right man.

"Are you two both there? Shaz, Lee, is the line dead?"

"Debs, we have fucked this up. We thought it was Kiff. Trouble is Kaye has gone into the building looking for Bruno and we don't know where they are."

"Listen, Sharron. Get in there, lock the place down, get everyone looking. The place isn't that big and it won't take you more than ten minutes to find them, do it now!"

"Right, I am on it."

"A quick question for Deborah before you go Sharron. Kaye said she spoke to Bruno early this morning, she left him gazing out of his office window. What time did you meet him?"

"It was about nine thirty. Evans said he couldn't make it - some early morning raid he had been put on. He mentioned it to CI Bruno and he said he would meet me. Evans thought it might be a good opportunity for me to interrogate him. Evans suggested to Bruno that I might be interested in an affair with him. That was sure to get his attention. Well, he turned up, bought me a coffee and that's the last thing I remember. I guess he must have slipped something into the drink before he brought it over.

Anyway, the rest you know. There is no doubt that Chief Inspector Mark Bruno is our man. Now get in there Shaz and find the bastard!"

There was no more talk. Sharron pushed the phone into her pocket, jumped out of the car and ran through the rain towards the main entrance of the station. I wanted to go with her, but I knew full well that they wouldn't let me anywhere near the place. Anyway, I was certain that the best people were now involved. In the next few seconds, the place would be secure, and Kaye Marie and Detective Inspector Mark Bruno would be found.

I sat back in the car seat. For the first time, a feeling of relief washed over me. Within a few minutes, both DC Evans and DCI Bruno would be in custody. The ACU would be here soon as would DI Deborah Smith and Gwen Walker. It had all come to a head rather quickly, but despite our screw up, it had all ended well.

Next time, I would simply hand it over to the local police and walk away. No more '*Mr stick your nose in*' for me. Leave it to the boys and girls in blue. -they know what they are doing, not me. Anyway, I still had things to attend to. There was Smelly Ken - goodness only knows what he was up to - leading Mike on a merry dance, I am sure. Of course, there was Tony Bianchi. I still owed him the 30k and he wasn't going to forget that in a hurry.

The one sad thing though was Ruth. She had died because of me and for no other reason. Someone, probably DI Bruno, had blown her brains out because she might know something she shouldn't. The truth was, she knew nothing at all, other than she had a date with an ex-piss head, Met Police cop called Lee Hunter!

I couldn't help myself. I banged on the steering wheel as hard as I could. I kept hitting it until the pain in my hand became unbearable. What was I thinking about? Who the hell am I? Why did I get involved? And all because I thought I had the answers. Well, I didn't. All I managed to do was to kill the one person who actually cared for me. What a selfish bastard I had become!

Tears started to stream down my face, blurring my vision. It seemed appropriate that I couldn't see properly anymore. At least I would be blinded to any other stupid ideas. The pain welled up inside of me. If I had a weapon, I would have turned it on myself. I didn't deserve to live.

I was just about to leave the car and go for a walk. Perhaps the cold wet rain would help wash away my overwhelming shame and remorse. Before I could leave the Fiesta, something caught my eye. Just as I reached the door handle, I blinked away the tears for just long enough to see a BMW X6 leave the carpark and speed past me, towards the main road.

The Chase.

I couldn't believe what I had just witnessed. How the hell did they get out of the station, let alone the carpark? There was no time to act. I started the car, turned around in the road and set off in pursuit. At least my little white Ford Fiesta would not really be noticed by the driver of the X6. Trouble was, if they put their foot down, there was no way I was keeping up!

My heart was pounding in my chest. I wanted to call back at the station, tell them what I was doing, but I had to stay on the tail of the BMW. I reached for my mobile, but I couldn't find it anywhere. It must be here somewhere, but it eluded me. There was nothing for it - follow the X6, stay out of sight. Once they stop, find the phone and call 999!

This would explain why they couldn't find DCI Bruno. He was already out in the carpark, just waiting for his chance to make a run for it. In that case, where was Kaye Marie? Then the realisation hit me - was she in the car with Bruno?

At least the driver of the BMW didn't seem to be in any kind of rush. I guess he wanted to just slide away unnoticed and it very nearly worked! The car moved relentlessly to the south of the town, out towards Woodvale aerodrome. I dropped back. My Fiesta was an innocuous car, but I didn't want to give the game away. Kaye's life would certainly depend upon it.

The pursuit passed without any major issues. The BMW was not an easy car to miss and I was determined not to let it out of my sight. We passed the aerodrome to the right and headed on towards Formby and the pinewoods. Winding our way through the town, we eventually arrived at a disused recycling centre about five minutes out from the centre. It seemed somewhat deserted - weeds growing everywhere, no signs of activity, just rusty containers and lots of broken furniture and general rubbish everywhere.

The BMW stopped at the barrier. The driver got out, unlocked the padlock and pushed the barrier up. The car then entered and disappeared around the back of four old lorry containers parked at the rear of the site. I parked my car down the road. There was no way I was driving in there, but perhaps I could slip in unnoticed elsewhere and try and ascertain who the driver really was and more importantly, was Kaye with him.

I finally found my mobile under the passenger seat. I looked at it for a few seconds. I knew full well what I would be told to do, *'Stay where you are and wait for the police units to turn up'*. Well, there was no way I was doing that. This guy had killed five people already. He wouldn't hesitate in putting a bullet in Kaye's head and then making a run for it. I had to act now. I needed to get in there and find out what was going on. Kaye's life might well depend on it.

I made the phone call to Deborah who was now safely in place at the police station. I appraised her of the situation and told her what I was about to do. Predictably she told me to stay put. Armed police were on the way, but there was no way I was sitting here waiting to hear that gun pumping three bullets into Kaye's head! I had to act and act right now. So, I left the relative safety of my little Fiesta and cautiously made my way towards the disused recycling site.

There was no way I would walk right in through the front gate. Not even I was that foolish. So, I decided to work my way around the dilapidated perimeter fence and see what I could discover. Fortunately, the weather had cleared and the late afternoon sun felt comforting as I approached the impossible tangle of brambles and nettles that engulfed the surrounding area.

I knew this was a bad idea. How long would it be before the armed police arrived? Thirty minutes at most? But I had to try. Kaye didn't deserve to die like all his other victims did. Then there was Ruth. Perhaps it was the thoughts of her dying alone in her car, wondering what the hell was going on as he pulled the trigger. Maybe these dark feelings were behind this madness, driving me on. I contemplated if I had to do this in order to somehow make up for Ruth's murder. Was this a misguided attempt to soothe my guilt and make things better? Of course, that meant my judgement had been clouded, and I was being controlled by thoughts and feelings not proportionate to the situation.

Despite every atom of my brain screaming to let this go and wait for the police, I found myself fighting through the tangled undergrowth. There were discarded bottles, old cans, the occasional settee, but I pushed on - on into what, I didn't know. From time to time, I stopped and listened. I wasn't quite sure what I was listening for, but I did. Of course, there was no sound at all. In fact, there was no sign of anything. From the back of the compound, I could see the BMW X6 parked towards the front of the old containers, but nothing more than that.

Eventually, I came to a gap in the fence. Looking down, I could see the remains of drug abuse littering the concrete compound within. It reminded me of Smelly Ken. This was just the kind of place he would hang out, risking his life with questionable substances coursing through his veins.

Pushing the rusty chain-link fence apart, I forced myself through the gap and into the compound. The level of fear inside me immediately jumped up 100%. Why this should be I wasn't quite sure. The chain-link fencing was never going to protect me if the bullets started to fly.

Crouching down, I scoped out the area. Apart from a couple of errant and scabby looking pigeons, there was no sign of anything. I slowly moved forward. Perhaps if I could make it to that first rusty container, I might be able to gain some cover and assess my position. It was precisely at that moment that the whole situation took a decidedly difficult turn.

I couldn't identify where the voice was coming from, but it was somewhere above me. The voice had a cold and uncaring tone, one that sent shivers down my spine!

"Can I assume you are Lee Hunter? I have heard a lot about you, Mr Hunter. Both from my colleagues in the force and other associates of mine. It seems that you have an unerring ability to stick your nose in where it's not wanted. Well, on this particular occasion, it's going to be your undoing. You see, I can't have any witnesses to my work. No one who might point the finger of guilt in my direction.

Anyway, I need you to walk towards me. Please remember that I have a loaded gun and that it's pointing directly at you. Oh, and your friend Kaye is tied up in the red container next to you. Perhaps if you move quickly, I might be minded to leave you both tied up here, rather than put a bullet in both of your brains, if you get my drift, Mr Hunter."

I slowly stood upright. Looking up onto the top of the red container next to me, there was a man I assumed to be Chief Inspector Mark Bruno. He stood tall in the afternoon sun, several feet above me. He looked strong and in control, not at all worried about the situation. He was ice cold, every bit the calculating killer. Waving the gun in my direction, he guided me toward the open doors at the other end of the steel box.

I of course complied. Partly relieved that the anticipation of what might happen was now over. I became focused on buying enough time before the armed police arrived. Entering the steel container, I noticed someone crouched down at one end. In the gloom I couldn't identify who it was, but I assumed it was Kaye. She looked up at me, but didn't speak. I guessed she just wanted this to end and hoped it would mean her leaving alive.

I heard a noise behind me and I quickly turned to see standing in the doorway, a man, tall with a pocked marked face and a certain arrogant air.

"Can I assume you are Chief Inspector Mark Bruno?"

"You can assume anything you like. It won't matter once I have drilled three bullets into your stupid skull. Thing is, should I kill the girl first or you? Ladies before gentlemen, Mr Hunter?"

He rocked back, laughing at his sick joke, waving the 9mm automatic pistol with alarming alacrity. This man was either completely insane or so far removed from the norms of a human being that any typical emotion was alien to him. This was how he managed to murder so many people seemingly with ease, despatching human beings like flies in a bedroom at night. The immediate problem here was that Kaye and I would be next!

"Why are you going to kill us at all? Just leave us here, lock the doors and make your escape. DI Smith and her team know about you. They are looking for you as we speak. Just leave us here and make a run for it. Killing us isn't going to change anything DCI Bruno. It's not going to help you, not now."

"I know Mr Hunter, but you see I am a bit of an obsessive, and I don't like untidy ends. I always like to leave jobs completed, all nice and ship-shape, if you get what I mean. Leaving you two alive would be, well negligent of me. I wouldn't be doing my job properly now would I, Mr Hunter? So, the question is: you first or the girl? What's your choice?"

"Not much of a choice if you ask me, DCI Bruno. Would you mind if I asked you a couple of questions first?"

"Fire away, Mr Hunter."

"There have been five murders and counting. I assume you killed all five?"

"Spot on, Mr Hunter. Enjoyed every one of them."

"Can I suppose it was all related to the disappearance of Mr Brau's money and Simon Walker? I assume my two friends, Jenks and Dell, just knew too much about you? Especially after you asked Dell to help with the kidnapping?

Adele and her husband were the launderers of the money, and my friend Ruth Davenport got too close? All these people died because of you DCI Bruno, and for what? A fat payday with Mr Brau? Was it all worth it?"

"You see, Mr Hunter. You are like all those fools in the police. They just assume it's all about money, but you are wrong, very wrong. It's about respect, power and privilege. Being someone important, free to live one's own life, unfettered by the rules.

When I joined the police force, I was all full of my own piss and importance, starry eyed, an upholder of the rule of law. My future was clear, I would catch the bad guys and protect the innocent, simple!

Thing is, it didn't take long for me to realise that it was a load of shit. The so-called bad guys were in fact the ones with all the good things in life. People like me just had the scrag end of what was left. Following rules imprisoned you into an existence of just trying to make ends meet, whilst Brau and his men laughed at me and spat in my face.

Every time I got close to busting them, there would be a phone call. I was told to back off, posted somewhere out of the way. It quickly became obvious who had all the power and which side of the tracks an intelligent man should walk on. So, as the old saying goes, *'if you can't beat them, join them'*, and I did.

That's why I am here, Mr Hunter. It's not the money. It's just the best place to be. You asked if it was all worth it? Well, it was and it is. I am going to kill you both, walk away from here, phone calls will be made and this time next week, I will be playing golf with some friends at the Royal Birkdale. Now, what could be better than that?"

"Surely you must have some vestiges of guilt about those five people you murdered?"

"Not in the slightest, Mr Hunter. To be honest, I rather enjoyed it. You see, they were not the same as me. They were part of the underclass. Simply here to make my life and that of the people I associate with easier. They had served their purpose, so they had to die. Why would you want someone who had no purpose in life hanging around? You wouldn't, would you Mr Hunter?

Oh, by the way, your friend...what was her name, Ruth? Yes, I really enjoyed killing her. She cried and begged for her life. She even promised to do whatever I wanted, if only I would let her go. I was curious, I must admit. I wondered what depraved level she would sink to in order to stay alive.

Anyway, I started with something quite simple - got her to strip off, knocked her about - that was fun. I thought about cutting her up. I had a good knife with me. I do enjoy watching the pain in people's eyes when I slowly push that blade into their bodies. I get a huge hard on. But that didn't seem right somehow. She deserved better than that, something real special.

I thought about it for a minute or two, and then it came to me, I wanted her to kill someone else. Yes, murder someone and she would live. What a great idea. So, I jumped into her car and we cruised around for a bit. There was a motorist at the side of the road - bonnet up, car fucked.

I pulled up and told her she had to go and shoot him, and I would let her go. She couldn't do it, she sobbed and eventually pissed herself, but she couldn't do it. That was a damn disappointment I can tell you. So, we called it off and drove to a quiet little spot. I told her to get dressed again and I shot her. A great fun evening, Mr Hunter. You should try it sometime."

I stood there enraged at the sick story. I wasn't sure of the exact moment when I lost control, but hearing about the end of Ruth was too much for me to bear. The next thing I remembered was diving forward at the sick bastard with the gun. There was a flash and a searing pain in my right side. The concussion of the noise made my head buzz as if an electric shock had been blasted through it. I pushed with all my strength. I remembered falling forward into the daylight and onto the concrete surface of the old recycling yard.

I could feel both pain and the warm stickiness of blood on my side. I instinctively knew that my time was short. I would either bleed to death or lose my strength as my life's blood ebbed away. Either way, this monster underneath me would win, and Kaye and I would be no more.

My eyes soon adjusted to the light, adrenaline pumping through my whole body as I looked down at him. His face was a mixture of surprise and anger. Maybe he felt fear, perhaps just annoyance that he had been taken like this. There was only one thing I could do. My right side was partially numb and my left arm trapped under his body. So, I arched my back as much as I could and brought my head down onto his face with every bit of energy still available to me.

I could both feel and hear the bones crunching in his face, like the ice on a winters pond. I arched my back again and struck for the second time. I felt his body relax under me. I couldn't take the chance that this was any permanent state, so I had to stand and get that gun.

I rolled out to my right and pulled my left arm free. The pain in my right side was almost unbearable, but I had to carry on. Pushing against the slick red surface of the blood covered concrete, I somehow managed to stand upright. The gun was some ten feet away, but my consciousness was fading. I knew in my heart of hearts that I didn't possess the strength to reach it.

As I stood, half bent over, I could feel the darkness overwhelming me. A cold shiver enveloped my whole being. I knew this was the end. I had tried my best, but my life force was spilling out over the dirty concrete and the red pool of blood surrounding me attested to my impending expiration. Detective Chief Inspector Mark Bruno had won.

Six Weeks Later.
Southport General Hospital.

It wasn't so much the bullet that had done all the damage, it had passed straight through. It was the subsequent infections that had nearly finished me off. There followed weeks of pain, sickness and half-consciousness, black dreams, nightmares and uncontrolled emotions. However, the doctors had finally given me the all clear and I could go home.

I must admit, getting out of hospital was the one thing I was really looking forward to. Well, that and a couple of pints down the Bold Arms, and perhaps a trip to the Peking Gardens. Don't get me wrong, the staff here have been great, especially Nurse Flores. A rather cute lady from Barcelona.

I had tried my best to get a date, but she was having nothing to do with it. I even laid on the wounded little soldier, saving the life of Kaye, but she wasn't falling for that either. Speaking of which, the visits from Deborah, Sharron, and Kaye had been a welcome break. They fed me with not so healthy snacks, bottles of coke topped off with whiskey - don't tell Nurse Flores!

Oh yes, Mike Giel dropped in too. Guess what? Smelly Ken had done a runner. I kind of guessed that would happen. At least he was safe now that lunatic Bruno was behind bars. Never mind, I will grab a coffee with Ken once I get out of here, at the soup kitchen, behind the old bus station.

Anyway, all's well that ends well. Detective Chief Inspector Mark Bruno was safe in custody and singing like a canary. I guess he didn't fancy years in jail mixing with those men he had locked up. So, he was on a special wing with all the other misfits, ex-police, sex offenders and inadequate human beings. Perhaps he didn't deserve that level of protection, but he wasn't getting out of prison for the rest of his life, so that wasn't so bad.

Mr Brau has been picked up and charged. His financial dealings were being taken apart as we speak. It wouldn't be long before he joined Bruno on that special wing in a Liverpool jail.

Of course, I couldn't forget Detective Constable Mike Evans. Turns out that he was a nephew of DCI Bruno, so we shouldn't be so surprised that he was working for Brau as well. He was on the same wing as Bruno in that Liverpool jail. Both of their trials have been set and both will be doing a very long time behind bars.

Then there were the Walkers - Kim, Simon and the daughter Gwen. He was in custody. Not sure what the outcome of that would be. He was being very 'helpful' to the officer in charge of the case.

Kim and Gwen have disappeared. They haven't done anything wrong of course, but there was still a lot of missing money. Well, that's what Mr Brau was saying. Makes me wonder if Kim was part of this all along? Now that she may have access to the cash and everybody else was languishing in jail, she could go and please herself. I have no doubt that she and her daughter were on a beach somewhere spending Mr Brau's money. Good on them.

The best bit of all was the visit from Fat Tony Bianchi. You might remember him - the local gangster to whom I owed 30k. Well, it seems he has profited greatly from Mr Brau being banged up. Seems that Fat Tony has acquired most of his businesses, so he was very pleased indeed. Anyway, he agreed to hold my debt in abeyance, with no further interest being added.

"Pay me when you can, Mr Hunter. You have done me a great kindness getting rid of that Mr Brau. I owe you a favour for that."

So, things were better that I could ever have expected. I was still alive, Fat Tony was no longer going to kill me and I was free to go. Perfect! Oh yes, just to cap it off, I won £500 on the local lottery. Talk about everything going my way!

The truth was though, things weren't perfect. There was the issue of Ruth Davenport. That lovely soul who had briefly entered my life. She ended up being murdered for no other reason than knowing yours truly. It made me feel sick just thinking about it. Why the hell did that happen to her? Why did that lunatic Bruno thought that she had to die?

I am not sure I would ever understand or accept that I wasn't, in some way, to blame for what had happened. One thing was for sure, I wouldn't let anyone put their lives at risk again. I wouldn't let anyone else get that close!

So, what was next? Well, I would shut the office for a while. The last few weeks have been a nightmare and nearly killed me - literally! I couldn't face any more calls or pleadings for help, especially from beautiful women called Adele!

Also, I needed to go back to the flat, but to be honest, I couldn't face that. Not after Ruth. Deborah said she would call in, pick up the post, make sure that place was secure. Oh yes, Deborah and Marcus. Seems once he had managed to convince his boss that he had Simon Walker in protective custody, he booked some time off. He and Deborah are now planning a walking holiday in the Lake District. Very nice.

I have my winnings of course, so I thought about a holiday. I've always liked the idea of a railway break. My Uncle Stan used to take me to the steam engine sheds to see the huge locomotives. So, I decided to combine the two - a holiday on a steam train. What a great idea!

After all, what the hell could possibly go wrong on a steam train? Absolutely nothing, right?

Printed in Great Britain
by Amazon

77428255R00102